Dancing *with* Kali

Dancing *with* Kali

Lalita Das

NIYOGI
BOOKS

Published by

NIYOGI
BOOKS

D-78, Okhla Industrial Area, Phase-I
New Delhi-110 020, INDIA
Tel: 91-11-26816301, 26813350, 51, 52
Fax: 91-11-26810483, 26813830
email: niyogibooks@gmail.com
website: www.niyogibooks.com

Cover Design: Nabanita Das/Niyogi Books
Editor: Madhuparna Banerjee/Niyogi Books

ISBN: 978-81-89738-60-0

Publication: 2010

Printed at: Niyogi Offset Pvt. Ltd., New Delhi, India.

There is a choice.

Either you can stay mired in your karma or you can
dance with Goddess Kali
who will wipe out your karma and release you to life.

Her boon is freedom.
Her price is bloody sacrifice.

PART ONE

1

The house was on the riverside on the outskirts of an inland village in North Goa. It was a large old house built in typical Goan style with a steeply sloping tiled roof, shell-fitted window shutters, and a balcao—a deep but short, almost square front veranda with red cement-finished benches on two sides, facing each other.

On the front veranda, Maushi sat waiting. She was dressed in a nine-yard old-fashioned sari that her generation still wore; her thick black hair – now sprinkled with grey – was pulled tightly into a bun on the back of her head and wound around with jasmine strings; her arms were loaded with wide gold bangles interspersed with green glass bangles—a symbol of her married status; and she wore two more symbols of her married status: a big round red kumkum on her forehead and a mangalsutra—a gold chain woven with black beads and with two tiny gold balls and a gold hollow semi-sphere in the centre—around her neck.

It was early morning; the golden dawn light was just changing to pale yellow as Maushi sat waiting. Flashing golden rays still played over the river and a golden oriole flitting over the river merged with them as it flew upwards. The river was still and dark, like molten lead, rippled by the cool breeze that also fluttered the leaves of the neem tree in Maushi's otherwise barren garden waking the little brown babbler birds that nestled in it.

The light changed to white while Maushi sat waiting. A woman's life is all about waiting, Maushi thought, watching the river change to a deep grey-blue. As a young girl she waited to get married, then she waited to bear children – especially sons, then she waited for them to get married, and then she waited for the arrival of grandchildren – particularly grandsons. On arrival of grandsons, a woman had fulfilled the purpose of her life. Then she waited to die saubhagyawati – while her husband was still alive.

The river turned blue-green while Maushi sat waiting. Now she could see the flow of water. Now she could see the reflections of trees in it and the shoals of little silver fish that darted through it just below the surface. A long-tailed shrike flew languidly across the river and a kingfisher skimmed its surface. A couple of reef herons landed for a moment on its bank and gracefully walked into the shallow waters. Maushi watched the river flow while she waited for Pundlik to come. He may come today, he may come tomorrow, or perhaps even after three days; whenever his work allowed him the time. Men did their own things; women waited.

Soon it will be time for her daily puja. Then she will get up and walk through the passageway to the internal courtyard, then along the veranda on its sides past all the rooms and on to the back veranda, and then into the gods' room opening off it. Sitting in front of the carved wooden temple she will make sure that there were no buds in the fresh flowers brought by the maid and that the little silver boxes were filled with kumkum and turmeric powders. Then she will rub the sandalwood sticks on the small slab of grey stone to make a fresh paste, serve the food for gods on top of the holy basil leaves arranged on a little silver plate and light the incense sticks and the little silver oil lamp in preparation. Her puja would take almost an hour.

Until then, she sat waiting, watching the eternal flow of the river.

2

In midmorning, the sun cleared the hill to throw deep shadows into the cove. Inside the cove, the ocean was almost calm in spite of the water churning furiously on both sides of it for though the crescent of the encircling hill was lush green, its ends, where they met the sea, were rocky and rock outcrops had continued into the sea almost a hundred metres away forming another crescent and breaking the force of the waves.

Within the cove, waves murmured on to the silver sands, palms on the beach bent and fluttered in greeting, and large, shady trees on the ledges of the hill whispered in cool breeze. A sparkling silver waterfall came cascading down the hillside through the greenery into a rock basin. Foreigners called it a paradise. Locals never went there.

In the seventies and eighties, hippies from the Western lands had appropriated it among other coves and beaches of North Goa that the locals had ignored, and made it their own enclave—secluded, isolated, protected. Nowadays youngsters from the same lands came here to become lotus-eaters for a while: to forget the daily grind, the urban stresses and the looming responsibilities. It was the land that did it to them—the sun, the surf and the sand.

The cove was not easy to get to. On either of its sides some strange upheavals of the earth had thrown up a kilometre-long- and a metre-high-plateau of rocks – a jagged, tilted jumble with hardly a horizontal foothold anywhere – requiring a long and arduous walk, hard but not impossible. Or it was a slide, slither, and climb down the steep encircling hill; again hard but not impossible. For the youngsters frequenting it, it was not even too hard.

Ronnie, not yet twenty-one, tall and rangy, came running down the hill like a young goat, jumping the last few feet to land on his feet in the sand. Then he threw up his hands, threw back his head, gave a big whoop of delight, bowed theatrically to the whistles and catcalls that greeted him, and ran into the sea. Swimming to a flat rock, he lay down with the warm sun beating pleasantly on his wet body and closed his eyes to the world beyond, to the memories, to the past. Nothing existed but here and now – the beat of the sun, the swish of the waves, the laughter and the music on the beach.

She was in the water clinging to the rock when he opened his eyes. 'Hi,' she said grinning. 'I am Hilary.'

Ronnie turned on his side shading his eyes to look at her. Honey blonde, tanned and freckled, pretty. Ronnie grinned back. 'Hi,' he said. 'I am Ronnie.'

'I know,' she said, 'Sir Richard Harrington-Wells' son,' and laughed as Ronnie raised an eyebrow. 'I have seen you around in London School of Economics. And who in London hasn't heard of Barrister Harrington-Wells?'

Ronnie gave a little self-deprecating laugh and rolled on his back. 'You never escape from under your father's shadow, however far away you may go,' he said looking at the sky. 'Even here in

Goa. Even now,' he added a little sadly. Around them the ocean rolled. Roaring waves came rushing to break on the rocks, sent metres-high sprays into the air, washed the rock, bubbled around their bodies, and then receded to make space for the next ones.

Hilary stopped laughing and sobered up. 'I am sorry,' she said contritely. 'He passed away rather suddenly a few months ago, didn't he?'

'Three months ago. It was a heart attack,' Ronnie said.

In silence they watched the beach for a while. There were young girls, blondes, brunettes and redheads, all in topless bikinis, all tanned golden, all pleasurably watchable, splashing in the sparkling waves. There were young men of all hues carousing about on the silver sands. Gathered in groups scattered all over the beach, some were just lying down soaking the warm sun, some were engaged in heated discussions – prodding each other in the chest and gesticulating to high heavens, others were playing games on the sand, and still others were dancing energetically to some crazy tune under the placidly wavering palms. On one side were the thatched shacks with rough wooden tables and benches – the beach dhabas – serving fried fish and curries. There were guitars being strummed and drums being beaten. There was gaiety, there was hilarity.

'Quite a scene!' Ronnie said laughing delightedly at this setting, at this carefree atmosphere, and turned towards Hilary, but she was looking at the boys on a nearby rock standing in a tight group straining their necks, watching the shore intently and gesticulating excitedly at the beach. They saw her looking at them and smiled down at her waving victory signs. She smiled back at them. 'Look, look,' they shouted pointing towards the beach and gesturing her to join them on the rock, one of them even bending down and extending his hand to help her climb. Hilary looked on smiling. Suddenly the water at the base of the rock that the boys were standing on churned and foamed and a redhead rose out of the foaming sea like a sea-goddess. As Ronnie watched fascinated, she caught hold of the shins of one of the boys, the one still bending down and extending his hand towards Hilary, pulled him thrashing into the sea, and started swimming off with him glaring at Hilary.

'Property rights!' Hilary said turning to Ronnie. They looked at each other and laughed. 'That's all I learned back there at the Law Department of LSE,' she added with a moue.

Ronnie looked at her with interest. 'That's all I learned there too,' he said. 'Rights and privileges and liens and debts.' They considered each other with a new regard, now united in their disenchantment with a system. A rushing wave dashed on a rock ahead of them and a lacy fountain rose before them.

The boys on the nearby rock were now cheering madly and splashing their feet in the water bubbling on the rock and their cheers echoed back from the beach accompanied by clapping. On the beach, a girl was walking on the sand balancing on her head a glass of water full to the brim, her arms spread wide like a tightrope walker, her back straight, her neck held rigid. Gingerly she placed one foot in front of the other, controlling her movements, taking her time, her eyes angled downwards, watching the ground. Others walked by her side, some stooping to watch her feet, some shouting encouragements to her. The drummer gave little taps on his drum to match her steps.

'She has to keep to the line drawn in the sand,' the boys told Ronnie, their eyes glued on the girl. 'She just crossed the halfway mark. Many have tried but as yet nobody else had managed it even up to there.' Ronnie and Hilary too forgot everything else and turned to watch her as intently.

'Keep to it, keep to it, you can make it!' Hilary, still in water, leaning her back against the rock and pumping her legs, shouted cupping her mouth.

Ronnie jumped up on the rock waving his arms. 'Attagirl! That's the way! Go to it! Go to it!'

'She's three quarters across,' the boys said now beginning to dance on the rock and wave victory signs. 'She is from our school,' they told Ronnie proudly. 'We all came together on this trip. Hurrah for Beckenham High!' they shouted suddenly, all together, their hands thrown high up in the air, fingers folded except two to make a vee, their cry taken up by others on the beach. A general excitement had enveloped the beach. Youngsters were running from all corners of it to join the crowd around the girl.

Even Hilary had got into the spirit of the contest. She was holding on to the rock with one hand and waving the other hand high up in the air, fist clenched tight, shouting encouragements. 'Yeow! Yeow!' she shouted joining her voice to other shouting, encouraging voices. 'Go on! Go on! Not much more to go.'

Ronnie too was shouting and jumping up and down on the rock and laughing, thoroughly enjoying this first foray of his into the wild freedom.

The girl, so close to the finishing line, now became overconscious of her movements, slowed her walk, and trembled a little.

'Almost there! Almost there! Watch out now! Watch out! Watch out! Oh no! No, no, no!' Ronnie said with total disappointment as the girl swayed slightly and the glass came tumbling down and a collective sigh went up. Ronnie sat down dejected. 'She almost made it! She was almost there!' he said watching the girl flop down where she was and being consoled by a young lad while the palms waved unconcernedly over their heads. At the other end, another lad was already starting down the line with another glass full of water on his head. The beach activities resumed. Ronnie subsided back on the rock and a subdued Hilary hauled herself up on it. The sun was bright on their faces, fine sprays cooled their backs. They sat watching people dancing on the beach with their shadows pooled around their feet.

'What bad luck!' Ronnie moaned.

'Karma,' Hilary said.

Ronnie turned to look at her and raised his eyebrows.

'What?' he said.

'Karma,' Hilary repeated.

Ronnie looked on blankly.

'You don't know karma?' she asked.

Ronnie shook his head.

'It's a Hindu word,' Hilary said. 'It means effects of your deeds in your previous life. Hindus believe that whatever happens to you in this life is all guided by your actions in your last life. For them everything, absolutely everything is written down long ago. Destiny and fate are the deciding factors for them. Luck or chance doesn't exist for them; they don't even have a word for it.' She grinned at Ronnie. He grinned back shaking his head incredulously.

Hilary planted her palms on the rock arching her back and looked up at him speculatively. 'Just come over?' she asked.

'Yesterday,' Ronnie, already a part of this scene, said with wonder looking at the beach. It seems like forever, he thought. It's as if I have always been here, will always be here!

'Been here before?'

'Eighteen years ago,' he said still watching the beach. 'I was not even three then.' And suddenly his face darkened, light went out of his eyes.

'What's it, Ronnie, what?' Hilary cried, frightened at the change in him.

But Ronnie didn't answer her. He stared blankly at her for a moment and then rolled away from her straight into a huge, curly-topped wave that came rushing over the rock, engulfed them both, and threw them off the rock. Ronnie rolled with the wave, tumbled into the ocean, swallowed a mouthful of salty water, and came up spluttering. Wiping his eyes he looked for Hilary, who was also just coming up for a breath, and there, clinging to the rock, they laughed together, a little too loudly, a little hysterically, and his black mood was dispelled. Memories were once again washed away in the waves. There was only here and now, laughter and music, sun and sand.

'Come and join us,' Hilary said.

Ronnie let his eyes wander around other groups. 'They are German,' Hilary said pointedly when he looked twice at a raucous, flamboyant group who were singing loudly and energetically in German. 'We are all English,' she added.

'Apartheid in Paradise?' Ronnie asked with amusement.

'It's always good to understand what others in your group are saying, don't you think so?' she asked arching her eyebrows, turned, and swam away as Ronnie laughed.

Ronnie lay under a leafy canopy on one of the ledges midway up on the hillside sharing a joint with Hilary and others and looked down on to the beach as into an arena. The sun was high and the activity on the beach was muted. But it was cool under the trees and dappled shadows played on the water. A cool green light enveloped the whole. Ronnie could hear the tinkling of the waterfall into the rock basin. He closed his eyes. There is only here and now.

3

In the harsh afternoon sun, the house showed its age. Its once yellow paint, the popular Goan colour for houses, had faded to an indistinguishable sickly hue dotted with grey where the paint had totally peeled off the plaster, many of the roof tiles, once terracotta red, had turned black, and some of the window shutters had warped and twisted in their frames.

The house still has a dignity, Pundlik thought as he approached it. As he put a hand out to unlatch the gate, he heard voices and turned with his hand still on the gate. Behind him the village moneylender's sons were crossing the road to the other side, sneering and throwing disdainful glances at the house.

Pundlik took his hand off the gate and stood glaring at them with his feet apart and his hands joined behind his back, unconsciously assuming his menacing stance that made even the worst of the offenders cower before him, and was gratified to see them look at him with fright and slink away hurriedly.

He smiled grimly to himself watching their hurrying backs and then unlatched the gate and walked through the garden to the veranda calling, 'Maushi, it's me, Pundlik.' Garden! Why had he thought of it as garden? For the last eighteen years there had been no garden; just a dusty, barren yard with patches of weeds and spiky nettles that were hard to dislodge once they got into one's clothing, and some old trees—mango, audumber, neem, tamarind, and a few coconuts swaying to the mild breeze—that had survived from Maushi's grandfather-in-law's time.

Maushi came out on to the front veranda just as Pundlik was climbing the steps to it.

'Pundlik! Come my Bhacha,' she said with a welcoming smile that Pundlik knew so well since his childhood, from ever since he could remember, and the way she always affectionately called him her bhacha—nephew—warmed his heart.

She wasn't really his maushi—mother's sister—in fact, he wasn't related to her at all, but in this land where every relationship is termed distinctly, 'maushi' is also a term of honour for all women. Children were taught from childhood to address all women as maushis unless of course they were atyas—father's sisters, or mamis—mother's brothers' wives. Even the grocers and vegetable vendors and fish-sellers in the market called out to women buyers shouting, 'O Maushi, here, come here, good bargain today.'

Pundlik bent down to touch Maushi's feet, and was, as always, suffused with deep filial feelings of affection and reverence for her. Though his family lived a couple of houses down the road, since childhood he had been far more attached to Maushi than to any of his aunts or even to his mother. It was to her that as a young boy he would come crying after a scuffle for turmeric and milk paste on his scraped knee and a sweetmeat to wipe out his tears. It was to her that he would come running with his school report card and stand proudly before her while she praised his marks and rewarded him with a laddoo. And it was to her steps that he had come carrying a sari bought with his first salary.

'Let the mother die but maushi should live,' so went an old adage. A maushi loved and pampered more than even a mother. All children learned at a very young age to go to their maushis for anything they wanted, whether it was one more laddoo or some new clothes or those particular toys that their mothers had always refused to buy for them. And maushis always fulfilled their expectations and more, and with love. 'Love like a maushi does,' was one of the first lessons taught to little girls.

And Maushi had lived up to that name. 'Maushi' to the whole village she was—always smiling, always helpful, always ready with a sweet, a story and a fond pat on the head for children, a sympathetic ear to the young girls' and boys' woes, and advice and practical help to any family in need. And in return she was loved, respected and honoured by the whole village. Respectful of elders, mindful of traditions and customs, she was held forth by all as a paragon of womanly virtues. The house would always throng with relatives and visitors—men in the front room, discussing and arguing; women in the inner room and later on, after Maushi had it opened out, on the back veranda, exchanging news and gossiping; and a multitude of children running around in the garden. And Maushi welcomed them all with a happy smile no matter however busy they kept her in the kitchen preparing her special snacks.

At least that's how it had been until eighteen years ago, Pundlik reminded himself. Eighteen years ago Anu, Maushi's daughter, had died of fever contracted in childbirth leaving a ten-day-old infant daughter behind and Maushi's husband, reverently called 'Baba' – father figure – by all, was bedridden with loss of muscular strength when a garden rodent bit him in the leg. Soon afterwards both her sons had left for big cities with their families—Gajanan for Belgaum and Vinayak for Mumbai—appalling the community at this dereliction of family duty. Maushi never complained, though now she had to bear the burden of making all the decisions and following them up for the household, of regularly checking the warehouses where the farm produce was stored, and also of bringing up her infant granddaughter all by herself. Her happy smile became rare now, mostly reserved only for her granddaughter. For some time there had been a strong wave of sympathy for Maushi in her misfortune with the whole community pitching in to help, but it had slowly waned as Meera—Maushi's granddaughter—started growing up into a wayward girl and scandals started shadowing this old and honoured family and as Maushi still steadfastly refused any help from the rest of the family in Meera's upbringing – calling it interference – with Baba silently acquiescing.

It was Baba's acquiescence that had shocked the community. It was a man's duty and responsibility to control his household and Baba had always been a strict adherent of proprieties except for the marriage of his daughter to a vilayati—a Western foreigner—something that the community had regarded with a mixed reaction of abhorrence and a begrudging pride. It was unthinkable that any decent family would marry their children out of the caste, leave aside out of the religion. And then to a vilayati? Absolutely not! Totally inconceivable! Especially a family like Baba's: of high-caste landowners, an old family, a leading family of North Goa, a family respected throughout the State. And the daughter—such a beauty! What a shame that she had been married to a vilayati! On the other hand, the vilayati was not only a white man but also an Englishman—belonging to the race of their past conquerors and rulers, one of those who had the power, the riches and the technology. They had seen highest of the high Hindus grovelling before an Englishman. Even now. After decades of independence! So it was but also a matter of pride for the villagers that one of them should want to marry the daughter of their landlord.

And now it was her daughter who was bringing shame on to the family name. Maushi, they said, pampered the motherless girl too much, but then Baba unquestioningly tolerating Maushi's indulgences? Tolerating Maushi allowing the young girl to disregard all Hindu traditions and customs? Tolerating Maushi letting her have her wishes and follow her whims without restraints, without propriety? Tolerating Maushi letting her mix with *Christians*, letting her make friends with *boys*, even allowing her to bring them to the house, and keep late hours? The community was too shocked. 'Poor man, what else can he do, bedridden as he is, dependent as he is on her ministrations,' they said and reduced their visits to the house to those required by absolute necessity. Now they crossed the road when passing the house and averted their eyes. Now no men came visiting Baba and then stayed for a meal. Now no women came to Maushi for advice and then stayed to gossip. And nobody came with any offers of help. The visitors' rooms on the upper floor remained empty. It was ostracism in practice; there was only the authoritarian, commanding presence of Baba, even if bedridden, and Maushi's powerful personality that demanded respect even in misfortune, and of course their status, that had deterred open declaration of it by the relatives and the villagers. Still, nowadays, Pundlik was the only frequent visitor to that huge and once crowded and noisy house now inhabited by only three of them: Baba, Maushi and Meera.

Now sitting opposite Maushi on the bench on the front veranda, he relaxed his tall, well-built frame, eased his rigid posture, took off his cap and wiped his face.

Maushi sat, as she always did, with her back resting against the wall, one leg folded and the other bent at knee and resting on the bench. 'Gauri, tea for my favourite bhacha,' she called to the cook inside the house but Pundlik put up a hand in refusal.

'I will just spend a few minutes with Baba and then I'll have to leave, Maushi,' he said.

Maushi looked at his tense face. 'You have come after a long time, Bhacha,' she said. 'What's the hurry?'

'Tourist season always brings problems, Maushi,' he said. 'Those hippies left a few legacies behind them when they were thrown out.'

'Hippies never bothered us,' Maushi said. 'They enjoyed their life in their own way. They kept to their beaches, never mixed with the locals, never interfered with us. And we never went to those beaches anyway. We hardly had any contact with them. Most of the time we were blissfully unaware of their existence.'

Except for Alec, Pundlik thought. He may not have been a hippie in the accepted sense but he had imbibed their set of values quite thoroughly. And combined them with his white man's contempt for those colonised.

'That's true,' he said. 'But they still instituted a way of life, a careless, irresponsible, immoral way, and a disregard for any values. Their sole aim in life was indolence. And indulging every whim of theirs. No discipline at all!' he added scornfully. Memory of Alec still rankled in his mind even after all these years. 'And the drugs that they introduced here! The hard ones may not be around much any more but marijuana is still commonly available on the beaches.'

But Maushi, though aware that this was the opinion of almost all the Hindus in Goa – 'subverters of the very foundations of our social order' as Baba had called the hippies when they had first started proliferating on Goan beaches and were tolerated by the seaside Christian communities – was still unperturbed.

'We have been drinking bhang for centuries now. Our sadhus use charas and ganja for meditation,' she said.

Before a shocked Pundlik could retort back, Meera—Maushi's granddaughter—burst out of the house like a whirlwind, as usual scattering restless energy and urgency upon everybody and everything nearby. 'Hello Pundlik Mama,' she said in greeting, briefly hugged her grandmother, announced she was running late and therefore would be back late, and ran out of the garden in the same whirlwind way, gathering surrounding vitality with her, leaving an emptiness behind her.

Pundlik looked at her back with a mixture of affection, pride, disapproval, and outright distaste. Anu's daughter. Such a bright and intelligent young girl. And so pretty too! But he strongly minded what he called her vilayati ways: her style of dressing, her greeting him with a hello instead of touching his feet, her habit of arguing with him instead of treating his word as sacrosanct – he being an elder, of her mother's generation. At one time he had tried to guide her upbringing assuming that Maushi would be more amenable to his rather than Baba's brothers' guidance but Maushi had told him too, politely yet curtly, to keep off Meera.

Now he looked with open disapproval at her jeans-clad backside and was suddenly reminded of another jeans-clad backside from eighteen years ago, exactly like Meera's, the same tall, slim, willowy figure, the same quick, graceful stride, the same long single plait of hair swinging on the back except that it had been jet black instead of light brown of Meera's. A fleeting glance over the shoulder, a startled gasp, and she had disappeared into the lanes of the bazaar near Calangute Beach while young Pundlik, a rookie policeman, had abandoned his beat and come running to Maushi in righteous indignation. 'Anu? On Calangute Beach?' Maushi had said with a smile, 'And in jeans?' and then had laughed outright on seeing the scandalised expression on Pundlik's face. 'You are so besotted with her, Bhacha, you see her everywhere,' she had admonished him. 'Stop this nonsense now.' And Pundlik had gone away chastened but not convinced.

'Why did they get her married to him?' he now asked of himself watching Meera's disappearing backside.

'Meera isn't married,' Maushi said with a smile.

Pundlik reddened and turned to look at the river. 'I was thinking of Meera's mother,' he said gruffly.

Maushi put her teacup down on the bench and looked at him speculatively. 'You used to ask that question a lot, eighteen years ago,' she said.

'Nobody answered,' Pundlik said still looking away.

'Then you stopped asking it.'

'Nobody answered,' he repeated stonily.

'What brought it back to your mind now?'

Pundlik turned and looked into Maushi's eyes. 'A lad came to Goa a couple of days ago,' he said holding Maushi's eyes. 'Ronald Harrington-Wells. Born in London, on 8 September 1983.'

Maushi stared at him for a moment, then turned her face away towards the river and sat watching its flow.

'It's a common name,' she said after a long while.

'Born on 8 September 1983?' Pundlik asked.

She then turned to face him. 'And how did you get to know that?' she snapped.

'I am a police inspector, Maushi. All foreigners have to register with the police.'

'And you study those hundreds of forms every day, do you Bhacha?' she asked with derision.

Pundlik was quiet for a while. 'I flagged his name,' he said at last. 'I have had it flagged for almost three years now, since he turned eighteen. I knew he would come one day. I knew he would come to Goa.'

4

For the next few weeks, Ronnie almost forgot everything else. He enthusiastically attached himself to Hilary's group. He swam, he sunned, he played ball on the sand with them. He went bungee jumping and wind surfing and water skiing with them. He went far out into the sea with them to watch the dolphins frolic. They zoomed all over the coast on their hired motorbikes, from cove to cove, from beach to beach, from dunes to dunes. Some evenings they loafed at one of the flea markets watching fire dancing, shopping for ethnic goods, guzzling beer, and listening to jazz and blues under a tree till early morning. Other evenings they bar-hopped, smoked and danced, explored hilltop restaurants and beach shacks for delicious food, went from one riverside café to another for coffee and desserts.

But every now and then that old black mood would come back over Ronnie. Then he would sit apart, alone on some rock, staring at the sea for hours at a time, staring with those eyes without any light in them, until Hilary could stand it no more. 'What's it Ronnie? What?' she asked him one day joining him on his perch high up on the rocks. 'Tell me.' But Ronnie didn't even hear her, just kept staring at the sea. Hilary watched him for a while, then held his face in both her hands, turned it towards her, and looked into his eyes, but all she saw reflected in them were the sea and the waves. 'Tell me,' she said.

'My mother died here,' he whispered at last.

Hilary stared at him dumbfounded.

'She was washed away while swimming at Baga Beach.'

'Eighteen years ago?' Hilary asked after a while.

Ronnie nodded, his eyes haunted.

'You were on holiday?'

Ronnie couldn't speak remembering Giles, his father's doctor and childhood friend, fuming at his father's funeral. 'I had been telling your father for years to take it easy. Since that first heart murmur of his eighteen years ago. I forced him to take a holiday then and so he went to Goa.'

'We all went, Dad, Mum and me.' Ronnie had reminded him.

'Elizabeth and you followed, after half a year or more.'

'Why?' Ronnie had asked in surprise. I never knew that, he thought, or that Dad had stayed so long over in Goa.

'Your father didn't want you there. He wrote that he had to recoup his spirit by himself. Learn to live, not exist. Plait the threads of his life. Just be.'

'That sounds almost hippie-like.' Ronnie had said unbelievingly.

'Yes. It frightened Elizabeth out of her mind. So she just picked you up and went there – that too in the midst of their monsoon.'

Ronnie, lost in his memories, stared at Hilary without seeing her. Hilary touched his cheek tenderly, brushed the hair off his forehead. 'You loved her very much?' she asked gently.

'I suppose so. I was too young. I hardly remember her,' he said thinking: except for all those photographs strewn all over the house. Wherever you looked, you saw Elizabeth. She was a constant reminder. But of what?

'You came to Goa only to visit your mother's grave, didn't you?' Hilary asked.

And also because he had thought that he would understand them a little better – his mother, his father, and their all-consuming love for each other that his father had tried to keep him away from. 'Also because my father didn't want me to come here,' he said again seeing his father's face before him, inches away from his own, contorted in anger, screaming, 'That place devours you. Why don't you understand?'

'He wanted me to promise him never to come to Goa and got quite unreasonably furious when I wouldn't,' he continued a little hesitantly, a little reluctantly, wanting to unburden himself but unable to talk openly to Hilary.

'Why did he do that?' Hilary asked in surprise.

'He was a strict disciplinarian,' Ronnie played it down.

But Hilary had no qualms about being blunt. 'He had a reputation of being an autocrat,' she said. 'They say he expected his word to be taken as Final Judgement.'

In spite of himself, Ronnie threw his head back and laughed. 'Yeah, he did decide for everybody what he thought would be best for them,' he agreed. Then he looked at her. 'And you know what? He was genuinely astonished to find that they wanted something else.' Me, for instance, he thought lapsing back into melancholy.

'You have to come to terms with it Ronnie. You have to get it out of your system.' Hilary said.

So much to come to terms with: a rigidly strict and contradictory father, an unknown mother, her untimely death, questions that went unanswered, questions that he couldn't ask.

'From childhood I had decided I will come here to Baga, to the place where my mother was lost, and pay my respects to her memory,' he said. All these years he had been obsessed with a vision of himself standing on the Baga Beach and saying, 'I remember you, Mum, I remember you still,' but the image of the seashore in his mind had been that of a cold, drab and treeless English seashore lit by pale sunshine; not this deep azure boiling sea, this shimmering air, this bright golden sunlight, and this lush green land where emotions rose to the surface. 'But now that I am here...,' he trailed off looking at the sea again, dreading it, feeling unsure of himself when faced with the watery grave of his mother.

'You will come?' he appealed to her.

'I will come,' she said.

Hilary stood waist deep in the sea off Baga Beach holding a reed basket full of flowers at her waist while Ronnie scattered them to the waves murmuring, 'I love you Mum, I love you still.'

Later they sat on the beach watching the oncoming and then receding waves that had taken his mother away.

'I was jealous of her also you know,' Ronnie suddenly said. 'My father loved her so much, so very much, that I had no place left in his life. Because of her. She occupied it all.'

'He talked of her all the time?'

'He didn't talk of her at all.' Talk to me Dad, tell me Dad, six-year-old Ronnie had pleaded with his father, tell me about my mother. But Dad never did.

'Except in the last minute before his death,' he said with that indelible image before his eyes—his father on his deathbed grasping Ronnie's hand, but looking through Ronnie somewhere far, far away, beyond the horizon. 'I loved her so much,' he had said with his last breath, 'I really loved her.'

'He just loved her too much, I suppose,' Ronnie said turning away from Hilary, watching the ocean.

'It's quite a love story, Ronnie.'

'He lost interest in everything after my mother's death, except in his career. He wanted to reach the top and he did. He was knighted.'

But knighthood had not brought happiness to his father. Ronnie had come across him the same evening sitting in a chair in his study staring out of the window with such terrible dejection on his face that Ronnie had not dared approach him.

'Is that why he never married again?' Hilary asked.

Ronnie had asked the same question of Giles after his father's death. 'Your father became impotent after coming back from Goa.' Giles had told him. 'We tried every known treatment. Nothing worked.'

It explained so much. Ronnie, as a four-year-old, remembered the night his father was escorting a baroness to a formal ball and was woken up later in the night by the loud slam of the front door. Creeping on to the upstairs balcony he saw his father enter the hallway alone, tug off his bow tie, bunch it into a ball and hurl it across the hall with all his strength. Never again did he go to any social function or ball – he, who according to Giles was a very good dancer, who enjoyed such evenings, was always seen leading well-dressed beautiful women on to the floor and murmuring in their ears to make them blush and smile – only to his club to keep up with the old boys' network. He also became much more aggressive in the court and much more short-tempered and strict with Ronnie. And Ronnie, who had always remembered his father as a dry, prim and prudish, strict, stiff-lipped Englishman, found it almost impossible to fit him to the portrait of a romantic charming dreamer who had once followed hippie philosophy, who had once enjoyed socialising and a good life, and who had once basked in the adulation that was showered on him at all those high-flown parties, that Giles described after his death.

Was it his mother's death that had brought this change in his father as everybody said? Was his love for her so strong that her death would make him a totally different person? 'I loved her so much, I really loved her'—a deathbed confession. A closed circle. Just his father and the woman he loved. His mother. What was she like, his mother? From childhood he had been trying to form a picture of hers pieced together from what Giles and others had told him, but the picture had refused to come real for him. It was always overshadowed by the figure of his father.

Ronnie hugged his knees and buried his face in his arms. Everything about his father had been awesome: his career, his reputation, his obsessive strictness, his temper, his love for his woman, and his rigid notions as to what his son should do and should be like. Ronnie had always had to battle him for his independence, for his identity, and now that he was gone, Ronnie suddenly realised that he was feeling lost and rudderless. I have to find myself; I have spent most of my life in fruitless rebellion without defining my real interests, my goals, my ultimate aims. I have to learn to let go of my father, of my mother, he said to himself and shuddered involuntarily, a shudder that turned into uncontrollable shivers and trembles. Hilary put her arms around his shaking shoulders and bent her head to his, murmuring soothingly. After a long time Ronnie quietened, looked up at Hilary with his eyes still puffed and smiled with the relief that comes after catharsis, that is felt after exorcism, the relief at having shared a pain. Hilary smiled back.

Then the guitars could be heard, candles were lit on the tables in beach cafés, crowds were gathering, joints were making rounds, and Ronnie and Hilary got up and scampered over to where the action was and danced and smoked and danced and smoked and danced, wildly, madly. In the early hours of morning, Hilary led him to a sandy depression under an overhanging rock and there they slept with their arms and legs wound tightly around each other.

Captain Rollo's Bar and Restaurant was a popular night place with the Indian tourists as well as with foreigners. Located right on the beach, it had a gurgling fountain in the middle of a luxuriantly planted courtyard with colourful plants separating the dining tables, a tiled dance floor, a large veranda, and a carved timber balcony at the upper floor level from where one could watch the dancers below as well as the dark ocean, the white-tipped waves and the silver beach. During the tourist season a six-piece band played under the eaves, a husky singer belted out popular romantic songs, and the dancers danced till early morning.

It was already bursting at the seams when Ronnie and Hilary appeared at a late hour. Manuel, the headwaiter, smiled at Hilary and laid a tiny table especially for them on the overcrowded balcony close to a group of young Indians with children. The band was playing in full swing overriding the noisy talk and laughter, dancers were spinning around the fountain on the brightly tiled floor, and waiters with full trays held high above their heads were rushing in between the tables with great dexterity.

Hilary squeezed in opposite Ronnie, next to one of the Indian men; there was hardly any space between their tables. Manuel plopped a bottle of Goan red wine and two glasses on their table without asking, smiled again at Hilary, and then disappeared in the crowd.

'Here's to Goa,' Hilary said clinking her glass with Ronnie's and eyeing the passing dishes. 'That green curry looks enticing.'

'You must try the kababs,' the young man sitting next to Ronnie at the adjoining table said picking up a plate and thrusting it at Hilary. 'Here, try this. Try it, try it.'

'No, no,' Ronnie protested and Hilary shook her head but he only pushed the plate further at Hilary. 'It's very good,' he said waving it under her nose. 'Take it, take it.'

Hilary took a piece of roasted spicy chicken. 'It's delicious,' she exclaimed smacking her lips and turned to the young man. 'Thank you. It's really tasty.'

Soon they had joined the tables eliminating the tiny gap in between and were sitting together. 'I am Raman and this is Ashok,' the man with the kabab plate said chomping noisily. 'We have come from north, near Delhi. On a week's holiday.' Raman was gregarious and talkative. Ashok sat silently next to Hilary with a silly smile on his face. They both were drinking whiskey.

'Here, have some tandoori fish, here, try it, try it, it's roasted on coals,' Raman insisted forcing another plate on Hilary. 'Ashok pass on those fried prawns. What are you drinking? Wine? That wine is for women, *our* women. Have some whiskey. I will get you some whiskey.' He raised his hand and clicked his fingers at a waiter.

'We are fine,' Ronnie said quickly. He looked at the noisy brats at the end of the table. 'Your children?' he asked.

'Those two are mine. That one is Ashok's.'

'Your wives?' Hilary asked.

Raman nodded. 'This is Kalpana, my wife. And that's Nisha, Ashok's wife,' he said without looking at them, gesturing dismissively at them. Nisha wore slacks and a tee shirt. Kalpana was in salwar-kameez. Neither greeted them but both looked at Hilary from under their eyelashes with suspicion and distrust. 'You are Americans?' Raman asked and continued without waiting for an answer. 'You are students? Your fathers must be very rich to have sent you here on a holiday. What car do you have? Do you live in New York? Kalpana's brother lives in New Jersey—mind the children, Kalpana,' he shouted as the table rocked.

'We should go. It's getting late for them,' Kalpana said trying to hold a struggling, wailing youngster. Neither of the men paid her any attention.

'Want to go swimming tomorrow?' Raman asked looking at Hilary. Raman did all the talking. Ashok sat quietly drinking his whiskey with that silly smile glued to his face, his hand never leaving the glass. 'There is a good pool in our hotel. Or we can go to that beach near Chapora Fort. You can go a long way into the sea there.'

'What about the children?' Ronnie asked eyeing the toddlers.

'Kalpana will look after them. She doesn't swim.' Raman said offhandedly, then turned to look at her and Nisha giggling together. 'What's going on there?' he demanded and then looked beyond them and frowned furiously. 'Why is that man looking at you?' He indicated someone sitting a couple of tables away with his chin.

'What can she do about it?' Ronnie asked with a smile noticing Kalpana's fallen face.

'Behave herself,' Raman said. 'Afterwards we could go to that floating casino on the Mandovi River again,' he continued with his invitations as both wives subsided back into silence. 'We had gone there last night. I won a thousand bucks. Ashok lost a few hundred.' Ashok's smile broadened. 'We didn't get back till early this morning.'

'You had said you will be back for dinner,' Kalpana said in an aggrieved tone. 'Nisha and I waited all night long without any food.'

'So?' Raman asked belligerently looking at her. She averted her eyes and busied herself with the children.

'Why did you wait so long?' Hilary asked Kalpana but she didn't look up.

'She is a Hindu wife.' Raman answered for her. 'A Hindu wife will wait forever for her husband if she has to.'

'Forever? Forever is a very long period,' Ronnie said with a grin.

'Tell them about the woman by the railway tracks, Ashok.'

Ashok drank some more whiskey and then turned to them keeping a hold on his glass and with that same silly smile still on his face. 'There is this old woman in our town. The townspeople tell that her husband left her, just got on a train and went away, forty years ago when he was thirty years old. She moved to this house by the railway tracks to wait for him, supporting herself by cleaning other people's houses. She waited and waited for him to come back and he did come back recently, when he was seventy, old and ailing.'

'What did she do?' Ronnie asked leaning forward, interested.

'What else? Fell at his feet, washed the dirt off him, cooked him a meal.' Ashok finished the story and turned back to his drink.

'Is he still there with her?'

'He is sick and he is old; where can he go? He needs her to look after him. Now she has to work double in other people's houses to earn enough to feed him also.'

'She is very much venerated in our town as a true pativrata,' Raman said and then added on seeing blank looks on Ronnie and Hilary's faces, 'A woman who is totally devoted to her husband.' Both he and Ashok nodded their heads in reverence and admiration. They were all silent for a while contemplating the story.

Ronnie turned to listen to the band that was playing a tune vaguely familiar to him but the singer was singing a Hindi song by popular request. Ashok had relinquished his glass and both his hands were under the table. With his smile still on and with his eyes half-closed, he was leaning forward and swaying his head in an enchanted manner, humming with the singer.

'Zarasa zoom loo main,
zarasa choom loo main,'

'What is he singing?' Ronnie asked Raman.

'Let me get a little high, let me steal a little kiss...'

'Hey!' Hilary exclaimed suddenly in indignant surprise looking into her lap and slapped both her hands down on her thigh with her talons extended.

'What?' Ronnie asked looking at her.

But Hilary did not answer. She just sat there with both her hands in her lap and a beatific smile on her face while next to her Ashok had retrieved one of his hands and was cooling the back of it on his whiskey glass and glaring at Hilary. He had lost his smile.

'What?' Ronnie asked again looking from one to another, his eyebrows raised. Ashok abruptly stood up. 'Let's dance,' he said to Nisha and walked away quickly.

Nisha, who was just picking up a piece of kabab, looked up, put the kabab back on the plate, and followed obediently. They squeezed their way through the tables and went down the stairs.

'Come on, let's dance,' Raman said to Hilary. He came round the table, pulled her up by arm, and walked her away leaving Ronnie and Kalpana at the table. Kalpana busied herself with feeding the children. Ronnie watched her for a while.

'Want to dance?' he asked after some time.

'My husband won't like me dancing with another man,' she answered concentrating on cutting the meat into bite-size pieces.

'But *he* is dancing!' Ronnie said.

She looked at him then. 'He is a man,' she said reproachfully and turned away again to separate two of the kids fighting over one piece of meat. Suddenly she turned back to him again. 'Don't you mind your girlfriend dancing with another man?' she asked.

Ronnie was taken aback. 'Hilary can take care of herself,' he said shortly and turned to watch the dancers.

There was quite a melee down there and it was some time before he could locate Hilary and Raman. 'What the heck!' he exclaimed as he saw them at last, Raman coming strong all over Hilary, groping and feeling her. 'Why the heck doesn't she move away?' he said jumping up but Hilary was intent on watching a waiter wend his way through the dancers balancing a tray full of wine glasses on his palm held high over his head. She timed her move perfectly. She was already out of the dancing crowd when the waiter, whom she had elbowed in the back as she had passed him, collided with Raman drenching him with the cascading wine.

'Attagirl, that was cool!' Ronnie said and laughed as he skipped down the stairs. 'Let's split,' he said grabbing Hilary by hand and pulling her away, both of them still laughing. Raman, his face as red as the wine, was cursing and screaming and prodding the waiter in the chest with his index finger. The waiter had both his hands on his hips, his jaws clenched and his face thrust into Raman's. Soon they would come to blows and the waiter would dunk Raman into the fountain. When Ronnie and Hilary, still laughing, passed Manuel, the headwaiter, he was studiously busy arranging and rearranging six prawns on a serving plate and didn't look up.

'I took a term off to travel,' Hilary said. 'I had planned to stay here for two weeks, then go on to Malaysia, Indonesia, Japan. That was two months ago and I am still here!' she laughed.

She and Ronnie were sitting with another English group under a large rain tree on Calangute Beach drinking beer. The composition of their group had changed considerably in the last couple of weeks. It had been alternately growing and shrinking as people came and went; nobody was here on a very long-term basis.

The rave had been going on for three days when the north-easterner joined their group that day. 'Hey Jimmy,' someone said kicking out a chair for him.

'The rave is being relocated to Anjuna today,' he informed them standing near their table. 'The cops closed it at Vagator yesterday.' They nodded. 'You will be joining it there?' he asked. They nodded again. 'You need sustenance then!' Sitting down he opened his cloth bag. 'You will be joining it today?' he asked laying out packets of pills and balls of marijuana. 'It may have to move again.'

Ronnie had never been to a rave before but Hilary was quite excited.

'Ecstasy, you have Ecstasy?'

'What is a rave without Ecstasy!'

Ronnie and Hilary joined a mass of people dancing in the coconut grove on the hill above the beach at Anjuna. In the purple sky the moon was a huge round disc of gold and the rippling waves were studded with bits of it shining like scattered diamonds. Over the palms the air was pulsating like a sheet of silk. Strums of guitars floated on it like streamers, beats of drums punched holes in it. Under the palms hundreds of youngsters swayed to the loud, mesmerising music interspersed once in a while by an insistent singer. 'Don't be fooled by the rocks I got,' roared the singer bending over the microphone and swirling, 'I am still Jenny...' he stopped, waiting. 'Jenny from the block,' the crowd exploded in answer jumping and swirling. Non-stop waves, non-stop music, non-stop dancing. Collective frenzy, collective madness, collective trance. 'Jenny from the block,' Ronnie screamed jumping high up in the air as he and Hilary exuberantly joined in the mad dancing.

A long time after when the little pieces of moon had moved a long way across the waves, exhausted Ronnie and Hilary stumbled down to the beach supporting each other, the madness still on them, the music still playing in their heads, their feet still dancing in the sand, and then flopped into the shallow waters. Silky sand cushioned their bodies; warm ocean licked them with little white-tipped waves. 'Let's just spend the rest of our lives here, hey Hils?' Ronnie said.

Hilary laughed. There was a tinkle in her laughter and a silvery tinge to her blonde hair. They slept under the palms secure in the knowledge that the sea, the waves, the music, the dancing, and the magic will still be there when they wake up.

After three days of dancing, sleeping, and dancing again, they decided to chill out on the rocks of Anjuna for a day. Far from the madding crowd, they lay on the high pile of rocks that stretched all the way to the Ozran Beach, the rocks that the waves had been battling constantly from time immemorial. Coming all the way from Arabia, undulating all the way, they sensed the barrier of rocks as they neared the shore and collecting speed and force surged ahead with huge curling foamy crowns to ram the rocks sending delicate lacy plumes metres high up in the air. Ronnie and Hilary lay beneath the undulating lacy curtain getting drenched once in a while but feeling too lethargic to move, each engrossed in his and her thoughts.

They felt sated with the sun, the sea and the sand. Both were coming to the conclusion that it was time to move on.

'Hils,' Ronnie said watching the waves.

'Ummm,' she mumbled drowsily snuggling against him.

'What are you planning Hils?'

Hilary sat up. 'I may travel around Asia a little—Malaysia, Japan—before I rejoin LSE,' she said pushing her damp hair out of her eye. 'We could travel together,' she offered tentatively.

'I hadn't planned anything beyond Goa. I will leave it like that,' Ronnie said. 'I want more time here, not on the beaches though; I want to see the interior. The hills, the rivers, the jungles... did you know that a third of Goa is forests? And then go back to London.'

'Back to LSE?'

Ronnie shook his head remembering the incredulous expression on his father's face as he had asked, 'Want to leave the London School of Economics?' and then he brusquely said, 'Nonsense!' that had closed the issue. 'Yes Dad, I do want to leave it,' Ronnie now said to himself. 'In fact, I have already left it.'

'I think I would like to study nature,' he said to Hilary watching a solitary sandpiper whirling overhead vibrating its wings, whistling its high-pitched song, searching for a stretch of sand to land on. 'Probably join the environmental studies, the ecology course at the University of London.'

'We have a relationship happening, Ronnie.' She was bending over him, her eyes searching his face, her expression questioning. 'Give it a chance.' Her face was barely a foot above his.

Relationship? A few weeks together in Goa didn't make for a relationship. He liked her, he cared for her, he would like to remain friends with her, but a few weeks together in Goa were just that. Soon they both will be going their own separate ways. 'Hey, hey,

Hils,' he said. 'Don't be so serious.' A wave broke over them washing over both their faces. Turning lazily on his side, Ronnie sat up. Looking down at Hilary, he traced the line of her cheek with his index finger and smiled at her. 'Let's give ourselves some time. Let's leave it till we meet in London, okay?' he said.

She looked at him for a long moment and then smiled back – a slow, small, sad smile. 'Perhaps Ronnie, perhaps,' she said. 'I am not one to wait forever like these Indian women.' She rose and stood watching him for a while and then walked a little way before stopping and turning to face him with decision. 'Hey, it has been great, hey Ronnie?' she said quietly but with determination. 'But I had better call it a day before I get too involved. Right now I can handle it.'

'Hey Hils, wait a sec,' Ronnie protested but she cut him short. 'I am a big girl, Ronnie, and you are right, we need some time apart. I will see you around.' She smiled again and gave him a little wave of her hand. 'Friends, okay?' she said and walked away.

Ronnie nodded in response. That's how it was. He was sorry to see her go like that; she had been a good friend and they had had some fun these last few weeks, but he just wasn't ready to make any long-term commitments. He felt too young. He had just got out from under his father's yoke and he had much to experience as yet – *they* had much to experience as yet: Japan and Malaysia for her, jungles and rivers of Goa for him. I will catch up with her in London, he thought.

He watched her walk away for a while, her figure receding, diminishing, and then turned to watch the roaring waves come crashing on the rocks, to marvel at their unending ferocity. It's such a hypnotic movement, he thought, they never give up, do they! Just then another lacy curtain rose before him and came cascading down drenching him again and Ronnie decided to leave this scene of perpetual battle between the rocks and the sea. Standing up he looked with fascination as a wave humped itself up curling its crown for a ramming attack, and sprang away on another rock as it came rushing in. Leaping from rock to rock at last he reached the last of them, jumped down on to the sand, and ran towards the gentler waves watching a flock of sandpipers skimming them. That lost and lonely sandpiper must have been searching for them, he thought. Each to his own.

Then he saw the girl rising out of the sea—tall, slim and willowy, glowing olive skin, long brown hair. There was grace of the waves in her movements and sparkle of the sun in her smile and magic of this land in her eyes – eyes that made you forget the rest of the world. The roar and crash of waves echoed in his head.

5

'How much does Meera know?' Pundlik asked sitting on the front veranda of Maushi's house where he always sat with her, sipping a cup of tea that Gauri always brought him as soon as he arrived.

Maushi looked at the dead grass, at the dried weeds in her garden. You have been asking me that same question all these years, you and Gajanan, both of you, she thought, so terribly worried as to what Meera will find out. 'That her mother died of fever ten days after her birth, that her father was an Englishman settled in Canada, that he went back right after her mother's death, that Baba had her last name changed to ours,' she repeated what she had been telling him for years.

'Does she know her father's name, his profession?'

'The whole village knows that!' Maushi said crossly.

'And how much more?' he persisted.

'Only what the family knows,' she said. What a question! she thought. How can I tell her anything more than what the rest of the family knows? At least until I tell her all the rest of it also?

'Didn't she ask to see his photographs?'

'You know there aren't any. Gajanan burnt the whole lot after Anu's death.' Except for the ones I hid under the sack of rice in the storeroom. You can't burn memories. And some day Meera has to be told.

'Didn't she ask why her father didn't take her to Canada?'

How much do you load a child's psyche with? Maushi was aware that as a child Meera had felt that her mother had willfully deserted her – how close she had been to the truth! – and was quite inordinately angry with her. How do you tell that child that her father too didn't want her?

'But surely Meera has not been satisfied with just that bit of information.'

No, of course not! Maushi remembered the days and weeks and months that Meera as a young girl had spent with her, with Vinayak, and with Vinayak's wife, asking, asking, asking and absorbing every detail of her mother's life and her father's brief sojourn with them. The two people she did not ask anything were Gajanan and Pundlik once she had noted their antagonism towards her father and their reluctance to talk about her mother.

'She cried when she fell out of the guava tree?' a six-year-old Meera had asked Vinayak with wonder. 'I don't cry when I fall down, do I, Vinayak Mama?'

No, Meera did not cry. Neither when she fell down nor when something went wrong with her plans and expectations. Just thought of another way to deal with the problem: of bandaging a knee and going back to play, of other alternatives. And only Maushi knew what a hard, uphill struggle it had been to instill that attitude in her, to imbue her with pride and confidence in herself with the whole family ranged against her.

She giggled when Vinayak's wife described how her father would follow Baba and Gajanan in the morning ritual of circumambulating the stone God Ganesha under the audumber tree wearing a dhoti and how he kept tripping on its pleats until Gajanan, in a fit of fury, had tucked it up high for him, the way working class men do. She listened with rapt attention when Vinayak's wife told her of the great love between her father and her mother and though like everybody else she too believed that Meera's father must have married again – after all a man needs a wife to take care of him – nobody mentioned it to Meera.

But the stories that interested Meera most were the ones of the days when she too was part of them, stories of their life together with her, and that was one area no one could tell her much about – in fact, there wasn't much to tell. Her mother had been around for only ten days after her birth, her father less than a month. 'Your father was staying in Panaji when you were born, pursuing his passport formalities,' Vinayak's wife told her. 'But he would come every evening to hold you, to spend time with you. Until your mother's death. He came only once after that – for her last rites on the thirteenth day of her death, just before he left Goa.'

Maushi would not talk of her father at all though she often told her about how much her mother had loved her. 'From the time you were born, she didn't let you out of her sight even for a moment. She held you to her heart all the time. Till the day of her death.'

'Tell me about that day, Aaji.' Meera had asked Maushi again and again cuddling against her and had cried with her every time.

That was a day Pundlik also would never forget. Though he lived just a short distance down the road, it was mid-morning when he got the news of Anu's death at dawn. Running to her house as fast as he could, stopping at the door to the back veranda, hanging on to the door frame, he saw that the women of the house had already bathed and washed their hair.

'She was already gone when we were woken up at dawn,' Vinayak's wife told him in between sobs, pulling her pallav—the loose end of her sari—and dabbing at her eyes with it, eyes that were already turning red with weeping. 'She suffered this high fever in the middle of the night. Aai poured a bucket of water over her but it was of no use. When we woke up, Aai was sitting holding her head in her lap and Baba and Gajanan-bhaoji were talking with Mahesh-bhaoji – Baba's doctor nephew. She had been sickly since the birth of her child.'

Pundlik had hung on to the door frame and just stared at her, totally unable to speak.

'And Alec is still in Panaji, getting his passport endorsed. They were to leave for Canada as soon as the baby was six weeks old.'

Running, gasping for breath and stumbling, but still running to the river ghat, past the compound where the holy cows were kept, past the burial ground where they buried infants, pregnant women, and those who had unnatural deaths, arriving at last at the cremation ghat, he saw from a distance that the funeral pyre was burning with full force and then breathlessly collapsed on the ground.

On the thirteenth day of Anu's death, right after the thirteenth day rites and meal were over, Baba went down with high fever. A wild rodent, one of the types that frequented the garden in the monsoons since it was so heavily planted, had bit him while he was in the garden, he said. He flabbergasted everybody by his unexplainable fury at his sickness, refused to let them get any doctor for him, would not let even Mahesh—his doctor nephew—come near him leave aside examine or medicate him. He lay in his bed glowering at them all, particularly at Maushi, as if about to blow up and controlling himself with great effort. He lost his temper on everybody in the house on small insignificant things, even throwing his cup across the room if there was more or less sugar in tea than what he liked.

After seven days, his fever abated leaving him too weak in the legs to walk but he still made Datta and Bhiku—the house servants—carry him to the front veranda and install him on a string bed there. Half lying, partly propped up on pillows, he made the three labourers, that he had especially asked Datta to get for the day, pull out every shrub, every plant, even those rare beautiful flowering plants that Maushi had cultivated with love, including even the blades of grass, and cut down and uproot every tree from the front garden in front of his eyes. Making them carry him to the back veranda and the side gardens, and even on the veranda running on all four sides of the internal courtyard, he had the same process repeated until only the trees planted by his grandfather—the audumber, the mango, the neem, the tamarind, the jackfruit and the few coconuts—and the holy basil in the internal courtyard were left standing in what had been a magnificent flower garden of Maushi's. Even Maushi's herb garden at the rear had not escaped the onslaught. Then he had the well filled up. 'He was right of course,' people said rueing the flowers and the herbs. 'Those rodents could bite others also.'

Maushi did not plant anything ever again.

It did not end with the garden though. Baba had the whole house cleaned out, not only the shelves and cupboards, but all the trunks and cloth bundles also had to be opened, all the saris and clothes unfolded for his inspection. 'It is almost like Diwali cleaning,' Gauri the cook said as she sat replacing tops of all the tins and boxes and bottles that she had had to open for Baba's inspection.

'Diwali cleaning, huh?' Gajanan's wife said in a cross tone, though she had not dared to refuse Baba. 'He made me unfold all the baby's nappies. As if a rodent could be hiding in them!'

One month afterwards Gajanan and Vinayak, both of Maushi's sons, suddenly announced their decision to leave the village, to leave the family house and farm, and to move to the big cities. Neither gave a very convincing reason for the move and no amount of counselling or cajoling by Baba's brothers and uncles could make them change their minds. 'Big city has advantages that this village can't provide,' was the only argument either would give. 'And what about the house, the farm, your father who is bedridden for the time being? Who will look after them all?' the elders asked.

'Especially the farm,' the elders said. 'Who will control the overseers, the foremen, keep a personal check on them, on the produce? Who will make rounds of the farm every day as Baba used to? Who will deal with the buying agents? Unlike other families with tenant farmers, in our family we ourselves look after our farms. You stand to lose the farms if you leave as you are doing,' they warned but nothing, absolutely nothing would make the sons stay. And soon afterwards, first one son and then the other collected and packed whatever they wanted to carry with them and left with their families. Throughout the days that the arguments, reprimands and pleadings from the elders for them to stay back went on, Baba did not utter a word of restraint to them, only glared with barely controlled fury and reproach at Maushi once and then kept totally silent. For the next eighteen years they visited the village only thrice a year – for Holi, for the Ganesha festival, and for Diwali.

Visitors crowded the house every day to sit with Baba, to keep him company, to keep him informed of village affairs, of farm problems, and to comfort him, to commiserate with him. Women came to spend their every spare hour to help in the running of the house since Maushi spent all her time looking after infant Meera, not letting any other woman – even a close relative – help in caring for her. Meera was beginning to focus her eyes and gave her first smile to Maushi the day her eyes focused on Maushi's face. Maushi's tears ran down her cheeks on to the chubby pink ones of Meera's.

'He will be back on his feet in no time at all,' visitors consoled Maushi on their way out after visiting Baba; but in time it was clear that Baba would never be on his feet again.

A few months after Baba's fever, after Gajanan and Vinayak had left for big cities, when it had become clear that Baba's infirmity was permanent and Maushi had in fact taken over the duties of the head of the household and had started making all the decisions for the house and was also helping Baba in dealing with the farm overseers, Baba's brothers visited him, all together, accompanied by his lawyer nephew Siddharth: a family council held at Baba's bedside.

They pointed out to him that since his handicap prevented him from looking after the farm properly, how the foremen and overseers were cheating him, and how the women were apt to run wild if the running of the household was left only to them without a check by the menfolk; even Maushi they said, 'She is a woman after all and to be trusted with so much responsibility...,' though reaffirming the great respect they had for her otherwise. They offered to take over the supervision of his household and administration of his farm – jointly of course – and got quite agitated when Baba firmly refused both offers. 'But the loss you are incurring could be avoided,' they argued. 'The loss is to be expected,' Baba replied.

Very much aware that though Meera's welfare was the first priority for Maushi, Baba also knew that as long as that was not interfered with, he could depend on her to take proper care of him, of the house, of the land, and of the interests of the family. He had always asked for her advice in private. Then one day he found himself calling her to his room to discuss the farm problems when the overseers were there and thereafter their joint discussions had become a routine. He still ruled from his wheelchair and yet, in many ways, after the initial hesitation and the frustration at its unavoidability and the shame of it had passed, he was greatly relieved at Maushi taking open interest in the farm—at her making the rounds of the store houses around the main house though of course not of the farms as her going out of the compound was just unthinkable—as long as she followed his orders. He could trust her implicitly to protect her sons' interests just as he had trusted her ministrations in his sickness. And it certainly was not his brothers' place to suggest that they meddle in his household.

'And you have no objection to a woman, even of Maushi's stature, dealing with those menials?' Siddharth, his lawyer nephew, asked and Baba glared at him until he hung his head in shame at having questioned an elder. Siddharth got so worked up about Maushi running the household by herself and taking an active interest in the farm that he even wrote to Gajanan to prevail on his father but to no effect. There was nothing anybody could do as the land had been subdivided amongst them nor could they say anything to Maushi; none of her decisions or actions in any matter at all could be questioned by anybody other than Baba while he was alive, incapacitated or not. She was safe behind her kumkum and her mangalsutra.

But neither did they accept the decision graciously.

The family breach widened into a chasm as Meera started growing up. Even her name, Meera, they found outlandish. 'What kind of a name is this for a Goan Hindu girl?' they said.

'It's an old Hindu name,' Maushi answered.

'Yes, yes,' they said, 'but it's not common in Goa. And don't forget that that Meera-bai in history was thrown out of the house by her family and was ostracised by the whole society!'

'And yet today everybody, even the priests, sing her bhajans in all the temples,' Maushi retorted.

Meera's upbringing was a major point of contention in the family. Surprised that the infant was still kicking in her cradle after Anu's death and Alec's departure, they had offered to take her off Baba's hands. 'We will take the responsibility since you are sick,' they had proposed, and were highly offended when Maushi had stared furiously at them with her lips clamped shut and Baba also had kept silent, and had not allowed their womenfolk to attend Meera's naming ceremony. Even after it was clear that the infant would survive, Maushi had refused all family offers of help in her care. For the first few years of Meera's life, Maushi had not let her out of her sight even for a moment nor had she allowed anybody to get within five feet of her. Whether Meera was sleeping in her cradle or crawling on the back veranda, Maushi would be there right next to her. If Maushi was attending to any household duties or discussing farm matters with the overseers, she carried Meera in the crook of her arm or on her hip. Or locked her in her room if she were sleeping. She had relaxed a little after she had forced Gajanan to leave the house but it still took her a long time to lower her guard totally.

She also overrode everybody in the matter of bringing up a girl child, especially Meera, who everybody felt should have been made aware of her low position in the family and taught to behave accordingly right from her childhood. Firstly, she was the daughter's daughter. Her place was in her father's house, not with her maternal grandparents. She was living here with them under duress, they stressed. Secondly, she was an abhagan—an ill-fated girl—who had killed her mother within ten days of her birth. She had to be made conscious of her shame and taught to live within more limits and with more restrictions than those normally imposed on girls, they felt. None dared to advise Maushi directly and their subtle hints not only went totally unheeded by Maushi, but she, on the contrary, was giving Meera the latitudes denied even to the boys in the family, giving her the freedom to do whatever she wanted, good or bad, right or wrong, clean or dirty.

'That wretch prefers to play with mud rather than her dolls like other girls,' one of Meera's aunts muttered on seeing the little girl sitting in the dusty backyard reaching for some nearby mud, and then, 'No, no, no! Get up, get up from there!' she shrieked.

The two-and-a-half-year-old shot up instantly on her chubby legs but her mouth was clamped tight and there was resentment welling in her eyes. Maushi went and squatted before her. 'Do you know why Mami said not to play with the mud?' she asked.

Meera thought about it. 'It's dirty,' she said.

'So what will it do to you if you play with it?'

'Make me dirty.'

'And what can you do when you get dirty?'

'Wash it off.'

'Wash it off,' Maushi agreed. 'So decide: whether you want to play in the mud now and wash it off later or come inside now and stay clean.'

Meera considered it, crinkling her forehead, tilting her head on to one side, and then sat down in the mud with a thump, a big grin lighting her face as Maushi smiled at her and her aunt glowered at her not daring to override Maushi.

And so it had been—the relentless training since even before Meera could walk or talk. Think, think, think. Don't say I don't know; find out; ask why. And then decide. Do exactly what you want to do.

By the age of six, Meera had learned to hold her own against the family, to fight for what she considered were her rights, and more importantly, not to curb her natural tendencies and to laugh and enjoy life.

And then Maushi had her enrolled in an English-medium school instead of a Marathi-medium school. That had created a furore in the family requiring another family council to be called by Baba's bedside. 'An English school! *And* it's a mixed school!' his brothers said appalled. 'What's more, most of the students there are *Christians*!' they added absolutely aghast at the thought of it. But Baba supported Maushi's decision. 'She must know her father's language,' he said tight-lipped and refused to discuss it any further though inwardly agreeing with his brothers, smouldering at his helplessness to control Maushi in Meera's upbringing.

Not that his answer came as a surprise to the family. For a long time now they all had become aware that as far as anything to do with Meera was concerned, Baba neither opposed Maushi's decisions nor did he ever question them. It was as if he knew what drove Maushi and kept clear of that one particular issue, though his word was supreme in everything else regarding the whole family including his brothers' families. As the eldest male of the family, all family decisions had to be cleared with him.

Nor did Maushi seem to inculcate any feminine decorum or values in Meera. If Meera didn't want to play 'house–house' or 'kavadis' or even 'hopscotch' with her girl cousins but instead preferred playing ball with her school friends, Maushi made no effort to dissuade her. She even got Vinayak to send her a bicycle from Mumbai which Meera rode up and down the road with her pigtails flying, watched jealously by her house-bound girl cousins, and in horror by her uncles and aunts. She gamboled along the riverbank with her friends, clambered up the trees, played gilli-danda —a rustic form of cricket—on the road, and Maushi let her do it all without blinking.

Even the way Meera moved, walked, ran, or just stood about, had an air of pride, confidence and abandon – she walks as if she owns the village, they said. Not the way other girls sat and stood and ran – constricting their bodies and restraining their movements. Her gestures were too open-armed. To the family she seemed to be running totally wild with neither Maushi, still in a shock at Anu's death, they said, nor Baba, bedridden as he is, they said, able to control her and so when Meera reached an age of seven, the family decided to take the matters in their hands.

First it was the women who tried to get her familiarised with the Hindu rites and rituals. 'Come to our house for the Pithori Amavasya vrat,' they offered on the next no-moon day. 'Then you will understand how to keep a vrat when you are married.'

Meera went. Dressed in a new silk long skirt and blouse embroidered all over in gold thread, wearing gold jewellery, with a red kumkum on her forehead and flowers entwined in her plaits, she arrived at her uncle's house.

That whole day all the married women of the house kept a fast without even a sip of water and spent all their free time after the housework in puja and prayers. Meera and her cousins kept sitting around and watching them, running errands for them and bearing part of their duties in the house. The concluding puja was done in the evening when the family priest came to officiate.

'A vrat is a period of austerity, self-denial and worship to be repeated regularly for attaining a particular purpose,' the priest told Meera when she asked what a vrat was. 'Once you vow to keep a particular vrat, you have to repeat it on that particular day of every week or every year as required for five or seven years or lifelong as required for that particular vrat.'

'What's this vrat for?' Meera asked.

'To ask God to give long lives to our husbands,' her aunts said.

'And that Mahalaxmi vrat that you keep, what is that for?' Meera asked.

'Also to gain long lives and good health for our husbands,' they said.

'Don't the men keep any vrat?'

'Yes, they do child. They too keep the vrats for acquiring wealth or for fulfilment of their other ambitions,' the priest said.

'But not for long lives for their wives?' Meera persisted.

The priest gave an embarrassed half-smile as he turned away and her aunts frowned and told her to mind her tongue.

'It's all for husband, husband and husband only,' she complained to Maushi when she came back, 'as if there is nothing else in life!' Not for women, Maushi thought; there isn't.

Then again they called her over to keep the Hartalika vrat. 'This is a vrat meant to be kept by unmarried girls and all our girls will also be keeping it. They do it every year. It's time you learned it too.'

And Meera went, again all decked up. Her aunts had put up a special worship platform in the inner courtyard and decorated it with banana plants at its four corners and set clay idols of Goddess Parvati and Lord Shiva. This time all the unmarried girls fasted the whole day without even a sip of water, worshipping the idols and singing devotional songs. Their mothers and aunts sat around telling them stories of girls and women who had kept different types of vrats and gained great boons—rich and honourable husbands, long life for husbands, good health for husbands... In the night, the family priest came over and narrated the story of Hartalika.

Goddess Parvati, daughter of the mighty Himalayas, had set her heart on marrying Lord Shiva and so had fasted the full day on this day of the year and had kept awake the whole night afterwards worshipping Lord Shiva all the time. Lord Shiva was pleased with her for practising such austerities for his sake and had offered her a boon. She had asked him to marry her.

'So all young girls must keep this vrat if they want to get the husbands they desire,' the priest said. 'Any girl who eats today will suffer widowhood in the next seven lives'—the worst fate a woman could imagine. He then blessed them all that they may get good husbands, blessed all the married women that they may remain akhand saubhagyawati—that they should never be widowed—and all the men and boys that they may stay happy and may enjoy long lives. At midnight he offered the fasting girls a little bit of curd to lick from a leaf.

Meera, like many of her young cousins, could not keep awake throughout the night and woke up next morning hungry, tired and irritated. 'Suffer, suffer, suffer! That's what women are supposed to do. And all so that good things may happen to the husband!' she muttered to her aunts who were preparing the clay idols to be immersed in the holy water.

'A woman's birth is for suffering, daughter,' they told her. 'And what better jewel can a woman have than a husband? And what better fate than dying before him?'

'Mine is not!' she told them hotly. 'And let my husband take care of himself! No more fasting and no more vrats for him! I will take care of only Aaji and Ajaa and myself,' and she flounced out leaving them shocked to the core. She walked home muttering to herself all the way and refused to go to them again for any further vrats or fasts.

Next it were Baba's brothers who suggested that Meera be sent to their houses in the evenings to learn to recite the shlokas, a daily ritual which Baba had discontinued in his house after his sickness and which had now been taken over by his brothers. 'It's time she imbibed at least some Hindu culture. After all she belongs to our family now,' they said referring to the fact that Baba – at last having unwillingly given in to the constant pressure by Maushi – had Meera's last name changed to their family name, a fact strongly resented by the family. So Meera was sent there in the evenings and for two days she sat with other children trying to chant the tongue-twisting Sanskrit words as one of her uncles led the recitation.

On the third day she wanted to know what the shlokas meant. 'They are chants of praise of God and of confirmation of our devotion to Him,' her uncles explained.

'Why do we have to praise God every day?' she asked. 'Does He need constant flattery?'

'Take care girl, watch your tongue! We have to constantly make Him aware of our devotion or why would He help us in our need?' her uncles said. 'It also trains your memory,' they added.

'My computer has lots of memory,' eight-year-old Meera said. 'And I have more interesting things to remember. Like compositions of air and water and earth,' she added importantly and refused to go to their houses again.

'That brash brat,' they said complaining to Maushi, but carefully, toning it down. Maushi, they said, was like a tigress where Meera was concerned, she will not listen to a word against Meera.

She will grow out of it, Maushi thought to herself philosophically. That brashness is a part of Meera now, a part of building up her confidence while you all belittled her. And what else will I be restraining if I try to curb that?

Meera's computer had been another major point of contention in the family. She had cajoled Maushi into buying her one at this tender age while the family had just bought one for one of her cousins who had turned eighteen and was nowhere as proficient at it as Meera. His brothers had complained bitterly to Baba about this wanton waste of money and about spoiling a girl – *a girl* they said – who would rather sit before her computer than recite the shlokas; or learn the housework. 'Just like her mother,' they said. '*She* was obsessed with her books, *this one* with her computer.'

'Gauri does the cooking, Shanta does other works, her Aaji looks after the house; Meera doesn't need to learn the housework; at least, not yet. There is plenty of time for that,' Baba said though he too had initially grumbled and fumed at Meera's acquiring the computer but now had secretly started taking pride in her prowess with it.

But this time his brothers insisted on calling the family council including all their cousins and nephews. They also protested very strongly about the exclusion of the rest of the family from Meera's care. 'Meera's upbringing and behaviour are going totally out of limit, completely against our traditions and customs and our dharma,' they claimed. 'What good is all this learning and knowing and all this freedom—freedom to play ball like boys, freedom to gambol on the riverbank and climb trees like boys, even to ride a bicycle—to a *girl*?' they asked. 'Girls should know no other world than the school and the internal courtyard of the house, have no interests other than housework,' they said. 'All this is going to bring shame on to our family name, blot on our family honour,' they said. 'And this mixing with boys! And that too Christian boys! Not only in school but she even brings them to the house! Who will marry a girl like her? Think of her future. You are letting her ruin her life. Time to control her and her behaviour is *now*,' they emphasised. When that did not have any effect on Baba – 'there is plenty of time for that,' he had repeated coldly – they played their trump card. 'Think of the family honour, if nothing else,' they said. 'Think of the harm that is being done to our family name,' they pleaded. Baba was the head of the family and they could protest only to this extent and no more.

'One must change with circumstances,' Baba said with an enigmatic smile and they all looked at him shocked out of their wits. 'Dharma doesn't change!' they said tightly but Baba only shook his head to signify that the issue was closed. After months of getting outraged at Maushi for allowing Meera's young school-friends, especially the boys, the run of the house and suppressing it, one day, in one of his rare upsets at her, Baba had vociferously and furiously upbraided Maushi. Maushi, in turn, had merely started containing them – boys included – in the backyard and on the back veranda, not banishing them from the house but not letting them go anywhere near Baba either. After a while Baba, lonely without Gajanan's and Vinayak's children, had found himself longing for their childish chatter and exuberant laughter reverberating throughout the house, and had grudgingly called them to his room and now – though he was still irritated and unhappy at their being *Meera*'s friends – had started enjoying having them around and encouraged them to the ire of his visiting relatives staying in the house.

It happened again and again. Baba suppressing his fury at Meera's ways, and then blowing up at Maushi one day; Maushi thereafter merely keeping Meera away from him instead of controlling her ways; Baba eventually, grudgingly, coming to accept them, until one day they seemed to him to be innate to Meera. With time he came to regard Meera as being quite naturally beyond the restrictions of dharma, a law unto herself.

And Maushi encouraged Meera. 'Show me on your computer how the sun rises and sets,' she would say to Meera sitting next to her. Or 'show me the shape of India on your computer.' And Meera would happily comply and more. 'Sit here Aaji, I want to show you how to make a rainbow,' and Maushi would shake her head in wonder saying, 'wahwah'. Then as Meera grew up it was, 'Check it on your computer how the plants grow' or 'how the clouds form'. 'Check it on the computer', 'check it', 'check it'.

And Meera did. Did it with diligence and intensity and complete concentration. But after she had managed to solve some tricky problem or whenever she understood a difficult proposition, she let herself go. She jumped about whooping and danced around Maushi and Baba, her pride in her achievements making her glow and burst with happiness. 'I am going to be a scientist, am I not Aaji?' a thirteen-year-old Meera once said proudly to Maushi and Maushi stared wordlessly at her glowing, excited face.

Visits of Baba's brothers and cousins and their families to his house dropped drastically. Now all of them, including the doctor and the lawyer, visited Baba's house just once a month and sometimes they brought their children and grandchildren. Men spent an hour or so at Baba's bedside while women and girls sat with Maushi, commiserating with her on her plight and extolling her courage. They left after tea and snacks, relieved that the duty was over for a month. Boys stole fascinated glances at Meera if she happened to be around and girls gave her fearful looks, sometimes being as bold as to ask her how she was.

Their visits were so much like those visits of their other relatives years ago when they would come to complain about Anu and treat Anu almost in the same way as they now treated Meera that Maushi at times had a strange feeling as if time had stood still. Time passes very slowly in a village, she thought, nothing much has changed in these last years. Except for Meera.

Nowadays Meera's gang—as she called her friends, both girls and boys—would invade the house to finish their schoolwork which they kept showing and explaining to both Baba and Maushi, and to play ball in the now barren backyard; and to the family's dismay, it didn't bother Maushi at all that the gang included Christians and boys. Nor did it bother her that they all – including Meera – wore jeans all the time that they were out of the school, or that they all went gallivanting together, on picnics and outings, or even swimming together in what her sisters-in-law called, covering their eyes with their hands at the horror of it, 'such skimpy dresses, as good as nothing'. Baba's house now was ruled totally out of bounds to all the members of his brothers' families. Other prominent families from the village stopped dropping in and relatives from outside the village, who customarily came to stay in his house, curtailed their visits.

Now Baba, who always used to be surrounded by men—men of the family, men who had come on business, men who had come with problems or for advice, men who had come to bring some news or discuss some event or just dropped in socially and stayed for a meal—lay alone in his room watching the road from his window and Maushi sat alone on the back veranda where once she had sat surrounded by the women of the family and of the community voicing their boasts and joys, confidences and hopes, disappointments and frustrations, and where she had presided advising and counselling, controlling them all, deferred to by all.

If it worried Baba, he did not say anything to Maushi, and if it worried Maushi, she did not show it; it certainly did not worry Meera as she sat before her computer with her friends excitedly discussing some topic or the other or frolicked with them all over the house. Very often after their games in the backyard, Meera and her friends would flop down on the back veranda demanding sarbats and bhajias from Gauri – just as Vinayak's friends used to do a long time ago after playing gilli-danda but out on the road in front. Later as they grew up and Meera finished school and started college, ball games were replaced by heated arguments about politics and environment and sports – just like in Vinayak's group though it had consisted of boys only – and demands for sarbats by demands for cups of tea, and Meera, busy with her friends and college, had hardly any time or inclination to worry about her disapproving relatives. Sometimes she met her girl cousins on the minibus while going to the college. They would all be sitting together dressed properly in saris or salwar-kameez, demurely constraining their bodies, going to the colleges in the nearby towns only, and strictly going only to the college and coming back home before the evening. And they avoided even acknowledging her. Even the villagers gawked at her as she strode to the bus in her jeans. But Meera did not seem to notice any of them. She came and went as she pleased, getting somebody to drop her home on the motorbike if she had to come back late and had missed the last bus, further shocking her uncles and aunts watching from behind the grilled windows. Her interests were expanding, as was her circle of friends, many of whom would drop in at the village house at all hours. She would take her new friends to meet Baba and spend time with him, and then bring them over to meet Maushi. 'Aaji, this is Cynthia from Panaji. She is studying music,' she would introduce, 'and this is Mario from Mapusa Group of Social Workers,' and they would sit around Maushi talking to her, marvelling at her ability to converse in English, even trying to pull her into their discussions.

And then one evening as Maushi and Gauri sat stringing beans on the back veranda, Meera walked in with a fair young lad in tow. 'Aaji, this is Ronnie,' she said pulling him forward. 'He is from vilayat. On a holiday over here.'

Maushi dropped the beans and slowly rose to her feet staring at Ronnie all the while. Elizabeth's son. Same colouring as hers from what Pundlik had told her; light hair, blue eyes. Laughter in those eyes but also a deep sadness behind it. Sensitive features. Tall and slim like Alec; Alec's bearing; Alec's cut of face.

'Namaste Aaji,' Ronnie said with his hands joined before him and Maushi was reminded of that day eighteen years ago when Alec had first stood before her just like this with his hands joined before him and looking down his aristocratic nose had said, 'Namaste Aai'.

PART TWO

6

Eighteen years ago, Alec was past thirty and so came down the hillside leading into the cove at a sedate pace, pausing at every ledge to admire the scenery and catch his breath, cursing whenever he lost his footing and slid on his backside. Landing at last on the sandy beach, he sighed with relief and then, did a double take. For Christ's sake, he had landed in the midst of a nudist commune!

He had arrived in Goa only a few days ago straight from London. 'Just drop everything and take off to somewhere remote. Alone! That's the only remedy,' Giles, his doctor and friend, had said after diagnosing the heart murmur that had brought Alec to him. 'You are in your early thirties and you have done extremely well. But you have also paid a price for it with all this accumulated stress. Complete change to a relaxed lifestyle for six months is the only answer to it. Get away from here. And I mean everything and everybody here.'

'Six months!' Alec had said shocked. 'I can't afford to take that much time off from my practice. I am still on my way up. Let's say one month, maximum.'

'Sure you can afford it. Otherwise there will be no practice, on the way up or down. Six months. Or I don't guarantee you more than a few years of life!'

As Alec absorbed the enormity of it, Giles added kindly, 'Go to India. Get into yoga. Find a guru and meditate on the bank of the Ganges.'

Instead, Alec had come to Goa.

A few days in a hotel in Panaji and he was already bored. Everything was too regulated, too organised, too tourist-oriented for his taste: a way of doing a place rather than relaxing in it, feeling it, absorbing it. A tedious boat trip, another fast-paced and tiresome visit to the churches, water cycling in the sea – for Christ's sake! In the hotel lounge where he met other groups staying in the hotel and on the outings with them, it was still shoptalk or inane accounts of other travels. People moved as couples, they went shopping and sightseeing, they drank aperitifs before dinner and liquors after dinner; it was all so patently respectable. They were on short-term vacations; he was on long-term recuperation. There were a couple of single women with one of the groups and he struck a friendship with them, even spent a night with one of them, but found it unsatisfactory. They left after a couple of days and Alec was not interested in any more one-night stands.

Then on one Fest day, as he watched the gay procession wending its way through the streets of Panaji with young girls singing and young boys dancing with abandon, he finally realised what he had been begrudging, what it was that he wanted. That he had actually been chafing under the pressure of striving towards the pinnacle of his career, of carving a high position in society and that he had been straining at the reins of conformity that went with it. For some time, just for a little while, he wanted to escape this yoke of organised respectability and all the rigidity that went with it. Just for a while he wanted to toss off his up-and-coming brilliant young barrister persona, dissolve his etched identity of a pillar-of-the-society in this warm air and water, and be free as a bird. He wanted the luxury of irresponsibility.

But his lonely walks in tourist areas brought him no respite either. He was constantly harassed by offers of girls, of drugs, trade for dollars or for any foreign goods he would want to sell. Boys not much over fourteen were smoking hash. Bars and wine shops sold drugs under the counter. 'What you do is get away from this sterile place; being here is the same as being in a hotel in any big city anywhere,' the assistant manager of the hotel advised him. 'Go live in an old, typically Goan place on a beach. There the life is very different. As it happens, my wife's brother's brother-in-law owns a small-little but beautiful hotel on Baga Beach...'

The hotel did turn out to be small-little and beautiful. It had a courtyard shaded with a large tree in the centre, open café-restaurant on two sides of it set in a lush garden and shaded by reed curtains, an open veranda with terracotta-tiled floor, and a narrow carved timber staircase leading to small but neat bedrooms on the upper floor. Whitewashed walls were hung with old Goan prints and wicker and wooden artifacts. Paper lanterns dropped from the trelliswork supporting flowering creepers over the café. The sea was just beyond the veranda. Alec lounged in a cane chair on the veranda watching the morning light spread on the waves in shades of pinks and gold.

'Hey,' said a bearded young man coming down the stairs. He was dressed in loose baggy pajamas and a short front-open vest, his long hair was tied neatly in a ponytail at the back, and his beard was trimmed and combed.

'Hey,' Alec responded.

'You new here?' he asked in German.

'Just arrived,' Alec said.

'Staying long?'

'Maybe six months.'

'You German?'

'No, I am English,' Alec said and added quickly, 'but going to settle in Canada,' as an afterthought, reminding himself that in law an intention was not admissible as evidence.

But the other guy didn't seem to care much about where Alec lived or was planning to live. 'You speak very good German,' he said.

'I studied it.'

'Want to come and chill out a bit?'

'Sure,' Alec said. 'Why not?'

'Willi,' the German said extending his hand.

'Alec.' A different persona for a different life, he thought as he shook hands with Willi. Am I crazy to have accepted such an invitation extended with this kind of informality? Alec asked himself as he followed Willi down the steps. Yet something in their exchange had captivated him. It's the informality, especially the introduction, he decided. Willi, Alec. First names only. No mention of one's profession or business. I like that. I am willing to give it a try.

But a nudist hippie colony in a cove was not his scene. Turning to go back, he looked at the intimidating steep hill in front and the jagged rocks on the sides and sat down to catch his breath before attempting either.

'How long have you been here?' he asked Willi resignedly.

'Some years,' Willi said indifferently pulling off his clothes.

'Some years?' Alec repeated incredulously. 'What did you do before?' he asked curiously.

'I was studying business administration at the University of Hanover. You know what business administration is all about?'

'Managing people?'

'Riiiight! Managing people. And to what end? To increase the production and thereby the profitability. Bottom line is the net profit. And who cares about the people as human beings or about their quality of life?' Willi said. Down to his swimming trunks, he planted his forearms and head in the sand and flipped his legs up into a headstand. Nobody paid any attention to him.

Squatting uncomfortably in the sand in his trousers and shirt and watching an upside down Willi, Alec thought it over.

'And you found it here? This way? The quality of life?' he asked.

'This is the only way left. I have tried all others.'

'Such as?'

'Campus rebellion. Dropping out. Heavy drugs. None of them were meaningful.'

'So you left?'

'So I started reading about alternative ways of understanding what life is all about. I read a lot of philosophy and theosophy. Kant and Hegel and Sartre and Russell. And J Krishnamurty.'

'Who?'

Willi laughed. 'Never mind,' he said still upside down. 'But because of J Krishnamurty, I am here in India.'

Alec looked around. Though majority of the youngsters were totally nude, there were a few who though topless, wore bikini panties. He looked towards the beach dhabas where modestly dressed Goan waiters, with total indifference, were serving fried fish to nude clients wearing only rings piercing most unlikely parts of their bodies – the navels, the nipples, corners of lips, ends of eyebrows; to those with matted Rastafarian dreadlocks; to those with bodies so covered with tattoos that you could not tell the colour of their skins. There were other Indian vendors, dressed equally modestly in lungis and short open jackets, moving with equal nonchalance in between nude women with young children hoisted on their hips dancing to some thunderous fast beat music and doped men sprawled naked on the sand, offering them henna tattoos and strings of beads and charms and talismans to light their way to nirvana. 'The locals don't seem to mind the foreigners living so freely on their beaches,' Alec observed.

'Not as long as you don't flaunt it away from the shoreline,' Willi said dryly. 'They have this live and let live policy. Also tourism is profitable to them.'

'Hey,' said a pretty redhead sitting next to Alec.

'That's Grete. She was in industrial chemistry,' Willi said. 'Tell Alec what industrial chemistry is all about, Grete.'

'Oh, killing!' Grete said. 'Killing the insects and the plants, and eventually, the people.'

Willi's group came as a surprise to Alec who had always associated hippies with filth, and drugs, and sexual deviations, and stupidity, and inability to make it in this world.

'Ach!' Grete said, 'You refer to those hard druggies and drifters! They are not hippies. They are not searching for an alternative way of living. They have given up on living.'

'They just laze about,' Bernd the youngster said frowning with disdain. 'It's just one unending party for them. Those vagabonds, those party animals and thrill seekers, and all those pushers and pimps and whores who feed on them. Parasites! But they keep away from us hippies.'

Not too far away, Alec thought wryly, looking at the crowd milling around the beach.

'We are the original hippies. We are not escapees from life but trying to live a meaningful life,' Willi said gesturing at others in his group. And they were too; they were also quite different from what Alec had imagined the hippies to be. Ernst was an engineer, Bernd an accountant, Inge had been a doctor. Lisl had been studying theology. They were all in their mid-twenties to early thirties rather than the late teens to mid-twenties that dominated the beach, and moved around proud, and they too wore bikini panties, and were clean and neat, which made Alec sigh with relief.

'What do you do?' Grete asked.

'I am a lawyer.' Alec said looking keenly at her. She looked intelligent and clear-eyed, obviously not on drugs – at least not on hard drugs.

'Is there any justice in law?' she asked.

Alec settled himself comfortably on the sand to discuss law and justice.

Alec, the Anglo-Saxon, joined Willi's German group; majority of the hippies in Goa were either German or French, he found out later. It was the age of the European hippie. American youngsters were already turning to God and Bible and employments with big corporations.

He was amazed at himself when he found himself still with them the next day. Not only that but he was eager to be with them. 'Spend some time with us and I will show you the fallacy of your mindset,' Grete had said, and Alec now laughed at how easily he had acquiesced. But then wasn't that why he had chosen to come to Goa instead of going to some ashram in the Himalayas?

This group interested him. What really made them tick? What impulse drove them? What could have influenced them so strongly as to make them give up their promising careers and rich lifestyles, to alienate themselves from the society and become pariahs? Clad in his bathing trunks he relaxed with them on the sand, ate fish curries, drank beer, kept strictly away from anything stronger than marijuana, and discussed the philosophy of life. Away from the beach he dressed like them: in baggy pajamas and a kurta, sometimes a headband to keep his hair under control in high wind, and found them comfortable in that climate. The pajamas or lungis – men wrapped them around the waist, women wrapped them around under their arms and tied the ends behind their necks – were some of the compulsory pieces of attire for acceptance in the tribe; then one could further improvise on them. And many did—tasseled vests, embroidered skirts or shawls, multi-coloured caps. And beads, as many as one liked, around the neck, around the waist, around the wrists or around the forehead. And then there were bells—little tinkling bells around the ankles. 'That noise keeps the snakes away when walking in the woods,' Willi explained to him. 'Walking in the woods? Where to?' Alec asked and Willi laughed.

He was amazed at their informality, their sense of total freedom, and even their disdain for the prevailing social values. They had chosen different commitments: the tribal ones. They just followed their own convictions and cocked a snook at the bourgeois of which Alec had been an acknowledged, cardholding, dues paying member. Alec had always been ambitious. Coming from a middle-class branch of the family, success had been very important to him. He needed to win, needed the professional prestige that went with it, and needed the trappings of wealth it brought. His life had been a daily battle to argue out the opposing council, to be on his toes to grasp that straw in the evidence that would advance his case, to make those judicious contacts outside the courtroom, to build a reputation, and bring home enough to meet his obligations—the mortgage on the house, the hire purchase on the car and gadgets, and some more, then some more, and then still some more. All my life I have been busy achieving, he thought to himself. I have never pondered on issues like purpose of life or questioned ethics of any system; nor did I ever feel the need to rebel against anything. I accepted the system as it is. *I* created all the pressures on me: pressures of making it within the system, of reaching the top, of being the best—a goal *I* set for myself.

But here, there were no pressures of any kind. None of them even wore a watch. 'Don't be tyrannised by time,' Grete had chided him. 'Learn to give up your linear perceptions of time, speed, progress. Experience timelessness. Learn to be still. Think infinity. Seek the shore beyond the darkness.'

'That sounds like Hindu philosophy.'

'It *is* Hindu philosophy. Why do you think we are here?'

During his stay with them Alec was highly impressed by how much of Hindu philosophy and also its practices they all had absorbed. First thing in the morning there was the sun-worship, followed by meditation and shloka chanting, and then yoga. They read a lot: philosophy and scriptures, as well as scientific and professional journals. Sometimes there were heated arguments about Gandhi and Marx and Sartre, about dialectic materialism and free will and absolutism. At night, every night, there were wild parties: there was bonfire and strange hypnotic wild music and everybody smoked grass and danced and danced. Without inhibitions, and without restraints. With total abandon.

'What exactly are you trying to achieve?' he asked Bernd.

'"Achieve" is exactly the word we oppose,' Bernd said. 'It brings to mind a destructive competition, a constant struggle to prove yourself superior to others, to set yourself apart on a pedestal. That word belongs to a materialistic world, the world we have left behind. Why don't you just try being? Being in harmony with yourself, being one with the surroundings, with the nature. Listening to your inner voice, discovering yourself, experiencing self-realisation.' But then Bernd had just turned twenty-four. He had yet to experience disillusionment. So Alec merely smiled at him and did not say anything even as they both stood watching a bloody fracas a distance away on the sand.

Still Alec had to accept that they genuinely disagreed with the existing social values in the world they had left behind and were genuinely committed to an alternative lifestyle, that they had decided that it was futile trying to change the world and that opting out was the only option open to them – opting out and creating their own different world. He admired their gumption, their commitment and their devil-may-care attitude; at the same time, he knew that he himself could never really be a part of them. Yes, now he admitted to himself, he did need to let loose once in a while to release all those pressures he kept accumulating within himself, but, as he had accepted earlier, he did function at his best under pressures and on tensions, and on competition. And his aim in life had always been success – success in all his endeavours. And power, don't discount power! You enjoy the power that follows success, he told himself.

Frequently the tribe was on move without any destination or any purpose. The first time that they all started moving, Alec asked Ernst, 'Where are we walking to?'

'May be Anjuna, may be Vagator. It's of no importance.'

'So it's the walking that's important?'

'You can stop if you want to.'

'So what's the purpose? Surely you are walking for something or to somewhere?'

Ernst laughed. 'Man, you still haven't got it, have you? The point is that you do exactly what you want to do. There is no custom here, no convention, no person who will set rules for what you should do and what you shouldn't. Nobody else defines the purpose of your life for you. You choose, man. Got it?'

'Yeah,' Alec said doubtfully. But he trudged along simply because there was nothing else to do. 'How long have you been here?' he asked Ernst.

'Six months. I move around. I lived in Thailand for a year before that. In my wife's house.'

'You have a Thai wife?' Alec asked in surprise. Ernst and Inge were an item in the tribe. 'Well, where is she?'

'You don't expect me to tote her along, do you?' Ernst said laughing at the expression on Alec's face. 'She didn't want to leave her house. I didn't want to stay there any longer. So we split. Simple.'

'Oh! Well, that sounds easy.'

'Separation is easy there. You ever seen a Thai wedding? It's nothing but just a feast. You decide to get married, you call your relatives and friends to a feast, and announce it; and that's it. How big a feast depends on how many marks you spend on it. And marks go a long way in Thailand. So do pounds. As they do here.' He added with a sidelong glance at Alec. 'Afterwards you may register the marriage or not as you wish,' he continued. 'Most Thais don't register them.' He shrugged. 'We also didn't. Then there was the bride price to take care of. And I provided for the child also though it was not expected. Once you get all that settled, parting is just a sweet sorrow for all concerned.'

'Child?'

'She was pregnant when I left.'

'And you lived in her house?'

'The trick is to marry the youngest daughter of the house. It's Thai custom that the youngest daughter has to care for the parents in their old age and in return, she inherits the house. So of course she can't move out of the house and her husband just moves in with her.'

'Ah!' Alec said reflectively.

'The marriage brokers arrange it all for you. She wasn't quite pretty, but what the hell – what a house she had! All those carvings and gilded doors and painted wooden birds perched on the gate. It was no surprise that she didn't want to leave it.'

'Don't you want to know your child?'

Ernst shrugged. 'It was her decision. She wanted the child.'

I would want to know, Alec thought. Actually I would quite like an Indian daughter: golden hued, smoky eyed, with all the graces of this land. A dark charmer!

'So what was it all about then?' he asked.

'An experience of a varied life,' Ernst said.

Alec enjoyed their walks. They walked from beach to beach, from one secluded cove to another, forded gentle rivers on foot or mighty ones in fishing boats, scampered over rocks and scaled high rocky bluffs that bordered the ocean's edge, climbed gentle wooded hills that jutted right into the ocean, walked under the waterfalls and through lush green jungles to the calls of exotic birds. So did everybody else.

The whole of North Goa coastline was one busy hippie highway. 'Path of enlightenment,' Grete said.

In Anjuna they lolled on the veranda of a house belonging to a Goan family eating delicious curries that they served. Like most Goan families with houses on the beaches, this family too had built two rooms at the back for rent and laid a couple of tables and chairs on the front veranda where they served curries and fried fish.

The weekly flea market was on at Anjuna Beach. Afterwards they wandered around under the coconut trees looking at the wares spread on sand—watches, cameras and trinkets, even secondhand clothes—mostly foreign, belonging to the hippies who needed the cash. Everybody was buying and selling something. Bernd was negotiating the sale of his Swiss watch to a middle-aged Arab with a shy young girl dressed in loose pajamas and a long shirt in tow. A long scarf was wrapped around her shoulders and her head and at times she kept pulling it to cover her face showing only one eye.

They encountered the pair again on the veranda of one of those houses where they had stopped for some cool fresh coconut water. Tony, the owner, knew Willi, Bernd and Inge and joined their table for a smoke. 'They have been here for only two days now,' he said indicating the Arab and the girl, 'living in the back room, but he is already regretting bringing her over.'

'I saw him towing behind those two touts who were trying to negotiate a deal with some white girls.' Bernd said.

'Yeah! These Arabs go mad seeing all that white female flesh lying uncovered on these beaches. Of course I blame our boys also. Touting for them!' Tony said with disgust. 'Well, it's a business for them.'

'Why has he brought that young girl with him?' Bernd asked.

'He married her in Hyderabad a week ago. You know it?' he asked Bernd who shook his head. 'It's northeast of here. It's a predominantly Muslim city and many Arabs come all the way to India and to Hyderabad to get brides for themselves. Only this guy made this stop in Goa on the way to Bombay and back home and now he wants to divorce her and send her back.'

'Can he do that so easily?' Inge asked.

'Sure. All he has to do is say "Talaque" three times and pay her the monies agreed in the marriage contract and she will go back, though if he were living in this country he wouldn't have bothered. They are allowed four wives at the same time. By law.' He gave a little envious smile.

'What will she do when she goes back?'

'She can always get married again,' Tony said shrugging his shoulders. 'As it is she wasn't keen to leave her family and friends and customs and a place she knows and go to some strange land. She will be quite happy to go back home.' He got up to serve some more customers who had just come in.

'Women here are so complacent,' Alec remarked to Lisl as they walked together towards the Vagator Beach and Chapora Fort.

'Yes? Like Parvati, yes?' Lisl said. 'But they can be like Durga or Kali too if a particular time requires it.' And she explained seeing Alec's blank face, 'They are Hindu goddesses. I am enamoured of some of them. Every year I attend their festivals. Originally I expected to find them all to be lusty, robust and exciting; like Greek goddesses; but ach! most of them are placid, all-forgiving and subservient to their gods. Yet when all the gods together could not kill the demon Mahisha, Goddess Durga emanated from Parvati—the loving, benevolent, all-forgiving Mother Goddess, consort of Lord Shiva—and this Goddess Durga rode a lion, carried many weapons, and slew the demon. And Goddess Kali, the most fearful of them all, is an emanation of Durga.'

'Why is Kali fearful?'

'Kali? Because she destroyed a whole race of demons, not just one. She cut off their heads, drank their blood, and then, danced in their blood. She is a contradictory goddess, Alec, a destroyer and a creator. A holy paradox of unimaginable horror and ecstasy; both intertwined eternally. A goddess also of absolution and abundant bliss. But she is not a gentle, compassionate goddess like Parvati. She is violent and wrathful and bloodthirsty. A goddess of retribution, of vengeance, and of cosmic justice; a generous dispenser of boons to the followers but also a dread to the wicked. So take care Alec, if you have any dishonourable intentions!' she added with a twinkle.

Below the Chapora Fort was a large hippie settlement—families with young children, who had been living there for years if not for a decade or so and had started schools, had established shops, bars, restaurants and small-scale industries—a sprawling residential and commercial hubbub; and all run by hippies.

'Do they live here all year long?' Alec asked in amazement.

'Some do,' Willi said. 'Like I do. But many others move to Hampi for the monsoons. That's a temple town on the banks of the Tungabhadra River – not too far from here. Monsoons are very heavy here and could be quite depressing too for some. It pours and pours and never seems to stop for four months at a stretch.' He grew morose and looked at the azure sea, at the silver sands and at the waving palms with nostalgia welling in his eyes. 'We all will probably have to move to Hampi or somewhere else soon... permanently. The Goan Government is coming down hard on us, making it more and more difficult for us to stay here much longer.' He looked at Alec and smiled sadly.

Alec smiled back with a little sympathy but not too much. 'So what's happened to the hippie philosophy? I see the same materialistic trappings here,' he asked.

Willi laughed. 'The difference is in attitude, Alec. Form is less important than the attitude. And we all have to make a living. But it has to be done in the right way; living in harmony with nature, respecting each other, valuing the quality of life. Living together, not destroying together.'

'Do you plan to follow this lifestyle forever?'

Willi smiled his patient, relaxed smile. 'Of course! That's why we all are here. To find ourselves and live our way.'

Hermal sand dunes sheltered another nudist colony. By now Alec was thoroughly disenchanted with the rebel society finding them as conventional as other societies except that their conventions were different: different in clothes that they wore, in the responsibilities or rather irresponsibilities that they assumed towards the society, in the lifestyle that they pursued. But they too stuck to them equally rigidly. They had started out by questioning the establishment but by the age of thirty most were beginning to question themselves. Most were rethinking their priorities and going back to the so-called square world. The few older men and women that Alec found sprinkled over the beaches were either diehard idealists, or drug addicts or pushers or pimps or loafers. Willi was one of the few hippies who was well over thirty and still accepted as a part of the tribe but then Willi was an idealist too. Everywhere they had strolled, many of the hippies, on recognising Willi, had come to talk to him respectfully calling him 'Professor', showing him the kind of respect reserved for a select few scattered all over the hippieland – the mature ones, but only those who spent much of their time in reading, writing, or in discussions, those who spoke their language but with scholarship and theory to back it up, like Willi.

No, though Alec now respected their philosophy of life, he couldn't see himself spending six months with them. 'I didn't quite bargain for this when I wished for something unconventional, nonrestrictive and carefree,' he said to himself with a laugh. He still needed something different in his life, something new to explore, but something a little more compatible with his values, his ideas, his style of life.

Surely there is something more to India than yoga and hippies.

Back at the Baga Beach hotel, Alec sat on the veranda listening to the waves come roaring on to the beach and feeling more lonely than ever. He was in paradise but a stranger to it and needed someone special to guide him through it, to share it with him, someone new to enchant, someone to whom he would also be new and fresh – not the same old jaded one. He was more than ready and willing to be charmed off his perch.

Joaquim, the owner of the hotel, joined him in a rum punch and they sat sipping their drinks and watching the sun reflect in a thousand fragments in the water. Joaquim was a gregarious, talkative man and he recounted in detail his problems of running a hotel to Alec.

'At last got a lad to polish the woodwork,' he told Alec. 'He is a Hindu and I am not sure he will stay. These Hindus, you don't find them working where the money is. Tourist industry is the biggest industry in Goa but will they have anything to do with it? They would rather live in their pigeonholes and follow the dictates of their ancestors. And they are the majority in Goa.'

'Hindus are the majority in Goa?' Alec asked in surprise. All the Goans that he had come across—the hotel owners, those who had those houses on beaches with rooms for rent, those who ran the shacks and beach restaurants and even those that ran the bars and cafés—had all been Christians.

'Sure. Christians are just about a third of the population here.' Joaquim said. Then he looked at Alec's face. 'You wouldn't think so, would you now? Perhaps you thought that the hippies were the majority in Goa.' He guffawed.

Alec laughed. 'Well, where are they?' he asked.

'In the interior. They are not beach people or water people. Do you know that most of their boys cannot even swim? And this is a land with this long, indented coastline and criss-crossed by a multitude of creeks and rivers. Water is the omnipresent force here. A land of water,' Joaquim laughed at his own witticism and sobered up as Alec raised his eyebrows disparagingly.

'Also they are not modern and cosmopolitan like us,' he said evoking a Christian comradeship. 'Do you know they still don't allow any mixing between their boys and girls? And dancing together like us? Oh no, no!' He threw up both his hands. 'They don't want to know the rest of the world. They have this frog-in-well mentality. Very clannish and traditional. Stick to their villages, their customs and their own people. Anyway, you are not likely to meet them,' he concluded. 'Even we, the local Christians, are not allowed to enter their houses. They don't mix even with us, leave aside mixing with foreigners.'

Alec, still under the spell of the little bit of Hinduism he had picked up from the hippies, tried to remember what he knew about

Hindus, their customs, their traditions. Not much besides that the women wear those beautiful flowing saris and that they have a thousand gods, and that they believe in rebirth, he admitted wryly to himself. And the hippies too had talked only of their philosophy, not of Hindus as people, not of their culture, not of their ethos, not of their lifestyle. So what do I know of the people of this mysterious India—India of yoga and gurus, of meditation and spirituality, of tiger hunts and snake charmers, of arts and crafts and music and dance and with those ancient temples with exhaustive erotic carvings on them? Only that all this has been around for ages. An ancient people. Ancient civilisation. Ancient culture. An ancient religion of cults and exotic rituals and mysterious practices.

Yet they were Aryans, of the same stock as his ancestors from Germany. Intriguing, he thought as he stepped off the veranda on to the beach wending his way in between the bodies sprawled on the sand, watching the waves come in with a roar and a crash before dissipating on the sand.

And then he saw the girl rising out of the sea – tall, slim and willowy, glowing golden skin, long black hair. There was the grace of the waves in her movements and sparkle of the sun in her smile and magic of this land in her eyes—eyes like deep dark pools, eyes that held you spellbound and made you forget the rest of the world. Butterflies flew in his stomach and the roar and crash of the waves echoed in his head.

7

Eighteen years ago, Anu had not even turned twenty. Slim and willowy with golden wheatish complexion, long jet-black hair, and kohl-enhanced deep black eyes, when dressed in a green sari with yellow border and with gold zumkas in her ears, she took the beholder's breath away as happened to Alec the first time he came to her house.

Born after two sons, Anu's birth was celebrated by the family with much pleasure and great relief, for didn't the shastras rule that kanyadaan—giving away of a daughter in marriage—was a necessary rite for the attainment of moksha—liberation from the cycle of death and rebirth—just as a son was necessary to light the father's funeral pyre? So a daughter after two sons was so much welcome that even Maushi's mother-in-law said, 'Today this house is blessed by the arrival of Goddess Laxmi herself,' and distributed sweets to the servants.

Gajanan and Vinayak were both named after God Ganesha, the family deity, but Anu – Anasuya – was named after the wife of a sage in Ramayana who was the epitome of wifely virtues, who had attained perfection through total devotion and service to her husband. Maushi, Vinayak and Pundlik, who had been her childhood playmate, were the only ones to call her Anu. All others including Baba and Gajanan called her by her full name as was the system and as if to infuse her with the qualities of the other Anasuya.

The house was overflowing with women dressed in their gold embroidered saris and laden with gold jewellery and men in silk kurtas with gold buttons on the day of her naming ceremony, the twelfth day of her birth. In the inner room, where all the women's functions were held, the cradle was bedecked with yards and yards of strings of flowers, and women vied with each other to rock the cradle and sing cradle-songs extolling the baby's virtues and beauty and predicting the honour she would bring unto the family by marrying a great man and bearing great sons. Bursts of laughter and animated talk could be heard from the men's area and every now and then someone would wander into the inner room and stand watching the proceedings. In a corner of the room a knot of young boys waited with bated breath for the singing to be over; Baby's horoscope had thrown up the initial 'A' and they had laid bets on the name that the baby's aunt would choose for her—'Anuradha, Annapurna, Aradhana.'

Then Baba's youngest sister, pushing her nose-ring on to one side, bent into the cradle, whispered the baby's name in her ear, and gave her a lick of sugar from her finger. Straightening up, she loudly announced the name she had chosen for the baby, 'Anasuya'. It was her prerogative to choose the name, just as it was also her prerogative to carry the baby into the courtyard that night to give her a glimpse of the moon.

Clapping from the inner room spread into the men's area as servants started serving trays of sweets and snacks and children started running around to grab the choicest bits. The gaiety spread even to the kitchens where harassed cooks were trying to cope with frying of fresh snacks and brewing of gallons of tea.

Afterwards all the young men accompanied by the servant boys went to the riverside to immerse the flowers from the cradle. Flowers used in any religious ceremony, even those from the daily worship of household gods, had to be thrown into flowing water, not just on any rubbish dump. Now young servant boys carrying brass thalis of flowers on their heads waded to the middle of the river before tilting them into the river to ensure that the flowers flowed to the sea with the current and did not get snagged on the banks as that would also ensure smooth flow of the child's life. For Gajanan's naming ceremony, he being the eldest son of the eldest son, Baba's father had hired a boat to carry the flowers deep into the sea.

As the first granddaughter in the family, Anu was much doted upon by all from the time she gave her first smile in her cradle. It was a joint family then with Baba's parents, his brothers and their families, all living together in one undivided house and there would always be someone around to coo to her as she lay happily gurgling and kicking in her cradle and there was always someone around to pick her up and cuddle her as she crawled all over the house giving big grins to everybody and there was always someone to hold her tiny hand as she started taking her first unsteady steps.

The main house—with quite a few smaller houses spread around it—had at that time consisted of two internal courtyards, the second one opening off the first. The first courtyard including all the rooms around it on both the floors was the men's area. All the women were confined to the inner courtyard and the rooms around it and came to the men's courtyard and the main door only on such occasions as going to their mothers' houses for the yearly sojourn of a month or on the rare visits to other relatives or to the temples outside the village. Even little girls had to keep to the women's area all the time. Except Anu. Always a naughty one even as a toddler, she tended to wander out of the women's area pausing in the doorway to the men's courtyard to glance over her shoulder, and then, with a gleeful gurgle, would run into the men's area as fast as her short chubby legs would allow if she saw anyone coming to stop her.

She was such a pretty toddler—chasing butterflies, toddling on her unsteady chubby legs behind Maushi as she tended her garden. Maushi's garden was famous throughout the area, with glorious flowers in the front and side gardens and herbs in the backyard. Maushi loved plants, especially the flowering ones, many of which she had got her far flung relatives to procure for her from far off places. She knew each and every tree, shrub and plant that graced her garden, the type of care required by each to bring forth those magnificent blooms – even though she was not allowed in the front garden, that being the men's area, and had to thereby depend on the gardeners to tend to it properly – and the qualities of each and every herb that she grew in the backyard.

Fame of her collection and her knowledge of herbs was as widespread as that of her flower garden. Relatives and villagers would come to her for herbal remedies for all kinds of ailments. Maushi would pluck some fresh herbs for them from her back garden or give them some of those dried ones from her tin box – the wild herbs that grew in jungles and which she bought from a jadi-bootiwala. They took the herbs and stopped to admire her flowers and all treated Anu also like a delicate and rare flower. 'A flower amongst flowers,' they would say and Anu, a pet of the whole village and apple of her grandfather's eye, would give them a charming toothy grin.

She also learned very young. By the age of three she had learned to flutter her eyelashes and speak with a pout to get anything she wanted out of her grandfather. 'Anasuya,' he would call as soon as he got up and a young Anu would run to get his daily worship flowers ready, to pluck the durvas – those particular three-pronged grass blades required for Ganesha worship – and to ensure that the fresh water lota was kept ready for his rounds of the Ganesha under the audumber tree so that later she could ask him for whatever it was that she wanted: a new dress or the red lac bangles.

And yet, she had also been a reckless child, flouting norms of expected girlish behaviour, disregarding all restrictions imposed upon girls, and expecting to get condoned for it by using her coquetries with her grandfather. She clambered up the guava tree with Vinayak and Pundlik and other boys instead of waiting underneath it like other girls, waiting for the boys to toss ripe guavas down to them. She sat by her grandfather's side in the men's room adding her impish childish prattle to their serious discussions. Her sassy talks and tomboyish behaviour only brought indulgent smiles from all the men and were even recounted fondly and with great hilarity by all.

But there were pre-defined limits. A little girl is not a child. The tolerable antics of a child became pre-proscribed activities for a girl. As Anu started growing up she found herself in total bewilderment as to the behaviour of the grown-ups. She was not allowed to climb the guava tree any more or sit chattering in the men's room. Not only were both the activities frowned upon but if she persisted, she was bluntly and furiously ordered to stop these activities and to go help in the kitchen. Kitchen was one place Anu avoided going into by using every possible stratagem, even though everybody fawned on her when on rare occasions and under duress she did find herself there. 'And what did you cook today?' Baba would ask her in a fondly patronising tone as he sat down for his meal – her grandfather having passed away by that time and Baba now being the head of the household. Anu was Baba's pet, and yet, too many times her expectations of pats on the back were answered by slaps on her cheeks and all her coquetries were totally ineffective against him at those times.

When was it that she realised that only if she followed the established rules as to the conduct of women would she be pampered and indulged?

Was it when Vinayak and Pundlik started excluding a six-year-old Anu from their games, pushing her away saying, 'These are boys' games. You go and play kavadis with girls.'? Anu though wouldn't go away but would stand in the front yard sulking and watching them play with her long skirt tucked up tight between her legs until one of the women servants came along and took her into the house untucking her skirt and scolding, 'Girls don't stand outside the house like that.' Complaints to Baba, which Anu had expected would redress the situation in her favour, only brought even more severe scolding to her.

Or, was it when she jumped into the well that first time, in expectation and excitement and not in desperation like the later time? A seven-year-old Anu had watched Vinayak and his friends frolicking in the well for many a summer days, watched them from a crack in the back door, and one day she ran from the back door straight towards it, grabbed the rope that was hanging from the pulley on one side of the well – the rope that was used to haul up buckets of water – grabbed it without breaking her stride, and jumped in straight as an arrow. Surfacing still holding on to the rope, she dog-paddled towards the edge and clambered up the steps, a little breathless, greatly excited and flushed with pride, expecting applause. Instead, she had received her first beating at Baba's hands.

Or, was it when she was made to wear saris at the age of twelve? 'They are so restricting, Aai. I can't run, I can't jump, and I can't play. I can't do anything,' a tear-laden Anu had complained to Maushi. 'I much prefer those long skirts that I can tuck up tight. In a sari I feel like a gajagamini.' And Maushi had laughed, recalling the fat Gauri and thin Shanta and every other woman walking in that unhurried, undulating way, the walk of an elephant, a sign of beauty in a woman.

Her rebellion against all feminine restrictions had been apparent to Maushi from her early childhood. While Gajanan accepted all conventions and traditions without a question, and while Vinayak didn't accept many of them and did not follow them either but also did not ask any questions, Anu questioned everything and followed only what she had been convinced of.

She also refused to follow any of the rules of deportment that her aunts kept dinning into her head: sit properly, walk properly, mind your hair, mind your tongue, eyes down, answer respectfully, learn to be coy. If anything, they only increased her rebelliousness. She skipped as she walked, laughed out loud instead of giggling demurely behind her hand, and argued with everybody. She managed to eat on the days women were supposed to keep a fast, broke rules of the vrats that the young girls were supposed to keep, teamed up with Vinayak to play pranks, and resentfully suffered the berating she got for it at Baba's hands. Baba, though, was careful not to say anything much to Maushi – this being Maushi's area of control – except to mutter, 'Teach your daughter some propriety.'

At eight years of age, Gajanan caught her riding Pundlik's bicycle, standing and pedalling, on the road outside while Pundlik ran behind her waving his arms. Gajanan pulled her off the bike screaming and struggling and dragged her to Maushi. Maushi knelt before her to reason with her as to why as a girl she couldn't ride a bicycle.

'Why not?' a frustrated Anu screamed. 'I ride it better than Pundlik. He keeps falling off all the time.' And Maushi sat back on her heels as she remembered herself asking the same question of her mother when her tutoring was stopped at the age of ten since that was the limit of the village school teacher's knowledge. 'Why can't I go to the town school like Dada?' she had asked her mother. 'Why not? I am better than he is at studies. He keeps failing in every exam.' 'Hush!' her mother had said, 'He is a boy.' And Maushi had begrudgingly accepted it just as she had accepted many other restrictions since then. Now sitting back on her heels she thought, 'Why not indeed?'

The more questions Anu asked, the more questions rose in Maushi's mind. As she tried to answer Anu, she realised that she too didn't know the 'whys' of many of them. 'It's always done like that,' was not a satisfactory answer to her any more than to Anu; nor was 'Girls don't do that,' or that 'It's the fate of women'. Many of the rules, she found, were there only to reinforce the established patriarchal social system. 'But why?' she asked herself like Anu. If men were naturally superior, then where was the need to affirm it over and over again? And were they really superior? Maushi wasn't so sure as she compared Anu with Vinayak and Gajanan, or even with Pundlik, or even with some of her other cousins. 'Hush,' she told herself as she had done since her childhood, 'They are boys.' There was nobody that Maushi could voice her confusion to though she didn't try to curb Anu's natural curiosity and independent tendencies either.

There was not much latitude for Anu for fulfilling either of those, confined as she was to the inner courtyard. Boys went to the primary school in the village; the village teacher came home to tutor the girls up to high school level when they all were sent there and brought back in a minibus. Rest of the time was to be spent in chores within the inner courtyard. Anu though took every opportunity to slip out of the back door and Maushi purposely looked the other way unless somebody else caught her at it. 'I am stifled in here,' Anu would sob as she was brought back into the courtyard and Maushi could not blame her. She herself felt restricted there at times, wanting to be outside in the open with the plants and trees that she loved. She too enjoyed the hour that she spent every day in tending her garden. She too found the courtyard too confining at times. None of the rooms around the inner courtyard had any windows to the outside at all; all that they opened on to was the internal courtyard and its contained space. I see the river in front of the house hardly half a dozen times a year, she thought.

'Why can't I go to an English-medium school instead of having English as a second language?' Anu asked at the age of eleven when she started going to the high school, already an avid reader. 'There is so much more interesting to read in English. And all good colleges need good knowledge of English,' she pressed. And though that was absolutely impossible for a girl, as only boys were allowed to go to those schools and that too sometimes only – Gajanan was still studying in a Marathi-medium school though Vinayak went to an English-medium school – Maushi turned a blind eye when she found that Anu had got Vinayak to smuggle in a dictionary for her and talked to him and Pundlik in English. 'Wahwah,' she said marvelling at the stories in the English books that Anu had smuggled in when Anu excitedly narrated them to her and never asked her wherefrom she got those books.

Anu had learnt her lesson by the time Baba started objecting to her reading. Obsessed with books from childhood, she always had a pile of them in the niche in the wall of her room, an unknown phenomenon in the house. Nobody could understand how she could immerse herself in a book from dawn to late at night, sometimes even through the night. She would have brought the book to the dining room even to read with the meal had she been allowed to. Even the boys studying for their exams were not allowed to read throughout the day; they had their duties and rituals to attend to. Neither were they allowed to read or study at evening time; that time was for them to be outdoors, for playing games, while girls helped with the preparation of the evening meal. Then at dusk Baba would collect all the children, girls and boys, on the back veranda to recite the shlokas, after which Maushi would narrate a story from one of the epics or the Vedas – part ancient history, part mythology. After that was the mealtime. Anu read throughout the day.

'Reading again? Going to be a scientist?' Baba would ask mockingly whenever he found her with a book, before roaring, 'Put that book away!'

Anu tried to hide the book whenever she heard his footsteps approach, tried reading sitting behind the well, tried hiding in the storeroom to read. Nothing worked. There was no place in that house crowded with men, women, children and servants, large as it was, for privacy or seclusion. All rooms were multi-purpose, opening on to the veranda running around the internal courtyard, and everyone bustled in and out of them all day. Anu's every action was open to the scrutiny of many; especially of Baba, who, as patriarch of the family, was aware of everything that went on in the house. No matter where she tried to hide while reading, the tall, lean figure of Baba habitually clad in starched dhoti and kurta inevitably materialised before her and that mocking tone asking, 'Going to be a scientist?' rang out wherever she was.

As she grew up, Anu incurred more and more of Baba's wrath. He was flabbergasted at all her longings. She wanted to go to cinemas, plays, concerts. She wanted to sit in beach cafés with a group of friends—more interesting, she hoped, than the ones she had now—heatedly discussing all the exciting happenings she had read about in the smuggled books, go to Panaji and walk around the shops, go on picnics and outings, swim in the sea. But whatever it was that she wanted to do, it was always refused with, 'Girls of our family don't do that.' Even her friends were a problem. The friends acceptable to the family had to be not only girls but only the girls of their caste, of their status, and therefore in the village, in essence, her cousins. Anu found them all dull and boring and far too conservative in attitude. None of them had any interest in reading, none had any new ideas to discuss, none wanted to know anything beyond the courtyard life, while Anu had an insatiable curiosity about other lands, other interesting occupations, other ways of life, further fuelled by the books she had been reading. She could hardly expect to meet an outsider herself but she kept badgering Vinayak and Pundlik to tell her about the people they met in Panaji and though Pundlik superciliously told her that he would not give even the time of the day to a foreigner, meaning a non-Goan, Vinayak's friends who came to the house sometimes did include outsiders. But they were boys and she obviously could not talk to them, and that only further whetted her appetite for a world denied to her.

By the time she became a teenager, Anu was at odds with the whole family. She could find none of her generation to relate to, even to talk to. Gajanan, much older than her and thoroughly steeped in traditions, was the one to be avoided. Vinayak, her companion in mischief when they were younger, though he still pampered her and brought her books on the sly, now had his own group of friends to play football with, to hold heated discussions on cricket and politics with, and to go out with, while Anu was confined to the house. Her girl cousins treated her as an oddity, suspiciously eyed her pile of books, shuddered at her rebellious ideas, and kept their distance. Pundlik, another childhood playmate, also could not understand her obsession with reading and looked equally aghast at her wanting to do something exciting, something beyond the housework.

Her school friends were no better. Her whole life was the school, her room in the house that she shared with her cousins, and the inner courtyard. She became morose and irritable and started snapping at Gauri and Shanta—the maids—and at the younger children for no reason. Her books became her only companions and the more she read, the more she hankered after a different kind of life.

'Whatever I want to do, wherever I want to go, whoever I want to be friends with, not allowed! I have got to get out of here to some place where people read and discuss and swim and dance and do all sorts of exciting things, where *I* can do exactly what I want to do and not just cook and sew and look after the house because that's all that is expected of women,' Anu, who hated cooking and sewing and housework, said to Maushi fuming with frustration.

When Anu turned fifteen, to Maushi's secret relief and to Anu's great pleasure, Baba's brothers insisted on dividing the farms and the houses amongst them and separating the family into smaller units. Left with a house with just one internal courtyard for her, Baba and the three children—one courtyard house but still very large with many rooms—Maushi immediately pestered Baba into breaking down the rooms that enclosed the rear part of the courtyard and creating a back veranda that opened out into the back garden. Women's work – all that cleaning of the grain and peeling and chopping of vegetables and grinding, all noisy, messy chores – require a separate rear area to replace the inner courtyard, she said.

The new back veranda now became a place of all activities for her. Now she could watch her herb garden and even part of the flower garden and the mango and tamarind and audumber trees and the well while sitting on the back veranda. Now she was in direct contact with her garden all the time. And Anu, who had been chafing at having to share a room with her cousins, immediately claimed a separate one for herself and – hurrah! – this having been men's courtyard previously, all the rooms had windows looking on to the outside.

A little relaxed now, free of all the aunts and uncles and cousins keeping a constant watch on her, she tried to find some outlets for her interests. Now, whenever Baba and Gajanan were out of the house, she would consciously ignore her girl cousins and go out to talk to Vinayak's friends gathered on the front veranda. But they too giggled uncomfortably at her interventions in their discussions and looked to Vinayak to send her back into the house. 'Just hold it,' Maushi wanted to say as she watched Anu flouncing away angrily. 'She probably knows more than any of you about whatever it is that you are discussing so heatedly. What books she has read!'

'There is a big wide world out there, Aai,' Anu said to her. 'With so many exciting things happening, so many different things to do. Here, I can't even breathe. I have got to get out of here.'

'I have got to get out of here,' became Anu's refrain.

What an eye-catcher she was even at sixteen. When she dressed in all the finery for the weddings and thread ceremonies and pujas, men would watch her enchanted and then talk to Baba about their sons, about their sons' interests, and about how good were their sons' prospects. Women would eye her and sidle up to Maushi asking, does she know cooking, does she know sewing?

Maushi knew they were all waiting for her to come to the marriageable age before making marriage offers for her. Discreetly, of course. Just a word through the local priest or the vaisin – the midwife. And though she concealed it, Maushi also took pride in that fact for normally an offer would be sent from the girl's side and the boy's side would see quite a few girls and weigh all the factors such as the family details and the dowry offered and the girl's looks and accomplishments in household duties before choosing one of them.

None of the men or women though asked about Anu's school performance, her interests, her aspirations or what she might want from life, while Anu, even then disdainful of her girl cousins who looked forward only to marriage, said, 'Surely there is something more to life than just marriage. Women do all sorts of things out there, Aai. They choose their friends, go out to restaurants, fall in love, marry whom they like, and live exactly as they want to. They are engineers and lawyers and big bosses and when they talk and discuss, people listen to them,' she added as she imagined herself doing something important – what? – well, something, something other than cooking and housekeeping; something that would get her accepted in that big wide world as someone worthwhile. 'I am stifled in here. There is nobody to talk to, nothing to do,' she would moan in frustration, 'I have *got* to get out of here.'

'It's all those books she has read that have turned her head,' Baba's aunt said. 'Give her a year or two and she'll forget the books and be mooning for a husband,' and she won accolades as a prophetess. By the time spring came and mango trees started looking ethereal being totally covered with delicate tiny creamy pale-gold blossoms and the mynas started singing and the cuckoos started calling their mates, Anu had started sitting dreamy eyed, swaying on the swing in the backyard that Vinayak had hung with two ropes from the tamarind tree watching the mango blossoms during the day, and in the night, the moon and the star-studded sky instead of reading in her room.

She became particular about caring for her looks, badgering Maushi for herbs for her skin, herbs for her hair, and bemoaning a solitary pimple or some imagined flaw in her body. She, who had hardly ever bothered to glance in a mirror, now spent hours in front of it trying out different hairstyles and twining different coloured flowers in her hair, saris that would enhance her colouring, and different pieces of jewellery in her ears and around her neck. She mooned melodramatically around the house unaware of all the activity around her and whenever Baba was out of the house, she would bring the radio from his room – the radio strictly monitored by Baba to play only the news and devotional songs and select Marathi programmes – on to the back veranda and hum with it the romantic songs it played while swaying on the swing under the tamarind tree with a wistful expression on her face.

In the mango orchard the cuckoo sings
a song of love to the spring.
On the newly opened buds the bumblebee flits
courting them with his hum.
Oh my love, I wait for you.

One tune of the cuckoo's song I have saved in my mind
to sing in your ear.
One blossom in the garden I have saved from the bumblebee
for you to fasten in my hair.
Oh my love, I wait for you.

Her cousins nudged each other watching her and giggled behind their hands and her aunts and visiting women relatives looked at her with fond smiles. 'She is just a young girl coming of age,' they said to Maushi. 'It will be years before you have to think of her marriage.' But Maushi was already on the lookout for the so-called modern families with sons, especially those in cities, who at a later time might cherish Anu as their daughter-in-law. For though the family thought that Anu's rebellious ideas were now a thing of the past, Maushi knew differently. She knew that in Anu's mind a romantic marriage and fulfilment of her intellectual pursuits were intertwined, one leading to the other. 'Someone I could talk to, someone I could love,' Anu had said.

'After I finish college, I will go to Mumbai to Sulakshana-atya's. May be find a job,' she said taking it for granted that she would be going to college.

'A job!' Maushi said shocked. No, nothing wrong in that, she told herself, but what job would Anu get, unskilled and unequipped as she was? And Baba would never allow it anyway. Nor would her atya's husband without Baba's permission. Baba would probably not even allow her to go to Mumbai.

'Unless...,' Anu said.

Unless! Maushi had watched her eyeing the boys at weddings and other family functions across the aisle separating men and women's sitting areas. And though a love marriage as such was just unthinkable – and how would she get to talk to and come to know a boy except from a distance anyway? – Anu knew she could always cajole Maushi into pressurising Baba to send the marriage offer to some chosen family. And of course she was more likely to meet someone she liked in Mumbai. Maushi asked Govind-bhatji, the family priest, to come over the same afternoon.

'Too young, too young,' Govind-bhatji said. 'Surely she still has much to learn about managing a house as yet. You wouldn't want to send a half-trained girl into another family. Think of your family's honour!'

'I wasn't proposing that we make an offer for her,' Maushi said stiffly, offended at his patronising manner. 'I only wanted you to get information about those families.'

'You don't have to go looking for a match for her. It will come right to your doorstep in due time. And why Mumbai? I know quite a few families around here who have their eyes on her.'

But Maushi knew what she was talking about. She knew that Anu would never settle down to being just a housewife in a village; that she would always hanker after what she called, 'something more to life'.

The problem that the family thought was now behind them came forth in earnest when Anu finished school and time came for her to join the college. Not all the girls from the family attended college; usually only those whose parents had already moved to a town or city did so. But Anu had taken it for granted that she will be studying further and had set her heart on going to the science college – she had always done well in physics and chemistry exams in school – though she wasn't quite clear about what she would do after that. 'College?' Baba said. 'What use is college education to a girl?' And that should have been the end of that. It was dinned in all their heads from childhood that one did not answer back to or argue with one's father or husband or any elder. But this time Anu used her childhood feminine tricks. With Maushi and Vinayak supporting her – 'Nowadays all good boys want college-educated girls, Baba,' Vinayak had said – Anu pouted, sulked, and let her big black eyes be brimming with tears, and used all her coquettish, feminine wiles until ultimately Baba relented but only to an extent.

'Girls' college,' he said sternly. 'And in the arts section. None of this science nonsense.'

Rumours and gossip about Anu started almost immediately. Once away from the village, she bloomed. Going to a college in Panaji, almost an hour's bus ride away, escorted there and back by Vinayak, and not really interested in the arts course, she thought she could use the in-between time as she liked without any supervision. College library was a treasure-house to be explored and read in the night in the privacy of her room. For the daytime, while she waited for her prince charming to appear and lead her to the exciting land of her books, she had other plans.

Changing into borrowed jeans, she excitedly roamed the beaches and frequented the dhabas and the sort of places where she didn't expect to meet anybody from the family with her newfound college friends, and watched the hippies from a distance. They, even the girls no older than she, swam in the sea, and played ball on the beach, and danced and laughed so freely – without any inhibitions. They went wherever they pleased, did whatever they wanted to, and cared two hoots for the family honour or for what people said about them. 'Those boys, they don't look at girls like our men do, Aai. They are friends with those girls. They talk together, they have long discussions, Aai, they laugh together,' she told Maushi with envy and jealousy bursting out of her. 'They are so free, Aai, nobody tells them what to do. They live exactly as they please without any of these restrictions. They could read books all day if they wanted to. They don't need anybody's permission to *want* something, Aai,' she said in such a hushed awestruck tone that even Maushi felt a catch in her heart. Frightened for her – 'young are so careless,' Maushi thought – she still was loathe to forcibly restrain Anu even as she cautioned her against these escapades.

'We have a thousand relatives in North Goa, daughter,' she told her. 'And that means two thousand eyes watching you.'

They did have a thousand relatives in North Goa and two thousand eyes did watch Anu. At times stories of her infraction of social rules reached Maushi even before she reached home in the evenings. Women relatives would come to visit Maushi in the afternoon and whisper that Anu had been mixing with Christians, she was seen with a group of them in places that she had no business to be in, in places where a Hindu girl from a good family should not be seen, and that too when she should have been attending her classes. Maushi listened tight-lipped and said those couldn't have been such bad places to be in since the menfolk of these women had also been there to see Anu anyway. Women looked at her aghast and quickly took their leave.

When it became apparent that no action was being taken to restrain Anu, menfolk started coming to talk to Baba – an extreme measure. After all, this was women's business. It was Maushi's responsibility to manage and train the young women in the house—the daughters, the daughters-in-law—and to ensure that they abide by the rules and regulations of the household. At dusk Baba would burst into the women's room raging at Anu. 'In this land of Sati-Savitri, my own daughter is putting me to shame!' he would fume. For some time the whole household would be in turmoil with everyone trying to find a corner to hide in, to be unobtrusive. Baba never asked Anu whether any of those incidents were true nor did he ask her for any explanations. He would vent his rage and depart with the standard threat of stopping her from going out of the house at all but Maushi knew he wouldn't. That would be a greater shame on to the family since it would make public what should have been tackled within the family. It would also raise unwelcome doubts and suspicions at the time of her marriage. But she doubted if Anu would be allowed back to the college after the term was over. She knew that Baba had also had Vinayak on the mat, had berated him severely and told him to keep a strict control on Anu's movements and friends. And also that he was now earnestly trying to arrange a match for Anu though she still had a couple of years of wait before reaching the normal marriage age.

'At least find her a Mumbai family,' she said to him. 'She won't be happy in a village household.'

'She *will be* happy in whichever household she is married into,' Baba thundered in reply.

'There is nobody I know in any of those families who I could talk to or look up to leave aside fall in love with, Aai. I will die if I have to marry one of them,' Anu cried to her with despair written all over her face and Maushi commiserated with her with a heavy heart but could think of no way out.

Anu, aware that time was running out for her, also aware that only she could find a way out for herself and that was to find an outsider who would marry her and take her away from here, now grew desperate. With Vinayak's connivance she spent most of her time on the beaches taking surreptitious dips in the inviting sea, trying to devise some strategy that would get her out of this dire predicament. It was on one of those clandestine jaunts of hers as she walked out of the water after one of the furtive swims, that she looked straight into Alec's eyes. He was tall and lean, handsome, patrician in bearing, well dressed, and oh those eyes! They were watching her with absolute enchantment in them and Anu looked back into them equally enchanted.

8

When Vinayak brought Alec for a meal at the house that first day as a fellow lawyer of Siddharth on a visit from vilayat, Anu, in her green sari with yellow border and with gold zumkas in her ears, was standing in the doorway to the back veranda leaning her back against the door frame. Alec looked from the door to the men's room straight along the passageway at Anu at the other end of it and looked again and then just couldn't take his eyes away. And Anu blushed.

Watching them both, Maushi intuitively surmised that this was not the first time they were meeting and also that it was Anu who – with Vinayak's collusion – had engineered this visit of Alec's to their house. And also that – recalling Pundlik's story about Anu in jeans on the beach – this probably was the first time he was seeing her all dressed up in a sari and jewellery.

Alec thoroughly enjoyed his visit. He was enchanted by the old house with its shell-fitted window shutters and with creepers climbing on the veranda pillars. Wide main doors panelled with narrow horizontal planks oiled black and studded with pyramidal brass studs opened on to the passage to the internal courtyard with the holy basil in its own planter at the centre of it. Fluted columns with lotus capitals ran along the veranda on all four sides of it, and carved timber windows of upper floor rooms looked down into it from two sides. And the men's room! It was an imposing room with high dark-raftered ceiling and moulded cornices, with floral designs painted on the walls around large gold-framed portraits of imposing, stern-faced ancestors, and with ancient bell-shaped etched glass shades for lights hanging on brass chains from the ceiling and brackets on the walls, and furnished with old carved sofas and diwans with embroidered cushions and bolsters and marble-topped tables, and with six-feet-high etched mirrors hanging on the walls. And oh the floors! Floors of all the rooms were laid with antique tiles arranged in patterns that glowed with the polish acquired over a century of use. The whole house bespoke of age, quality and status.

It was a cool day and the garden was a riot of colours with flaming red gulmohars and yellow laburnums and purple jacarandas along the compound wall forming a backdrop for other colourful trees and shrubs. Alec, Baba and Siddharth sat under the partial shade of the neem tree surrounded by flowers with bumblebees humming and butterflies flitting around them, talking lightheartedly about casual topics. Alec enjoyed the relaxed discussion about British political system and law with Baba and Siddharth so much so that he even managed to ignore Gajanan's sporadic barbed comments. He enjoyed the cool rose petal sarbat that Maushi had made from the roses in the front garden. He enjoyed the mild curries with coconut milk that Vinayak's wife had especially cooked for him and he was totally enamoured by the dining-room setting. They sat on low individual wooden platforms just a couple of inches off the ground with individual foot-high wooden stools in front of them arranged with a silver thali, silver bowls and a silver water lota and glass each. All the sitting platforms called paats, and the dining stools called chaurangs were painted in bright colours and inlaid with polished brass flowers. Designs made with rice powder encircled the thalis. Men and boys including Siddharth's three and five-year-old sons ate first. Women and girls served. Alec was so enrapt in watching Anu bending over before Vinayak's thali to serve him that he missed putting up his hand to contain Vinayak's wife who was serving him jilebis—fried gram flour spirals soaked in sugar syrup—and she, after a naughty glance at Anu, kept piling his thali high. But Gajanan, who also had noticed Alec's interest in Anu, brought his attention back by maliciously informing him that 'in a Hindu home it is good manners to leave a clean thali' and Alec blanched on seeing the pile of jilebis on his thali. But Baba was annoyed at this levity and made them all quail before him with a stern look and reminded them of what the Vedas said – 'atithi devo bhava' – a guest should be treated as God.

For the next eight days, Alec was a constant visitor to the house at the invitations of Vinayak. Many of Vinayak's cousins would also drop in and they would all loll around either on the diwans in the men's room or on cane chairs in the garden drinking tea or sarbat and plying Alec with questions about the Western way of life in general and about England in particular. They were all highly curious to know about London society and at times found it difficult to believe that the outrageous scenes that they had seen in Western movies were in fact a normal way of behaviour for the vilayatis. 'Are women really so outgoing in London? Doesn't it make them mannish and overbearing? Doesn't it make them lose all sex appeal?' they asked. And then the real questions: 'Do men and women really kiss on the public streets? Do women really go to the offices in those short skirts, showing their thighs? And wear those low-cut evening gowns to dinners? How can they appear in public without proper dresses? How do their husbands allow them to be so shameless? No Hindu girl will ever be allowed to appear in public dressed so sparsely,' they said virtuously, trying to mask their lust for white women behind a show of morality.

They too had noticed Alec's infatuation with Anu. His forgetting to drink his tea or burning his tongue with hot bhajias while trying to catch glimpses of her—in the garden, under the tamarind tree, by the well; his total lack of attention to their discussion while watching Anu stretch upwards to pluck chameli flowers from the creeper climbing on the front veranda pillars or when she bent over by the gate to feed rice to the cow brought there by a village woman. They smirked knowingly catching each other's eye and derisively said, 'This guy is hooked,' to each other behind his back.

Quite often Siddharth and at times even Baba would spend part of the day in discussions with Alec though Gajanan avoided him, throwing disparaging looks at him whenever he passed him. It was not an accepted practice to entertain a Christian, and that too a vilayati, in one's home but Baba liked having Alec around since he avidly drank in Baba's discourses on the essence of Hinduism.

'It's a misconception that we have thousands of gods,' Baba told him once. 'There is the pure consciousness above all, the One Absolute, the Brahman who is omniscient, omnipresent and omnipotent yet formless and without attributes, who can only be described in a negative way: neti, neti, neti—not this, not this, not this. All other gods and goddesses are only manifestations of the different aspects of the One Absolute. Such as Vishnu the Preserver,

Shiva the Destroyer, Saraswati the Goddess of Learning and Laxmi the Goddess of Wealth. The aim of every Hindu is to realise the Brahman, to merge with this pure consciousness, to attain moksha.'

Alec found this concept very impressive. With his Anglo-Saxon ancestry, he could understand and also appreciate the need for different deities for different forces of nature, for different attributes, for different functions. A destroyer Shiva, a bountiful Laxmi: something tangible to fear; something visible to worship. An atavistic memory of pagan festivals and ancient rites stirred in his subconscious.

He was particularly attracted to the concept of the holy Troika: Brahma the Creator, Vishnu the Preserver and Shiva the Destroyer; three separate deities as well as one deity with three aspects, three faces.

'It's the right religion for such an ancient, multifaceted society,' he said.

'No,' Baba said another time. 'Religion is not the right word for dharma. Dharma encompasses much more than that. Manav Dharma, which is the dharma of people, includes moral and ethical duties also. But basically dharma is a way of life, a way of being, essence of an entity – whether animate or inanimate. So there is the dharma of the human beings but also of the animals and of the rocks and the mountains and the rivers. They all have a way of being. That's their dharma.'

'Does Hinduism then advocate a rigidly regulated, ascetic, pleasureless way of life?' Alec asked Baba one day after Baba had explained to him the Code of Dharma—the duties of every person and the rituals he has to follow.

'Not at all,' Baba said. 'Hinduism accepts that it's natural for men to seek worldly pleasures. Our scriptures include artha, that is accumulation of material wealth and kama, which is satisfaction of sensual pleasures, as two of the legitimate pursuits in man's life along with the following of dharma and attainment of moksha.'

'Ah!' Alec said.

Baba would even sit around nodding his head while Siddharth explained the Hindu customs and talked of how everybody's behaviour and the whole society were controlled mainly by the elders through the social mores rather than through the laws made by the lawyers. They treated him with respect and only Gajanan snickered at the blush on his face when Anu, with her eyes demurely downcast, came to the men's room with trays of snacks to serve them.

One morning a village boy came over reverently bearing an exquisite deep pink lotus in both his hands, followed by an admiring crowd chattering excitedly. 'It has more than fifty petals,' he proudly told Baba.

'Wahwah,' Baba said looking at it enchanted. He told him to wait, went to the well and washed his hands and feet and face, and only then accepted the lotus with both his hands. 'It's a highly revered flower for us,' he told Alec. 'In the beginning when there was nothing, when everything was unmanifested, Lord Brahma rose out of the milky ocean seated on a lotus and created the universe. It's also a symbol of the spiritual journey and enlightenment of mankind. It's born in mud, rises out of murky waters, and spreads its petals to the sun. That's the meaning of life's quest.'

Alec found this enjoyment and worship of beauty everywhere: in the rangolis—rice powder designs—made around the thalis and at the main door and filled in with powders of other bright colours, in the colourful way the thalis were arranged with specific places for sweets and curries and condiments, in the yantras—those geometric designs—hanging on the walls of the gods' room and which were worshipped and meditated upon. Sometimes Vinayak and his cousins would take Alec to the seashore. They didn't swim or frolic on the beach but just sat on some rocks watching the waves or the glorious golden-red-purple winter sunset and exulting in it. 'On the full moon day in the month of Ashwin in autumn, we offer coconuts to the sea to keep it happy and satisfied,' Vinayak said.

If his talks with Baba and Siddharth were heavily philosophical and legal, his afternoons with Vinayak and his cousins were of equally lighthearted banter with tea or many glasses of cool sarbats and hot bhajias. Alec was beguiled by their easy relationship with each other—calling each other brother even though as he understood some of them were distant cousins, some even in-laws having married their sisters—by the bonding and the camaraderie amongst them and yet the way they respected the elders even within their peer group. They referred to themselves quite nonchalantly as Bhau-log—Band of Brothers. They supported each other in anything and everything.

One day, on arriving at the house, he found all of them gone to the help of one of their cousins who had had an accident with his motorcycle leaving a youngster to await and entertain Alec until their return. The cousin had hit a bullock cart. 'All of them?' Alec asked. 'What will all of them do there?'

'You never know what help he might have needed,' Vinayak said when they all came back. 'It was better that everybody be there. Just rally around him. Kind of moral support, you know.'

They candidly discussed all their problems, even the business or marital ones, among themselves and though Alec was embarrassed to hear personal details, none of them showed any awkwardness at his presence. They freely told him of their misfortunes and their good-luck stories and their future hopes and expectations, and with equal candour bluntly asked him everything about himself: his family—father, mother, uncles, cousins, and grandparents—and what each did, his age, and his income. 'How much? How much do you earn per month? How many rupees?' Narayan had persisted in spite of Alec pointedly ignoring him and desisted only when Alec turned to look at him down his patrician nose with his lips set in that English hauteur and his eyebrows raised superciliously.

He also squirmed uncomfortably at the sentimentality they so openly displayed during their talks in the group. From his childhood, his father, teachers and priests had dinned it into his head that Englishmen do not wear their feelings on their sleeves. Here they all became misty eyed at the romantic tale that Kashinath narrated and had tears running down their cheeks when Ananta described his plight. 'What your parents must have gone through!' Vinayak said wiping his eyes. They don't dissemble; they are much more honest with their emotions than we are, Alec decided, and without any false pride either.

He also noticed and envied the confidence this sharing and togetherness generated in them when dealing with the world outside the family. They approached everything with the sure knowledge that there would always be someone around to share their happiness, or provide with a shoulder to cry on if required. Well, I guess it must be a relief not to have to bottle-up one's emotions and put up a stiff upper lip, Alec thought, not to be always on one's guard. Moreover, a stiff upper lip can get strained a lot. And it must be a comfort to openly seek and get succour.

A family here is like a club in London, he thought with sudden insight, with a lot more openness and interdependence thrown in. Alec found himself relaxing his English guard in their company, even admiring their casual approach to everything.

He was amazed to know that they all met at least every second day. If they happened to be there at mealtime, they all filed into the dining room without hesitation, without waiting to be invited, and if there were too many of them, they just sat on long durris—thin cotton carpets—spread on the veranda floor outside the dining room. Nor did the household ever seem to run out of food. They were equally amazed to know that Alec had no brothers or sisters and that he met his cousins mostly just once a year – usually for Christmas dinner at his grandmother's who lived alone, by herself.

One day sitting in the garden with Vinayak and his cousins, he saw a middle-aged woman come through the gate, all decked up in a new sari and jewellery, with flowers in her hair and a big happy smile on her face.

'Ah Parvati-bai, so Dayanand-bhau has come, eh?' Vinayak said in a bantering tone. 'Those bangles look new to me.'

She blushed and bashfully covered her mouth with her pallav before scurrying away towards the back veranda and Vinayak and his cousins laughed.

'She has come only to show off her new bangles,' someone said.

'Is she happy that Dayanand has come or that he has brought her new bangles?' someone else asked and they all laughed again while Alec looked on perplexed.

'Her husband is a contractor working in Pune; comes over three–four times a year. They are trying to collect enough cash for their three daughters' dowries,' Vinayak explained.

'Doesn't she want to go over there and live with her husband?' Alec asked and they all laughed loudly at his question.

'Catch Parvati-bai going and living anywhere outside this village,' one of them said and others nodded in agreement.

'He probably has a second wife in Pune,' someone said.

'Possibly. Brahmanand from the next village has one. And two children also. My sister-in-law's brother has visited him there.'

'He would of course need one if he is going to live there most of the year.'

Alec, surprised at their casual acceptance of this way of life, repeated the story to Baba and Siddharth in the evening when Siddharth had dropped in after the courts had closed. 'That's bigamy,' he said. 'His second marriage is totally illegal. Does the first wife know?'

'Sure she does,' Siddharth said. 'But he hasn't deserted her. It would be different if she were one of the deserted wives. They have no life to speak of. But then there are hardly any of them around.'

'Why?' Alec asked. 'What happens to them?'

Siddharth flicked his hand to indicate that that was absolutely of no importance. 'Dayanand maintains his wife and children, comes down every once in a while. After all, this is *his* village and *his* children. And also the house belongs to *him*. He wouldn't want to give that up.'

'And she doesn't mind what he does otherwise?'

'How can she? Manusmriti, that's Manu's Laws, written two thousand years ago, clearly states that though he may be destitute of any virtues, debauched or of bad conduct, or devoid of any good qualities, yet a husband must always be worshipped as God by a faithful wife.' Baba said quoting verbatim.

'You don't mean to say women here still follow that!' Alec exclaimed in amazement.

'Of course they do. That's our dharma,' Siddharth said.

Alec mulled over it and was still thinking about it when just two days afterwards a young couple came over, the wife still in her wedding finery. She went around the house to the back veranda while the young man squatted on the ground in front of the front veranda facing Baba.

'So you have given up the idea of going to the night school and taken up that road worker's job in Satara?' Baba asked him.

'Yes, Sarkar.'

'Good,' Baba said nodding his head. 'It's said in the Gita that it's not right to take over another's dharma however good you may be at it. One should always follow one's own dharma.'

'Yes, Sarkar,' the young man said looking at the ground.

'When are you leaving for Satara?' Baba asked.

'Tomorrow, Sarkar,' he said.

'Taking your wife?'

'How can he?' Gajanan said. 'Who will look after his old parents?'

'That's right, Sarkar,' the young man said. 'She has to stay back to look after my parents.'

'Your parents can move in with your uncle's family,' Vinayak suggested. 'They live right next door, don't they? They will care for them. Sadanand's parents did. That's what families are for!'

'Yes, Sarkar. But until they do so it's their daughter-in-law's duty to stay with them and serve them,' the young man said.

'Why did he get married if he wasn't in a position to take his wife with him?' Alec asked after the couple had left having touched everybody's feet including Alec's who didn't know the right way to respond and was terribly embarrassed and Vinayak had explained the situation to him.

'Who would look after his parents with him away?' Gajanan said. 'His other brothers are dead; sisters are married. It was necessary that he marry and leave a wife behind to care for them.'

'Is this a common system here? Wife staying back in the village?'

'They belong to low caste,' Baba said with a dismissive gesture. 'And of course it's a man's duty to care for his parents. So if a wife has to stay back in the village, she stays.'

'We are not like vilayatis. We look after our parents,' Gajanan said sardonically and though Baba gave him a sharp glance, he didn't say anything.

'Hinduism is very mystifying,' Alec said to Baba once, after Baba had explained him the different spiritual paths to the realisation of Self. 'There are so many contradictions in it. It is holistic in its approach encompassing all elements, its emphasis is on self-exploration, on free inquiry into self-knowledge, and its goal is spiritual liberation; yet it's rigid and restrictive in practice especially in caste system and in many of the societal controls especially over women.'

Baba nodded appreciatively. 'Yes, those are two totally different aspects,' he said. 'Shrutis, that is, the revelations of the Supreme Knowledge and the philosophic treatises such as the Vedas and Upanishads, are the exponents of free inquiry; their philosophies have been debated upon; they advocate the exploration of a spiritual path to self-realisation. But all of that is a personal quest that every man must follow individually. In the meanwhile, the society must function. And so there are the Smritis, such as the dharma shastras, or the Manusmriti, which specify the codes of conducts, the rules of behaviour, the system for organising the society. And they necessarily have to be strict to ensure the smooth functioning of the society.'

'But then how do you explain one's expectation of different ways of behaviour from different people in similar circumstances?'

'It's not confusing at all. Rules for every action to be taken by each one of us have been codified a long time ago. Manusmriti has categorically stated everyone's rights and duties by caste and gender and their relationships for every stage of their lives, for every age, and for every situation. Everything falls in place when you follow those laws. Surely even in your country you classify people according to their status? You wouldn't expect a Lord and a footman to react in the same manner to a particular situation, would you?'

Just then Anu came into their view, plucking flowers in the garden with a basket held at her waist. She chose a particularly glorious red rose, put the basket down, and stretched backwards to fasten it in her hair.

'Yes, yes, of course we do,' Alec said absentmindedly, all his attention glued on Anu and Baba glared at her. But when Baba went to the back veranda to give strict instructions to Maushi not to send Anu to the men's area for anything – 'Send one of the maids: Gauri or Shanta,' he said – Maushi looked up blankly at him. 'How can I send a maid to serve a guest?' she asked and Baba turned and came away tight-lipped.

9

When Gajanan came to his room, Baba was standing at the window looking out with his forehead furrowed and his lips compressed in impatience. Outside, the large shady trees in the compound had created a green filigree that filtered the afternoon sun streaking in through the window. Gulmohars in their burning red splendour stood in a group near the front wall—a burst of fire against the green filigree. Under the window, bumblebees hummed on red roses and on golden-yellow sunflowers, and butterflies flitted in between them. But Baba hardly saw any of them. He was watching the road partially visible through all the greenery, in between the gulmohars. He could just see the people passing on the road – it being a few feet below the level of the garden – the river beyond being much more visible, its blue-green waters shimmering in the afternoon sun.

'Baba, may I talk to you?' Gajanan asked respectfully standing on the threshold of Baba's room.

Baba turned from the window to look at him and nodded, well aware of what was on Gajanan's mind.

Gajanan came nervously into the room and stood uncomfortably before him clenching and unclenching his hands. Baba raised his eyebrows and stared at him without a word, further unsettling him, unnerving him. Gajanan fidgeted, shuffled his feet, looked at the floor. Baba leaned his tall, lean frame back against the windowsill and waited, watching him.

At last Gajanan gathered his courage and looked up at Baba. 'You have to forbid Vinayak from inviting Alec to the house, Baba,' he said in a rush. 'Already there is some gossip in the village.'

Baba frowned and kept staring at him. Gajanan flushed and dropped his eyes to look at Baba's feet. 'He looks too much at Anasuya,' he mumbled looking at Baba's feet.

Still without a word Baba turned back to the window and stood looking at the road, at the people walking on the road that were fleetingly visible through the trees. Gajanan raised his eyes to Baba's back and waited. The gulmohars outside rustled in a sudden gust of wind, a bumblebee floated in through the window, made a round of the room and floated out again, but Baba neither turned towards him again nor did he say anything. At last Gajanan could contain himself no longer. 'He is a vilayati, Baba,' he burst out at Baba's back. 'Our family honour is at stake.'

'You may go,' Baba said without turning around.

Gajanan stared at Baba's back for a moment and then dropped his eyes, turned on his heel, and walked out still simmering with anger.

Baba kept standing at the window, watching the road for Govind-bhatji, the family priest. He had been waiting for quite some time now, getting more and more impatient, his mood now further aggravated by Gajanan's untimely outburst though he had already known about the gossip in the village. He pushed Gajanan out of his mind; all his thoughts now concentrated on the news that Govind-bhatji would bring, the news that would settle everything.

'How many messages do I have to send to that son-of-a-priest before he will come to see me?' he muttered to himself annoyed at the priest. Normally Govind-bhatji, subservient to the family, would come running on receiving a message from the house. At times he would even drop in uninvited to read from the Gita or other holy books to Baba and the family. Today Baba had just sent him his third message when even a single message should not have been necessary. Govind-bhatji should have come by himself to report to Baba as soon as he came back from the village where Baba had sent him; and Baba knew that he had come back the afternoon before.

Now he saw him come scurrying down the road dressed in pure white dhoti and kurta, his white uparne—the long cotton scarf—neatly folded and draped on one shoulder, three finger lines of sandalwood paste drawn on his forehead, carrying his bundle of papers wrapped in white cloth, his pure white form flitting in between the red gulmohars. Baba waited till he had come through the gate and then went on to the front veranda to receive him and usher him into his room.

Govind-bhatji took his time. He sat cross-legged on the divan, opened his cloth-wrapped bundle of papers, wiped his forehead and shaven pate with the end of his uparne. Baba pulled a chair and sat facing him.

'Well?' Baba asked impatiently, bending towards him.

'Their second daughter will come of marriageable age in three–four years. They want to wait till she is married before considering a match for their son,' Govind-bhatji said looking down at the open bundle of papers in his lap, still dabbing at the sweat on his face with the end of his uparne even though the day was not warm and the room was cool.

'How old is she?' Baba asked.

'Sixteen.' Govind-bhatji said nervously.

More like five years, Baba thought sitting back in his chair, anger now replacing his impatience. He had been so sure of a positive response from this family that he had been merely awaiting a confirmation before starting the formal procedures. A bumblebee flew in towards his face and he swatted at it angrily, ineffectively.

Govind-bhatji looked up and saw the anger rising in Baba's eyes, his lips pressing into a thin line. 'That Mangal in Anasuya's horoscope is the problem,' he offered as a palliative even though he was well aware that the Mangal was quite mild in its aspect.

'Didn't you tell them of the puja we have done to appease the Mangal?' Baba asked belligerently.

'Yes, yes, I did, b-b-b-but,' Govind-bhatji started stammering.

'Didn't you tell them of the one-eyed rudraksha bead that Anasuya has worn around her neck for seven years to counteract it?'

'I... I... did...'

'Didn't you tell them of the dowry she will be bringing with her? The farmland by the riverside and the gold?'

Govind-bhatji nodded miserably.

'The answer is still no?'

Govind-bhatji hung his head unable to look at Baba.

'It's not only the Mangal in her horoscope, is it?' Baba asked bitterly, glaring at Govind-bhatji.

Govind-bhatji raised his head and looked Baba in the eye. Startled, Baba stared into his eyes, seeing in them scorn mixed with pity. He got up and went to stand by the window looking out, his back turned to Govind-bhatji, his temper beginning to rise to the boiling point.

The wretch of a girl! Her infamy travels ahead of any marriage offers I send for her. No family in Goa would have ever dared to refuse a marriage offer from our family in the past; in fact, it would have been a great honour to them. Till recently. Only a couple of years ago *they* all were lining up to make offers for her at the right time!

This had been his last gamble after the rejections from a couple of prominent North Goan families—rejections couched in very polite language, accompanied by plausible excuses, but rejections all the same—with that barbed query at the end: 'Isn't she too young for marriage as yet?' It had been a great shock to Baba. He had not expected to find the gossip about Anasuya so widespread and had also assumed that their family name would override the youthful capers of an immature girl. This family that he had just had Govind-bhatji approach was in a village in South Goa, quite a distance away, and not in a predominantly Hindu area. Nor was it quite up to their status.

'How dare they insult our family like that? My bad karma! What sins did I commit in my last birth to have a wretch of a daughter in this birth?' he asked himself in a rare bout of self-pity.

What now? No decent family is going to consider a marriage offer for Anasuya.

What if he were to get some impoverished family to accept her as a daughter-in-law because of the farmland and the cash and the gold she would bring in dowry? Could he entertain such a family in his house? Treat such a family with the great honour and respect due to a daughter's in-laws throughout her lifetime? Could he bow down to such a family? And it will certainly be a blot on their family honour. It will also affect the marriage chances of other youngsters in the family – not only of the children of his brothers but even of far removed cousins. They all will have to marry beneath them.

What then?

Have an unmarried daughter living in the house all her life? Impossible! Absolutely unthinkable! Not only will it mean a great loss of punya—merit which one has to accumulate to attain moksha—but, and much worse, an unbearable shame on the family name. A daughter has to be married, at any cost, to any groom. No matter if it impoverished or enslaved the rest of the family. No matter if the family had to bend their knees to everybody or even endure terrible insults. Even the poorest of the labourers mortgaged everything including themselves for a daughter's marriage. Also, having an unmarried daughter in the house will not only not improve the situation for the rest of the youngsters in the family but will make it far, far worse.

'Didn't the stupid girl realise that her behaviour would affect the whole family?' he muttered to himself seething with rage and frustration. Soon their family will be objects of scorn and pity of the whole village, of the whole community, of the whole of Goa—the scorn and pity that he had just seen in the eyes of Govind-bhatji.

'I will *not* tolerate an unmarried daughter in my house,' he said aloud to the roses and the sunflowers below the window, already tasting the bitter taste of shame in his mouth.

Laughter and voices floated in from the garden and Baba turned his head to look towards them. Alec was sitting in the garden under the neem tree talking to Vinayak and Siddharth.

Alec!

Of course Alec is thoroughly enamoured of Anasuya and that stupid girl is also making eyes at him! I can either deter him or give him that little nudge that is required to push him into making a marriage offer for her.

What is more harmful to the family honour? To have an unmarried daughter in the house who people will point fingers at for a lifetime, a constant reminder of the shame on the family name, or one married to a vilayati? Once she is out of the village, people will forget.

A vilayati! We consider them inferior—spiritually, culturally and morally—and yet we also worship their white skin; we feel inferior before them; we can't forget that once they were our rulers. Today theirs are the developed, powerful, rich nations. They send men to the moon. They were rajas in our recent past and they are rajas today. But our family is the aristocrats of this State. We are expected to hobnob with the vilayatis of the white skins, vilayatis who were our past rulers, on equal terms. And so though the whole community will be shocked for a while, there will also be jealousy, envy and admiration. It may even enhance our prestige. Alec has aristocratic looks, a haughty manner; he is well educated; he is obviously rich: hasn't he hired a car with a uniformed driver to bring him to the village and take him back every day? And the way he dresses! He could be projected as a prized catch rather than as a last resort.

Baba was the eldest son, the head of the family. And it was his daughter who was bringing this disgrace on to their family. He would have to have a solution in hand before calling the family council.

He went out into the garden to talk to Alec.

'A Hindu girl is brought up to consider marriage as her natural destiny; for her it's self-dedication, the true fulfilment of her womanhood,' Baba said. 'She is taught to treat her husband as god. She will do everything for him, his children and his family. With love. With selfless love. Hindu girls do not seek equality with men as Western girls do. They seek fulfilment within the marriage. Their role models are Sita, Sati and Savitri. They consider the husband's welfare and upholding of his honour as the supreme purposes of their lives.'

'But in law they are equal,' Alec said.

'This is the land of ancient dharma. Of Vedas, of Gita, and of Manusmriti. Here age-old conventions still rule supreme and social customs are followed more than the law,' Siddharth said. 'Here, in practice, a husband has total rights over his wife and no Hindu girl will even *dream* of going to the court against her family.'

Just then Anu came out into the garden dressed in a rose-coloured sari with roses in her hair and holding a tray of glasses full of rose sarbat and Alec was lost.

For Alec, those days were wonderfully exhilarating as well as tormenting. That sprawling, breathtaking old house, that blooming garden with rainbow-coloured flowers, those vibrant people in flowing bright dresses, their touchingly emotional yet easy-going manners, their enviable family bonds, that exotic way of life! London seemed far away, far back in time, a dead memory in the back of his mind. When he did try, with great effort, to evoke his memories of the city, of the courts of law there, of the family and friends, they all came to his mind in faded colours, grey and rigid, dull and vapid like cardboard cut-outs without any vitality of life in any of them. This sun-drenched lush land, this pulsating, exhilarating atmosphere, and these ebullient, intense people were the only reality to him. This was where he would live, this was where he would belong, and this was what he would possess. And Anu – he was haunted by her. She was in his view all the time—stretching, bending, moving with that indescribable grace of hers—and yet, now, here in this house that she had enticed him to, she was totally unapproachable. The more distance she put between them, the more he wanted her, wanted her badly, at any cost. He was willing to take any chances, sacrifice anything, to possess her again. It was a torment to him to have her so close yet so inaccessible. All the time that he spent there he had been trying to catch her eye, to hold her hand, to arrange a tryst but Anu was being elusive, playing a teasing, tantalising game. She would only throw him flitting glances from those deep, dark, bewitching eyes of hers, or give him secret, enticing smiles over her shoulder, or at the most, brush against him briefly in doorways and passageways – touches that sent goose pimples up his spine – but she painstakingly maintained the decorum required of her as a young woman in a traditional Hindu family.

On the eighth day of his visit to Anu's house, a thoroughly bewitched Alec asked Baba for Anu's hand in marriage.

The family council was called the same night. This being an issue of marriage, all elder women—Baba's aunts and brothers' wives and Maushi—also were asked to join in.

'A vilayati!' Baba's brothers said, shocked. 'They have no culture, no dharma and no spirituality. Their lack of any ancient civilisation has left them unrefined, decadent, and without any family ties.'

'Alec is very cultured and very highly educated.' Vinayak interposed and Baba's brothers scowled at him. Young men could be present in family councils but were not expected to open their mouths in front of elders especially to contradict them.

'He is a Christian!' they said disgustedly in answer to him. 'Does he expect Anasuya to convert to Christianity?' they asked Baba.

'He is very much interested in Hinduism. He is studying it seriously and already knows many of its doctrines. He may even convert himself,' Baba said. 'He also wants the ceremony to be according to Vedic rites.'

That mollified them a little.

'Is he proposing to take her to England?' Baba's aunt asked.

'Canada,' Baba said. 'He is English but settled in Canada.'

'Where is that?' Everybody wanted to know.

'Farther away than England, near America. It's as developed and prosperous a country as America. Alec owns quite a lot of property there.' Baba improvised; he hadn't dared to ask Alec too many personal details in the fear of losing this highbrow vilayati as a prospective son-in-law.

'There have been so many offers for her from high-caste landowning families in nearby villages,' Gajanan said. 'Those will be more profitable alliances.'

'There will be no dowry to pay if she marries this vilayati. She can't carry farmland with her to Canada,' an old aunt of Baba's reminded him pointedly.

'He doesn't want a dowry in any case. He is very well off in his own right,' Baba said.

'Being well off has never stopped anybody from asking for a dowry,' Baba's uncle observed knowingly.

'Alec wouldn't. He is a gentleman. I like him. And Anu does too.' Vinayak spoke voicing the sentiments of his cousins also and then blanched as Baba threw a scornful glance at him to let him know that neither his nor Anu's likes and dislikes were of any importance to the decision to be made.

'What do we know of his family?' Baba's uncle asked.

'He is an only son. His parents are dead and there is no family to speak of,' Baba informed them. 'They have a different family system in England. Everybody lives separately over there—even unmarried girls and boys; they all leave the house when they grow up. They do not have joint families like ours.'

They all looked perplexed at that. No family to speak of? There were always uncles and aunts and cousins. How can there be no family to speak of? And what about his father and grandfather and great grandfather? Who had they been?

'Then what do we know of him?'

'He is a very well-known lawyer. They respect him highly in the Lawyers' Club in Panaji. Even Judge Sardesai has a high regard for him.'

That impressed them greatly as Judge Sardesai was not to be taken lightly.

'He is also registered with the Bar Council in London,' Vinayak spoke again risking the displeasure of his elders. 'Siddharth has asked him.' He looked at Siddharth for confirmation and Siddharth nodded in agreement.

'It is an honour to our family that he has made an offer for one of our girls,' Baba said rubbing it in.

'These vilayatis have no moral sense. How can we be sure that he will treat our Anasuya properly?' someone asked and others gave him withering looks. Once married, a woman became her husband's property and how he treated her was nobody else's business, unless, of course, it reflected on the family honour.

'Has anybody checked his horoscope?' the old uncle asked.

'I got Govind-bhatji to prepare it from his birth date,' Baba said. 'It matches Anasuya's.' He elaborated what Govind-bhatji had said: that in both their horoscopes the marriage houses were in the oblique sight of the Mangal planet but its ill effects were cancelled by each other. Of course Govind-bhatji had hastened to add that since the marriage house in Anasuya's horoscope was in the oblique and not in direct sight of Mangal, the consequences anyway would have been trivial for her husband.

There was an uncomfortable silence after that. Mangal planet in the horoscope was the worst thing that could happen to a girl. It always foreboded a danger to the husband, even fatal if it were strong. It was not easy to marry off a Mangli girl. Only a family with Mangal in their son's horoscope would consider such a girl, whatever other virtues she may possess and irrespective of the family background. Though there were pujas to perform and jewels to wear to counteract its ill effects, families still hesitated to consider a Mangli girl. The oblique sight of the Mangal was not as bad though, quite weak in fact, and a good match could still be found if one persisted.

'It's not too difficult to find a Mangli boy,' Gajanan insisted.

The discussion went on and on.

Though Maushi didn't say anything, her heart was fluttering within her chest. Her keen experienced eye had already noted that Anu was pregnant. It was in her eyes. For the last few days, Maushi's mind had been in turmoil. This was a totally unthinkable thing to happen to a Hindu girl from a good family. They were trained to not even look at a man in the eye leave aside even a flitting touch, and flirting with one was totally out of question. It went against all norms of their religion and of their society. On the other hand, these things did happen and there were all sorts of potions available to avoid and also to get rid of unwanted pregnancies. The fact that Anu had not asked for any help in the matter or that she had even got pregnant, had made Maushi understand what Anu was undoubtedly trying to achieve. With an almost unbearable shock she had realised what it meant: that Alec had not yet committed to marriage and that this was Anu's last gamble, a gamble that could lead to disastrous consequences though she had to concede that it was the only recourse left to Anu in the circumstances. Almost against her will she found herself admiring her daughter's gumption to find a way, any way, to get out of here and not just sit back and be sacrificed on the marriage altar to someone chosen by the family. On her part she had been abetting Anu as much as she could: plying Alec with good food and sending Anu on errands that would put her in Alec's way.

The clinching argument was put forth by Baba's old uncle. 'I have been hearing that the girl is totally wayward: she has *Christian* friends and was seen on Miramar Beach wearing *pants*. It seems to me that she is attracted to vilayati culture and that the family cannot control her,' he said looking at Baba and Baba reddened and hung his head in shame at this rebuke. 'Either you have to find her a strong and Mangli husband very quickly or...' he paused and with his age-old but still sharp eyes stared at each of them, particularly at Gajanan, until each dropped his eyes, even Gajanan. 'In my opinion, it's best that she be married to this vilayati who will take her far away from here,' he continued, 'before she gets into any mischief that will bring shame on to our family name.'

The marriage date was set just a few days hence at the behest of the old aunt who said, 'Get her married quickly before this vilayati changes his mind. He has no family here to control his behaviour.' Maushi hastily agreed saying that she had been preparing for her daughter's wedding for years now, collecting saris and jewellery and silverware, so there was no reason to wait any longer.

10

Anu's marriage was performed with a pomp and show the like of which had never been seen in that area. The house was painted and decked out, garden festooned with coloured lights, and the front gate, main door and the veranda eaves were hung with yards and yards of garlands of marigolds interspersed with mango leaves. Upright banana trees were tied to all the doorposts, veranda pillars and the gateposts. There were two large tents erected—one in the front garden and another in the backyard—both covered in silk with silk hangings, and shehnai players in their traditional garbs and wearing plumed safas on their heads sat on red durris at the gate playing their music throughout the day. Baba's, his brothers', cousins', and even neighbours' houses were bursting with relatives who had come from outside the village. And the feasts! A couple of hundred women and girls were present just for Anu's turmeric ceremony and the feast after. The ceremony took hours as each woman in turn dipped the two mango leaves, one in each hand, in the turmeric paste and dabbed it on her forehead, cheeks, shoulders, knees, and feet while her cousins smeared it all over her body purifying her for the wedding ceremony. On the wedding day, Anu was gorgeous in her yellow turmeric-coloured wedding sari, Alec impressive in his silk dhoti-kurta, and the men of the family strutted around wearing red pugrees on their heads.

Anu and Alec left for South Goa immediately after spending the wedding night at one of Baba's uncle's home. There had been quite a shocked flurry in the family when Alec had announced that he had booked a hotel in Panaji for the night. It just wasn't done. Nor could they stay in Baba's house as Anu had to be sent away from there. And so the old uncle had graciously offered his house for the night. That brought another problem to the fore. Anu would have to upset a lota full of rice kept on the threshold of her new home symbolising the plentitude and prosperity that she was bringing to her new and now the only family, and then dip her feet in a thali of red kumkum powder before crossing the threshold – her imprinted footprints denoting the good fortune that she was bringing with her to her married house. Only all this good fortune should have been brought to her father-in-law's house or at least to Alec's house. Anu giggled at the thought of all this good fortune pouring into the old uncle's house and Alec fumed at the thought of having to spend the night in an old, dark and dank house with a cranky old man and his family while the rest of the family deliberated on this unforeseen problem.

However, Govind-bhatji rose to the occasion. He decreed that wherever the young couple stayed for the night would be deemed their temporary home and the good fortune would travel with them to their permanent home. And so Anu, with henna designs on her hands and feet and green glass bangles in between the gold ones on her arms, entered the married state by delicately nudging the lota full of rice with her right big toe and scattering the rice on the threshold of the uncle's house.

That night Maushi stood at the door of her house and watched Anu and Alec leave for Baba's uncle's house with Gajanan and Vinayak and other cousins escorting them and then sat down exactly where she was. Anu will at last be free and happy. She will at last escape here, be part of that big wide world that she had hankered after so much, with a husband of her choice. She will at last do what she had always wanted to do – something exciting. Maushi felt fulfilled but also empty and exhausted. The hustle and bustle of the marriage, the hordes of relatives that had descended on the house, the tension of all the arrangements as well as the exhilaration of the marriage itself had taken its toll on her. Sitting in the doorway she wiped the flow of tears from her eyes with her pallav and unaccountably, a chill passed over her. Shivering, pulling her pallav tightly around her shoulders, she got up and went into her room, and bolted the door. Everybody understood that. The daughter that she had brought up, cared for, nurtured, loved and cherished, had now become a stranger; now she belonged to another family.

On Anu's departure, Maushi's life reverted back to the routine. Her life was guided by the seasons: cleaning and storing the year's supply of grain in autumn, making jams in winter and pickles in spring, grinding and storing spices in summer. The house was always full of people. There was a natural spring near the village renowned for its curative properties and many of their relatives would come to take its waters, and naturally stay in Baba's house. The upper floor visitors' rooms were always full. Baba as the eldest son had inherited the mantle of the head of the household as well as the responsibilities of hospitality that went with it and he fulfilled them meticulously. Every summer his sisters, their children, and sometimes even their husbands – though for a very short period only – would come for the yearly sojourn to the Maher—mother's house—which now meant Baba's house. All religious festivals were celebrated at Baba's house with the whole family gathering there. Then there would be seventh month celebrations for expecting mothers, naming ceremonies of the newborns, and in spring, haldi-kumkums – women's get-togethers – when the special snacks and drinks made of raw mangoes were served to celebrate the arrival of spring. Besides all these were the fasts and vrats to be kept, the special pujas on special days to be performed, especially in the month of Shravan in the monsoons when it seemed to Maushi as if every day had a special significance requiring special pujas and special foods and special arrangements. The management and the supervision of it all were up to Maushi and she revelled in it.

Her days were busy. Mornings and evenings were devoted to the needs of menfolk and children. Midmornings, after the menfolk had left to pursue their occupations and children for the schools, she would spend in the garden with the gardener and personally supervise care of the more delicate plants and herbs. Now that the family had separated, she had started caring for the garden in the front yard also when the menfolk were not around and would even stand around at times watching her garden, watching the river, and the passers-by on the riverside road. Then it was time for her pujas. First the main puja of the gods in the gods' room and then the puja of the holy basil which grew in lonely splendour in its own three-feet-high square planter built with bricks and plaster, with ears at the four corners, and swastikas—the signs of sun—painted in saffron on all four sides of it, in the centre of the inner courtyard. After that she read from one of the holy books for an hour before the hustle-bustle of lunch started.

The hour that she spent every day in reading the holy books had always been viewed with suspicious mistrust by her women-in-law: Baba's mother, his aunts. 'A woman should devote herself to the wellbeing of her husband and children and the care of the house and nothing else. Reading holy books is men's privilege,' her mother-in-law had muttered soon after Maushi's marriage but had not objected openly to it since neither her husband nor her son seemed to mind it. It had been a daily routine of Maushi's since her childhood and she enjoyed it as much as looking after her plants.

After dinner, she spent time in Baba's room when he discussed the day's happenings with her—problems with the farm, events in the village, family situations. Baba took Maushi's advice seriously and more often than not followed it also though it was inconceivable that she should involve herself directly in any of these matters and of course she could never be expected to attend the family councils.

Maushi was very much aware of the respect with which Baba treated her but then she herself also never overstepped the limitations that society had imposed upon her as a woman. Her opinions were sober and judicious though she always deferred to Baba and his opinions. Baba, on his part, trusted her advice far more than that of the men in the family.

She knew that in almost all the families, including Baba's brothers', menfolk never talked to their wives about anything other than domestic matters and that too only occasionally. Neither did Gajanan, which saddened Maushi. Most times, opinions or questions or even explanations from women were called 'answering back' or 'being insolent' and were quite often answered with slaps or beatings. During the days when the whole family was staying under one roof, some mornings Maushi had watched her sisters-in-law come red-eyed into the kitchen, sometimes even with bruised cheeks or forearms and give some inane explanations and then burst into tears without any reason when the menfolk were not around. Once, after noticing her youngest sister-in-law futilely trying to cover her bruised arms and neck for a week, Maushi had mentioned it to Baba. He was the eldest in the family; he controlled other men. But Baba had shrugged it off. 'He is the husband. He has the right. And a few slaps never hurt anybody,' he had said. 'And she must have provoked him with all that chatter of hers.' And, Maushi had looked at him startled.

Of course she must have provoked him, Maushi admitted to herself, the way he ignores her. Even a slap or a beating was a touch, an acknowledgement of one's existence. Even hatred was preferable to total disregard of one's being.

Early evenings Maushi again spent in the garden while the boys played outside and the menfolk were either out on work or discussing weighty problems in the men's room and the women were getting busy with dinner preparations. Women's work would carry on till late in the night.

But the afternoons were women's own. Afternoons were the time for relaxation and socialisation. There was of course the housework still to supervise—cleaning of grain, grinding of spices, making of snacks, sewing, stitching, polishing silverware and brassware and on occasions, the afternoon visitors to look after—but still, it was a time for women to be together, to also chatter and gossip. That was the time to let their hair down and discuss their problems, seek advice and assistance. Many times her sisters-in-law, since they lived so close by, would cross over to Maushi's house for the afternoons with their servants bearing their work: the grain for cleaning or the clothes for stitching. Used to spending all their time in an enclosed courtyard, they were not much at ease on Maushi's back veranda where Maushi now spent all her time except when she was in the kitchen or the gods' room or when the women who *had* to be entertained formally in the inner room came visiting. Even Baba's brothers had protested strongly at this 'Christianisation' of the house when he had the rooms at the back broken down. 'No Hindu house has ever had a back veranda,' they had said. 'Only Christian houses have them. Our houses have always had internal courtyards.'

'The house has been Christianised from the day our great grandfather built it more than a hundred years ago,' Baba had retorted referring to the fact that the house faced the river like the Christian houses did and had not turned its back to the river like the Hindu houses. But facing away from the river would have meant facing south, the direction of Yama Raja—the God of Death, and on the east, the most favourable direction, were the cremation ghats. 'Nor is it a Hindu system to sub-divide a main family house,' he had continued.

But he had understood the reasons for it. In other families with tenanted lands, sons and grandsons moved to other places, to towns and cities, to find other jobs. In the families with other occupations, sons and grandsons graduated to something modern and also moved out of the village. Moneylender's sons joined banks and trader's sons became businessmen and schoolmaster's sons became government officers.

But in Baba's family majority of them stayed back in the village because of the untenanted land; just as he was sure that Gajanan would stay on in the village even if Vinayak moved out. Gajanan had already started making rounds of the farms and orchards with him and attending the meetings with supervisors and buying agents. And so the main house had become too crowded, the extended family too unwieldy as a single unit. Especially the women's courtyard had become rife with jealousies, petulancies and intrigues.

In time, after the initial uneasiness had passed, and since Baba had high compound walls built around the house before breaking the rear rooms thereby separating it and securing it from the rest of the estate and from the housing of the craftsmen and the artisans and the foremen that surrounded the house on three sides, all the family members had started enjoying the back veranda. In the mornings the audumber tree with the red-stone Ganesha underneath now became part of the house rather than the 'outside' for the men and in the afternoons, Anu, Maushi's younger daughter-in-law, and even visiting young girls enjoyed swaying on the swing that Vinayak had hung from the tamarind tree with two ropes.

Some afternoons other women relatives from nearby villages, always escorted, would drop in to discuss family matters and problems – those that were women's concern. Maushi's decisions in these matters were supreme. Nobody dared to contradict her or oppose any decision she made. It was as much due to the respect Maushi had earned as an individual as her status as the wife of the eldest son of the family. Even village women came to her for advice and young girls and boys sought her support against their families knowing that her word will be respected.

Maushi always had visitors dropping in in the afternoons though by custom women hardly went out of the house except on special occasions such as marriages, thread ceremonies or major pujas, or to visit expecting or newly delivered women relatives, or in sickness and death – and that too only of the close relatives. They were too busy in their kitchens otherwise to think of visiting anybody, they said. And for what? They had enough company in the women's courtyard with this joint family system, they said.

Some days Govind-bhatji would drop in to read them stories from the Pothi—scriptural teachings told through a collection of parables and mythological stories. Sometimes, though not very often, there would be bhajans and sometimes even kirtans in one of the nearby temples and then all the village women would be escorted there for the afternoon. The temples were always located outside the villages in some scenic place, either on top of a hill or by a riverside, and always in a glade. This was one of the few outings allowed to the women otherwise confined to the house and no woman would want to miss this chance of a get-together with other women besides the legitimate entertainment the afternoon would provide.

There would be a harmonium player, a tabla player and other musicians accompanying the priest clicking little cymbals tied to his fingers, sitting in the main open-sided pavilion of the temple outside the sanctum and the women would sit around them, listening to them, singing with them, and gossiping in between bhajans—devotional songs in praise of gods—sung mostly in a monotone. '*Gopala, Gopala, Devakinandan Gopala,*' the priest would sing and '*Gopala, Gopala,*' the women would chorus, swaying and clapping to keep the beat, almost lost in a trance.

Kirtans were different. Aimed mainly at men, a kirtankar would choose a moral or a philosophical principle from the scriptures and give a discourse on it. A good kirtankar's skill lay in making the topic understandable and interesting to the lay public and some kirtankars used parables or even musical renditions of stories from one of the epics or the Vedas to illustrate a point. A kirtankar would then stand before the audience and partly sing, partly recite with gestures to create the story. Discoursing on the good qualities that people should cultivate, he would give the example of Lord Rama and narrate incidents from Lord Rama's life—Rama, the most virtuous, principled, conscientious, courageous and exalted; Rama, the Dharma personified; Rama, who had accepted fourteen years of banishment into the forest to honour his father's promise to his stepmother; Rama, who had so bravely fought a war against the demon-king Ravana. 'And thus Rama led his army to slay Ravana and destroy his capital Lanka to rescue his wife Sita whom Ravana had kidnapped,' the kirtankar would recite in his baritone voice and then, '*Rama re Rama*,' he would burst into a song with all the musical instruments keeping pace with him and all would sit enthralled.

'He returned triumphant with Sita flying on the back of the great Garuda bird to reclaim his kingdom and establish Ramarajya.'

Ramarajya—Rama's rule, which signified a rule founded on justice, righteousness, mutual love, affection and respect amongst the populace.

Except for women.

After the devastating war, Rama told Sita that he couldn't take her back at all, contaminated as she was by having been held as prisoner for a year in Ravana's palace. She was free to go wherever she liked, live with whomever she pleased; his sole reason for the brutal war had been the vindication of *his* honour, not *her* rescue.

Sita, humiliated by both Ravana and Rama, the detested kidnapper and the loved and honoured rescuer husband, went through an ordeal by fire to prove her purity, and so Rama brought her back with him. But the citizens of his kingdom were not satisfied. And so Rama asked his brother Laxmana to take her back to the forest and desert her there – this time for life.

'On this earth born of the creator
should we learn of anyone but Rama?
So concerned for his people was the great king Rama,
that his honour and thereby theirs be not blemished,
by doubts raised of Sita.

'By the populace, questioning whether she could have stayed chaste while held for a year in captivity in Lanka by Ravana who was besotted of her...

'And so he sent her to the forest,
though to him it was a torment.

'But great kings are expected to make great sacrifices. And the great king Rama measured up to them.

'But a man must prefer fame and glory
rather than a wife, who after all is only
like sandal-paste or garland of flowers
an object of sensual pleasures.

And so to the forest he had her sent,
forever he abandoned her there.
For he was the Dharma incarnate,
the great king Rama, Lord of all men.'

So the kirtankar would sing in his baritone voice throwing up one hand to the sky, other placed on his breast, over the heart.

Gauri and Shanta also sang, though in a low monotone, whenever they were grinding anything on the grinding stones. The grinding stones were two huge big round slabs of stone almost two feet across, placed one above the other, the one on top with two holes in it, one hole in the centre for pouring in whatever they were grinding which they kept on doing in handfuls every now and then, and the other almost at the edge which had a foot-high round piece of wood sticking out of it and which they used to rotate the top stone over the lower one, sitting on the floor on opposite sides with their legs stretched out on two sides of it, and passing the wooden staff from hand to hand and to each other. And they sang to keep up the tempo:

'The shade, shade, of my love
follows behind, behind, Sita-bai
into the forest and into the jungle
a second time.

Rama re Rama,
what kind of a king were you?
Who knew not any dharma, dharma,
nor felt any qualms, qualms,
to banish a pregnant Sita-bai
to the jungle by guile?

The loyal wife who refused, refused,
her freedom from Ravana's jail
at the hands of the monkey king,
so as not to, not to,
deprive her beloved Rama of the honour
his own victory would bring.

Though cruelly spurned by him,
his honour, honour, she upheld,
his praises, praises, she would sing
my loyal Sita-bai.

Rama-re-Rama,

not worth of Sita-bai.

She a diamond chip,

he a weakling.

The great king Rama,

Lord of all men.'

So sang Gauri and Shanta as they ground the grains and the spices on Maushi's back veranda but they were only servants and of low caste and nobody paid any attention to what they sang.

In the evenings, after tending her garden again, Maushi sometimes stood watching the boys playing gilli-danda or ball on the road along the riverside. They were totally unconscious of themselves at those times, immersed in the spirit of the game with no elders dictating any rules of conduct. They jumped and kicked and ran and shouted and laughed without any restraint and Maushi disliked coming into the house to supervise the young girls helping with the preparation of the meal, all of them taught to walk demurely, to perform all their tasks delicately, all their movements so very restrained and controlled. She had never heard them laugh out aloud; come to think of it, she mused, she had never heard any woman laugh out loud except Anu who was always hushed instantly by all. Maushi preferred to stand watching the boys until Baba called all the youngsters in for the shloka recitation.

There were different shlokas—the chants of praise of gods and goddesses—for different days and for different times of a day such as at dawn, during puja, bath, or at meal times, which Baba and Gajanan regularly chanted, or when the lamps were lit. Every dusk, as soon as the lamps were lit, everybody in the house would join their hands in namaskar and Gauri would go from room to room with an incense pot, taking it to every corner of every room, fanning its smoke with her hand while chanting the prayers. But for the youngsters only the dusk time recitation of shlokas was compulsory in all the households with an elder male leading them. As soon as the shloka recital was over, the children would scamper in Maushi's backyard like young goats let out of the pen until she came out on the back veranda. 'Listen, I have a story to tell. Are you listening?' she would call and 'Hooooo' they would respond, rushing on to the veranda to grab the choicest seats, sitting cross-legged, leaning forward in expectation, already excited.

'There was this Raja, very rich and very powerful, living in a palace of gold, studded with many jewels,'—her stories almost always started like this. Then would follow a story from an epic or a Veda, a story of love, or of war, or of great penance, or of great sacrifice, of great wars won and honours gained through penance by men, of great love and devotion and sacrifices by women.

'And his name was Prajapati Dakshya and he had many beautiful and accomplished daughters but his pet was his eldest daughter Sati. And she was resolved to marry Lord Shiva even though her father opposed the marriage.'

'Why?'

'You see, Sati was very beautiful and many rich and powerful kings had asked for her hand in marriage while Lord Shiva was an ascetic who wore only a loincloth made of tiger skin, his hair was all matted and piled on his head and a great snake lived in it, and he wore garlands made of human skulls. He frequented crematoria, demons and ghosts were his followers, and he drank intoxicants and danced.' All the children sat goggle-eyed, listening spellbound.

'But she still wanted to marry him? Why?'

'The great sage Narada once sang his praises to a young Sati. That he was also a supreme yogi, a great renounced, self-realised, transcendental soul, free of all enmity, beloved of all entities. He was also the God of Destruction who had the power to dance our world to atoms.'

'Wow!'

'So Sati was totally enamoured of him but her father was not pleased with her choice and so when he called her swayamwar—an assembly of all her suitors for her to choose her husband from—he didn't invite Lord Shiva. Not finding him there, a disappointed Sati threw the garland that she was supposed to put around the neck of the chosen suitor high up in the air and lo! Lord Shiva manifested himself and caught it.'

'Wow!'

'So her father got her married to Lord Shiva but did not invite him to any functions. Then he arranged a great yajna in honour of all the gods and though he invited all the great sages and rich and powerful kings and Sati's sisters and their husbands, he did not invite Sati and Lord Shiva. Sati heard about it and assuming that she would always be welcome at her father's place, tried to pressurise Lord Shiva to accompany her. Lord Shiva said, "Sati, you are his pet, but neither you nor I will be honoured there. You also should not go as due to being my wife you too could be insulted and the results will be very sorry indeed." But Sati said, "A daughter needs no invitation to her father's place", and went anyway.'

'And then?'

'None came forward to receive her. Instead her father and all the guests belittled and scorned Lord Shiva in the most disparaging ways, calling him many names.'

'Oooh.'

'Sati couldn't bear to hear them talk like that about her husband and so striding to the main area of the yajna she said, "Let all who sit here give ear to the Mistress of the Universe. My husband, the Lord of Lords has been insulted for no good reason. It's said in the scriptures that those who defile the Lord are great sinners."

'Turning to her father she said, "Father, the scriptures also say that a wife who hears such defilements and does not act is the greatest sinner and that devotion to the husband must supersede all other feelings, even filial piety. You are my father but you have blasphemed Lord Shiva who is my husband. I am ashamed of this unworthy body of mine which is born of you and I shall no longer bear it." And there in the sacrificial arena, Sati strode to the sacrificial fire and bowed to it reverently.'

'And then?'

'She jumped into the sacred fire.'

'She burnt herself?'

'Yes, she burnt herself.'

'Ooooooh!'

Another time she told them the story of Savitri. Savitri, the only child of king of Madra, loved and cherished, and brought up to fully explore and blossom her potentialities.

'Beautiful like Laxmi, learned like Saraswati, talented and accomplished, radiant like an angel and graceful like a nymph, all eyes followed her when she moved, but men were scared of Savitri's learning, intelligence and beauty, and none dared to ask for her hand.

'"You yourself choose some youth as your Lord, daughter," the old king said to her. "Whoever will be dear to you, shall be dear to me. For the rule is, as the sages have said, that he who does not give his daughter in marriage, is debarred from attaining moksha."

'Accompanied by ministers and sages, Savitri journeyed through kingdoms and holy places, over the mountains and through the forests but found none to pleasure her heart, until...

'Narada, the greatest of great sages was sitting with her father when Savitri came back to Madra. "Living in the forest like a hermit in dire poverty is Satyavan, son of Dyumatsena, the blind king, who was betrayed and dethroned by his enemies," she said. "To him is my choice given."

'"Evil is this choice," Sage Narada said. "Noble is the prince – like the sun for grace and glory, like Brihaspati for counsel, like Mahendra for might – but, he is fated to breathe his last in one year as of today."

'"Choose another for your Lord, daughter," cried the old king. "How can I consent to give you to one whose days are numbered?"

'But Savitri looked him in the eye and said, "Only once can a daughter be given away, Father. I have wedded Satyavan in my mind. How can I choose another?"

'"What must be, must be," so said the king and ordered the nuptials to be prepared with all the rich gifts. But the moment his party left the hermit's hut, Savitri put away all the gifts, stripped the jewels and silks from her body and lived the life of a dutiful daughter-in-law dressed in a robe of bark.

'Many moons passed and for three days and nights before the last day, Savitri fasted and sat praying before the holy fire, motionless as if carved of wood. On the last day she accompanied Satyavan into the forest where he went every day to chop the wood and collect the fruit.

'At noon Satyavan was fatigued and said, "Oh dear wife, let me lie down a little. I cannot stand on my feet." So Savitri cradled his head in her lap sitting under a banyan tree when before her rose a majestic shape garbed in red, dark of body and mien, eyes burning like fiery suns, and with a noose in hand.

'"I am Yama Raja, God of Death," he said. "You are a faithful wife, true to your vows, pious and dutiful, and this was a prince unparalleled; so I have come myself to collect his soul instead of sending one of my minions." So saying he collected Satyavan's soul and started towards the South—his domain, the Netherworld. But Savitri, holy by her ascetism, followed him.

'"Go back, Savitri," Yama said. "You have come too far already. The paths are dark and rough and your feet are tender."

'"How can I weary when I walk with my Lord?" Savitri said. "Nothing is too tough for me if I am with him."

'Yama said, "Return. Yet I am moved by your words. Ask for any boon except the life that I bear away. It shall not be denied."

'So Savitri asked that the eyesight of her father-in-law be restored but still followed Yama.

'"Turn back, Savitri,' Yama said. 'My road is long and hard. Turn back, lest you endanger your life also.'

'"I must go where my lord goes," Savitri said. "That's my duty. The seven steps around the holy fire bind a wife to her husband forever and the sages say that doing one's duty is the only path to moksha."

'Pleased with her answer Yama offered her a second boon and then a third and then a fourth and Savitri asked that her father-in-law be reinstated as king and then, that sons be born to her father and lastly, that many sons be born of her own body, and Yama granted them all. Yet she followed him. At last Yama offered her one last boon. "You are the greatest pativrata, Savitri; your devotion to your husband is an example and inspiration to all women. So ask for something incomparable and then go back lest you too die."

'"Oh Yama Raja, mighty God, I do not crave great wealth or heavenly bliss," Savitri said. "But how can your last boon of sons born of my body come true if my lord does not come alive again?"

'Thus Savitri freed Satyavan's soul from Yama's grip and brought him back to life again. It was her chastity and determination to follow him even into the kingdom of death, even at the cost of her own life, that ensured a long life for her husband.'

'So you see that's why Sati and Savitri are considered as the greatest pativratas.' Maushi ended the story. 'They lived only for their husbands, would do anything, sacrifice anything including themselves for the sake of their husbands and to defend their husbands' honour. And that's why this land of ours is also called the Land of Sati-Savitri.'

11

'Yama Raja visited the village on the other side of the hill yesterday, Maushi,' the vaisin said while kneading Maushi's calf. 'Bhagwat's younger son – such a nice young man. Hit by a truck in Mapusa. His poor wife is still in a shock,' she sighed. 'Only God knows what is written in whose karma.'

The vaisin had dropped in as she did many an afternoon to massage Maushi's legs and pass on the gossip from this and also from the neighbouring villages. Like all others of her ilk, she too was more than just a midwife. Massaging a new mother and bathing a newborn baby for the ritual forty days was her job; as was washing and dressing a female body for the funeral. She also prescribed and supplied jadi-bootis—herbs and roots—for every feminine ailment as well as for conceiving and for abortions.

Maushi was sitting with her back to the wall on the back veranda, one leg laid out straight, other bent at the knee, as the vaisin pressed her shin and kneaded the calf. Nearby Gajanan and Vinayak's wives were cleaning rice; at the other end of the veranda Gauri and Shanta were grinding spices on the grinding stones.

Nobody remembered the first names of Maushi's daughters-in-law even though they were given new first names with due ceremony during the marriage rites. A woman had to leave her first and last names, her total identity, her whole personality behind her when she got married and adjust herself to the systems of her married family. Only her husband called her by her new first name, that too sometimes only – other times calling her just 'she' or mother of his children. The rest of the family called her by the relationship, such as elder or younger daughter-in-law, or uncle's or brother's wife. Outsiders called her as her husband's wife.

'Truly, what a tragedy! I remember him very well as a young boy,' Maushi said. 'He was married only recently, a few months ago, I think. Isn't the girl from your village?' she asked Vinayak's wife.

The young girl nodded silently. 'Poor Chandralekha,' she said with heartfelt sorrow. She had been a childhood friend of hers. They had gone to school together, played kavadis together. They had exchanged confidences, dreams and expectations while giggling behind their hands in the corner of the backyard when their marriages were arranged one after the other. They had attended each other's wedding, helped arranging each other's hair and entwining it with flowers. She could just imagine her friend's life now: that beautiful long thick hair shaved off, no more dressing up – only white saris now, no jewellery, not allowed to laugh or participate in any social or religious functions, eating the leftovers, if any, after all the others, relegated to the lowest of the housework. It would be a lonely, hard and joyless existence for her friend.

'Poor who?' Gajanan's wife said raising her eyebrows, 'It was she who brought this misfortune on her husband. Ill-fated girl! The boy's family should have checked her horoscope thoroughly before agreeing to the marriage.' She added flicking her neck disdainfully.

Gajanan's wife had been in a greatly exhilarated and aggressive mood since she had come back a couple of days ago from her mother's house where she had gone for her yearly sojourn. Within a couple of days of her going Gajanan had contracted a head cold and had started complaining about her absence. He needed someone to rub his head all the time and to help him drink the infusions that Maushi prepared and be at his beck and call which neither Maushi would tolerate nor Bhiku or Datta—the house servants—could spare time for. In ten days, he had made Vinayak go to his wife's village to fetch her back instead of allowing her the usual one month's stay at her mother's and Maushi, who was expecting a disgruntled daughter-in-law, was surprised to see her come back beaming until she heard her gloating to her sisters-in-law. 'My husband can't live without me,' she was saying. 'He told me never to go away again leaving him alone like that. He said he just can't manage without me.'

Now, as the elder daughter-in-law and keeper of the family traditions, she lorded it over Vinayak's wife. 'It was her karma that has brought this calamity on to her husband's family,' she said.

'Still, her life is finished.' Vinayak's wife was crying silently, resting her head on her bent knees, wiping the tears running down her cheeks with the sari covering her knees. This was very much closer to home for her. After all they were of the same age. She could very well imagine herself in that situation. The young girl's life was truly finished. She may even jump into the well one of these days and finish it forever. 'It's so unfair,' she burst out suddenly. 'Chandralekha will have to suffer for no fault of hers...' she broke off remembering her position in the household and bent back to her rice cleaning with her cheeks reddening. She knew she was still being assimilated into and trained to the ways of the household and was under the watch of the elders. And that though Maushi was lenient, considerate and easy-going for a mother-in-law, who even allowed her daughters-in-law to bring the radio from Baba's room on to the veranda to play Hindi movie songs whenever Baba went out of the house, yet she also had a terrible temper. Luckily, she lost it only rarely. But when she did so, everybody quavered and scurried out of her way. Even Baba found some excuse to leave the house.

But Maushi didn't reproach her. She was silently wondering about the same. Widowers led a normal life, didn't give up anything, in fact got married again as soon as possible. Otherwise who would look after them and their children and their houses? But a widow? Well, how else could a widow live? She couldn't be allowed to dress up and look pretty or laugh or sing or enjoy life since she certainly couldn't be married again. For wasn't it said that 'A man is like a metal vessel – scrub it, wash it, and use it over and over again. But a woman, she is like a mud vessel – once used, it has to be broken.' So a widow had to spend all her remaining life mourning the death of her husband – without any fault of hers, as Vinayak's wife had said. Something is not quite right, Maushi thought.

Now looking up she saw the vaisin covering her mouth with her hand in shock at this sacrilege by a young daughter-in-law and staring saucer-eyed at the young girl and Gajanan's wife watching Maushi like a hawk waiting for Maushi to take the lead in trouncing the girl. Pitying this young girl, who with her eyes downcast and trembling like a sacrificial lamb awaited the onslaught, Maushi tried to change this contentious subject.

'Has Naik's elder daughter-in-law delivered as yet?' she asked the vaisin.

'Has she!' The vaisin gave another huge sigh and turned back to pressing Maushi's legs disappointed at Maushi's indulgence of her younger daughter-in-law. She straightened out the leg she was working on and bent the other one. 'Another daughter! Fifth daughter she would have been, just imagine. Some families would tolerate one daughter, if she were not the first born. But five daughters? One after another? What bad karma she must have collected.'

Maushi also sighed. 'Poor Jagannath's wife!' she said. 'How much abuse has she borne because of that! And so many vows she had made to so many gods for the boon of a son! Even went on a pilgrimage to Vithoba at Pandharpur. Walked all the way.' She shrugged in resignation. 'Devachi Leela,' she said. Game of Gods.

'You speak truly,' the vaisin agreed. 'She had even vowed a puja of five thousand rupees to Vithoba to let this child be born a boy.' She said starting to work on Maushi's foot, kneading each toe separately. 'Of course this poor girl also didn't survive,' she added with a quick sly glance at Maushi's face before bending down to the foot again. 'The old man himself sent for me.'

Gajanan's wife looked up with a pinch of rice still in her hand. 'What did you use this time?' she asked curiously. 'Husk of rice? Or pillow on face?'

'Heh, heh, heh,' the vaisin cackled. Sitting back on her haunches, she pulled out her tin box of betel leaves, thinly sliced areca nuts, lime, and some flavoured seeds and started folding a paan for herself. 'Of course he wasn't there when I arrived. Jagannath's mother supervised me.' She looked up to see a red flush beginning to spread on Maushi's face, her lips pressed tight, eyebrows crunched together, her temper about to blow. Vaisin froze. 'What now?' she muttered to herself at the same time bracing herself against the burst of anger that she knew was coming.

She wasn't wrong. 'How could you, a woman, do that sort of a thing?' Maushi lashed into her. 'Haven't you nurtured a baby for nine months in your stomach? Borne the backache, the morning sickness, the nausea? Borne the labour pains for hours, sometimes for days? Given birth to the baby tearing yourself in the process? And to have that life snuffed out just like that, in a moment...'

With great difficulty Maushi controlled herself. She was really angry at Jagannath's mother, but then perhaps she too had no say in the matter, Maushi thought, perhaps she had just been ordered to supervise the vaisin. Perhaps. Or perhaps she too believed in this system, in perpetuating the family name – girls' names were changed on marriage, weren't they? Didn't most women believe in it too? 'Light of the family line' that's what they called the newborn male babies. In any case there was no point in berating the vaisin. She only provided the service that the families asked of her, that the society condoned. But when had God ever said that daughters were unwelcome? Many of the great sages and kings in Vedas and in the epics had only daughters. Lord Rama's wife Sita was an only child; so were Princess Lopamudra of Vidarbha and Princess Sulabha, daughter of King Pradhana and also the most revered pativrata Princess Savitri, daughter of King Ashwapati. They were all loved and cherished. Men vied for their hands in marriage and the girl chose her husband herself from an assembly of suitors called by her father. Then, at some time much later, the system changed. Men chose their wives, dowry became the norm.

That's when it all changed: when men started demanding dowry and are now finding daughters to be burdens, she thought and then, suddenly sat up straight. No, that can't be the only reason, can it? Even in the old days daughters were married off by their parents with pomp and show and with rich gifts for the in-laws, weren't they? she asked herself and sighed. And did a girl really choose her husband from that assembly of suitors? She was usually just a prize for the man winning the competition set by her father for that occasion. Lord

Rama had won Sita by being the only one to bend and break the heavy bow that her father had hauled to the hall and made it a stipulation for winning Sita; Prince Arjuna had won Draupadi by being the only one to shoot an arrow through the eye of a fish revolving overhead while watching its reflection in the water which was her father's required condition for winning her. No, women had always been pawns in men's games, either to be traded as prized possessions or to be discharged as unpleasant responsibilities. And hadn't the Atharva Veda called a daughter a misery? Even the Rig Veda—the oldest of the Vedas—had prayers for being blessed with ten sons in its marriage hymns but no mention of daughters. Maushi sighed. The bias was obviously an old one; and man-made; not God-proclaimed; and loyally acted upon by women. Maushi sighed again. 'Men make these rules to suit themselves and we women enforce them,' she said sadly.

'But of course,' Gajanan's wife said puzzled at this outburst, 'men know the best.'

'I have given birth to sons only,' the vaisin said with virtuous justification. 'It is to Jagannath's wife's shame that she has given birth to girl after girl.' She firmly believed it in spite of what all the doctors had been telling her. 'Now she hasn't stopped crying,' she added in a derogatory tone, 'but what's the use?'

Gajanan's wife, back to carefully sorting out husk from rice, gave her a smug smile. She had a daughter *and* a son; son the first born. But Vinayak's wife, a newly wed, looked worried.

She caught hold of the vaisin under the tamarind tree near the well as she was leaving. 'I want to ensure that my first born will be a boy,' she whispered pulling the vaisin under the foliage.

'How right you are, daughter!' the vaisin said, nodding her head. She was still chewing the paan and now she spat the red juice at the root of the tamarind tree. 'Don't you believe those big doctors from Mapusa and Panaji. It's *you* on whose head the shame will be should it be a girl.'

The young girl's anxiety increased. 'Will you give me some jadi-booti?' she asked in some trepidation. They were both aware of Maushi's firm opposition to such potions.

'Your mother-in-law knows all the jadi-bootis,' the vaisin temporised. 'She has them growing all over the backyard. She even buys from that old jadi-bootiwala from the ghats who comes here every few months,' she said knowing that such selective fertility potions were hers and only her forte.

The young girl knew it very well too. 'I would prefer one of *your* concoctions,' she said.

The vaisin peered into her face. 'It's expensive, daughter, very expensive,' she said. 'But, for a son, what's money and what's gold?'

12

The jadi-bootiwala came a couple of days later. He was a thin old wiry tribal from up in the hills, his face weathered, his legs muscled and scratched from the constant forays in jungles, dressed in a once white loincloth tucked tight between his legs and a sleeveless short vest, and a black cloth band tied around his head. His wares he carried in a tin box wrapped in another black cloth, which he also used to spread them on. He was accompanied by a young boy – his grandson whom he was training – carrying a jute shoulder bag from which a multitude of dried sprigs poked out. The old tribal squatted on the back veranda laying out roots and tubers and dry stems tied in bunches with dry straw, dried leaves and flowers wrapped in paper, seeds and fruit pulps and gums and powders in plastic pouches, and little bottles of oils. His grandson sat cross-legged on the ground below, intently watching the old man.

Maushi, her two daughters-in-law, her sisters-in-law, and a dozen other women relatives crowded around him as he explained and Maushi guided them on which herbs to combine with which others for a particular sickness, and whether to powder them and mix them with honey, or boil them to make a potion, or make a poultice of them.

One of Baba's old aunts called to Maushi from near the wall where she was resting her back. 'Do find me those same roots you did last time, will you? They worked wonders in relieving my joint pains last monsoon. The rains will be coming soon, and they do play havoc with my joints!'

'Do you have anything for curing jaundice?' a cousin of Baba's asked impatiently pushing to the front of the group.

'Yes, Bai,' the jadi-bootiwala said. He called all women as Bai—lady—qualifying it with Mothya for elder and Lahan for younger. He rummaged through his collection and put forward a few bundles of roots and packets of leaves.

Vinayak's wife, keen on learning about the herbs and roots and beginning to differentiate between them, bent forward to study them closely and picked up one of the bundles of roots and then looked up at Maushi for approval before passing it on to Baba's cousin. Maushi smiled and nodded.

'Take these kutki stems also,' Maushi told her sister-in-law taking a bunch of thin dried brown stems that the jadi-bootiwala was offering. 'Powder them with those pithori roots and give your son those powders with hot water twice daily. And don't forget the decoction of those chachinga leaves with coriander seeds that I have already given you.' She looked at the woman's drawn face. 'Don't worry,' she said. 'Just give him all these potions regularly and he will be perfectly all right for his exams in two weeks.' Her sister-in-law smiled weakly in relief.

Vinayak's wife looked admiringly at her. 'You are so knowledgeable about all these herbs, Aai,' she said.

'So will you be. You are already learning well. A few more years and I will make you an expert also,' Maushi said fondly patting her on her back and Vinayak's wife flushed with pleasure.

'I want something to whiten my complexion,' a young girl, whose parents were trying to arrange a match for her, said nervously to the jadi-bootiwala. The boy's family was coming to see her in ten days and she had heard that the boy's aunt was very keen on a fair-complexioned girl. She prodded a bunch of roots. 'Something that will work wonders and very quickly too.'

The jadi-bootiwala wrinkled his forehead in thought and then searched through his collection and hesitantly laid some leaves and strips of barks and oils before her but Maushi shook her head.

'Nothing works better than turmeric powder mixed with fresh cream of milk and applied every night at bedtime for improving the complexion. Just take that kahu bark to clear your pimples. Mix its powder with honey and apply it on those spots. And drink some juice of neem leaves.' The girl made a face and crinkled her nose. Maushi smiled at her. 'I know it's bitter, girl,' she said putting her arm around the girl's shoulders. 'But try it with a lot of water and a spoonful of jaggery. You will be pretty in ten days. No aunt is going to disapprove you.' She caressed the girl's cheek and pinched her chin. The girl blushed and put her head down and busied herself with inspecting the bundle of roots she was holding. 'And leave those roots alone,' Maushi said lightly slapping her hand. 'They stop you from conceiving.' The young girl dropped them as if they had burned her hand and other girls tittered behind their hands.

'And what do you want?' Maushi said smiling down at Gajanan's daughter who had crawled up to her and now putting one chubby paw on Maushi's lap was grinning toothlessly up at her. 'My darling doesn't need any of these herbs. My darling is fair enough already,'

Maushi said picking her up and holding her up. The little girl gurgled and grinned. 'That's right,' Maushi said seating her on her lap. 'And what a marriage we will make for my darling. You think your Atya's marriage was grand, do you? Wait till everybody sees my darling's marriage ceremony. It will be the wedding of the century!'

After the purchases were made and remaining wares packed and all others except Maushi had left, the jadi-bootiwala relaxed on the floor gratefully slurping the tea that Gauri had brought him and his grandson in steel glasses.

'You have a good collection of herbs growing here, Mothya Bai. And properly cared for too,' he said casting an approving eye on her back garden.

Maushi nodded as she looked at her herbs with pride: green and purple and yellow, shrubs and grasses and plants. Some covered with netting to protect them from birds, some propped with little sticks tied to them, some allowed to bloom, some pinched in bud, some prepared for drying. Maushi knew her herbs. 'I need to grow some kantakari and some mulethi,' she said.

'Yes,' he said agreeing with a nod. 'Those are necessary for children's sicknesses.' He slurped some more tea. 'But I would get rid of that kadua tree by the gate,' he said uneasily looking in the direction of the gate. 'How did you get it Mothya Bai? It's a wild tree that usually grows only in the jungle.'

Maushi thought back. Somebody had brought her some saplings, the kadua one amongst them, but had also warned her saying, 'Its flowers are very pretty but the roots are bad.'

'Its roots are bad,' the jadi-bootiwala echoed her thoughts. 'Bad for men. They make them lose strength where it matters.'

Maushi laughed. 'I have heard that before,' she said. 'But that's a rumour.'

'No, no, Mothya Bai. It's true,' he said emphatically.

Maushi looked at him thoughtfully for some time and then nodded. 'Yes,' she conceded. 'Yes, it may be true. But it's a tree, not a shrub; who is going to dig up its roots?' she stopped suddenly remembering that some of its roots were actually spread above ground. 'Also I am told that they are very bitter.'

'Yes, Mothya Bai. That is true.' He put his glass down preparing to leave. The young boy stood up with alacrity, tied his headband, and slung the jute jhola over his shoulder.

The old man tied his tin box in the black cloth, stood below the veranda, and looked unhappily at the kadua tree as he tied the black band around his head. 'And in monsoon it will have that tree fungus covering it and all that wild fungi growing at its base, Mothya Bai,' he said insistently. 'They look so attractive, but they are all harmful. Some make you sick in stomach and some make you go blind and others make you go weak in limbs.'

Maushi smiled. 'I know all those fungi and what they do. They have been growing around that kadua tree for years now,' she said as he hoisted his box on his back, bowed his head and he and the boy joined their hands in servile namaskars.

She walked to the edge of the veranda and watched them to the gate and then turned to look at the kadua tree near it. It was a small tree with a thin scaly brown trunk with delicate branches fanning out like an umbrella and thin, delicate roots, some of them starting at the ground level and spreading around before burying themselves in the ground. It was so very pretty now in early spring. Loaded with bunches of small trumpet-shaped white flowers with orange centres that covered all its branches, it lorded over the tall sky flower trees and the shorter peacock flower trees and competed with the temple champa and the golden champa in glory. In the morning, its flowers would carpet the ground underneath while new buds opened on the tree. In the monsoons, when the cascading rains had washed off all the flowers in her garden, it were the tree fungi that covered it and the wild fungi that grew at its base that lent the only touch of colour and brightness to her garden—brilliant white, deep pink, bright red and orange, yellow, blue, dark green and black, some spotted and streaked, some smooth and some pitted, some button-shaped, some fan-shaped, some palm-shaped, some umbrella-shaped, some saucer-shaped, some flat, and some round. All were inedible, all were harmful. Some were poisonous, some were emetic, some caused cramps and some attacked the liver and the kidneys and the brain cells and some caused loss of strength in the muscles of legs or arms. Once set in, these harmful effects cannot be reversed. In Marathi, these wild fungi are called crows' umbrellas.

13

Anu and Alec came back after more than two months of honeymoon in South Goa just in time for Holi and it was now obvious to all that Anu was pregnant. There was a glow to her cheeks and a sparkle in her eyes and a smile on her lips and a new grace in her movements. She danced while picking flowers, hummed while shelling peas, and laughed with Gauri and Shanta as they sat grinding the spices. She exuded so much happiness that even Gajanan's wife smiled fondly at her. 'See what imminent motherhood does to a woman?' she said to Vinayak's wife.

But Maushi saw more. She noticed how it were now Anu's eyes that dwelt adoringly upon Alec and followed his every move, how it was she who now touched him surreptitiously when passing him in the doorways, and how she jumped up with alacrity if he only happened to raise his eyebrows to run errands for him. She spent more time in the kitchen than she had ever before. 'Teach me to make those spicy bitter-and-sour methi wadas, Aai. Alec likes those,' she said bustling about.

That full moon day, being Holi, she too happily fasted the whole day with other women of the family. The villagers who had been dancing and revelling in the temple courtyard since the eleventh moon day now came to the house dancing and beating drums and blowing flutes all the way, dressed in their most colourful clothes, and bearing bright coloured cloth flags with gay embroideries, and a long decorated pole that they called Holi. They danced around the holy basil planter in the courtyard of Baba's house with all the youngsters in the house joining them in dancing, and Baba and Gajanan and even the women watching from the doorway to the back veranda laughed merrily with them, all affected by this gaiety and revelry. At last they stopped exhausted, and Baba handed a thali heaped with coconuts, rice and a pile of coins to the leader, and they went away grinning happily. In the night, Alec went to the temple compound with Baba, Gajanan, Vinayak and other men of the family to watch them plant the Holi pole decorated with coloured pieces of cloth and paper streamers in the ground, surround it with other poles, build it into a chimney, and, after a short worship of it, set it ablaze. Young boys kept running around it throwing in other pieces of wood, old clothes, cardboard boxes, anything they could find to make it blaze higher.

'The priest will tell you the story of Holika, how she, an evil woman, was got rid of by throwing her in fire and how this is a celebration of triumph of good over evil but actually this is a festival to celebrate the change of season, a preparation for the new year to come,' Baba said when Alec asked what Holi signified. 'Winter is over and spring has arrived. Today they say farewell to winter, tomorrow they will welcome the spring with colours. Today is the day to discard everything that's old and useless – to burn it off and start afresh. You have come back at the right time.'

Village families kept on coming, throwing some puffed rice and coconuts into the fire, and circumambulating it three times before sitting around to drink sarbat and eat sweets. Alec sat with Baba on the string cot placed by the riverside. The villagers surrounded Alec, treating him like a guest of honour, and he sat around basking in the attention being bestowed on him, thoroughly enjoying himself.

Next day, boys from the village played the colours, throwing red, blue and green powders on each other and drenching the unsuspecting with coloured water. They came to the house dancing and singing, and to respectfully put a red kumkum dot on the foreheads of elder men and women and Maushi distributed sweets to them. They pulled Vinayak and Alec to play the colours with them and soon they were all fooling around in high spirits, playing games, and laughing at each other's multi-coloured faces. Then they all sat down below the riverbank to drink some bhang. The boys had been plucking hemp leaves all day before to grind them with cashew nuts and mix the paste with milk. Alec took a sip, found it cool and refreshing, gulped some more, found it exhilarating, and finished the glass. The boys laughed and cheered. Alec beamed at them, loving them, loving this country. This is better than marijuana, he thought. 'My body feels so light,' he said to Vinayak. 'As if I am floating. Now I know what it means to walk on air.'

'Just don't start laughing,' Vinayak cautioned him. 'Because if you do, you won't stop for a very very long time.'

In the afternoon Baba invited Alec into his room to ask for his passport so that the marriage could be registered and to discuss the procedure of obtaining a passport for Anasuya. If Alec was momentarily flummoxed at this, the lawyer in him covered up immediately. 'Best way is to get Anu's name entered on my passport,' he said. But it turned out that Alec's passport was about to expire and therefore needed to be renewed first and then he would have to get his visa also renewed and extended before the marriage could be registered and Anu's name entered on it. 'On her own she won't get a long-term visa leave aside a resident's one very easily. The Canadian Government has become very strict about admitting Asians,' he said and Anu resigned herself to a few more months of living in the village.

Actually Alec had been shocked to learn that Anu and the family expected him to take her away almost immediately. 'I thought Asian women never wanted to leave their homelands,' he said to Vinayak.

'A Hindu wife will follow her husband to the end of the world,' Vinayak said.

'But then, Parvati-bai and that other couple that had come over... ' Alec said hesitatingly, not wanting to mention his experience with the hippies.

'That's different; Parvati-bai stayed back to look after her in-laws and then felt too secure here to risk going anywhere else. Also by then Dayanand already had another wife in the city,' Vinayak said off-handedly.

These Hindus confounded him in other ways too. When he had offered to pay for the marriage expenses there had been a totally shocked reaction from the family. 'What does he think of himself? And who does he think we are? Beggars?' Gajanan had said seething with rage. '*We* spend in the marriages of our girls. *We* will also give Anasuya everything that should be given.'

And so Anu and Alec made themselves at home in Baba's house while Alec's passport formalities were being attended to. 'It's just for a short while,' Anu said to Maushi. 'And once I am out of here, I will never come back. I will have my baby in Canada.' And Maushi sadly agreed that that would be best for her.

Anu knelt in front of Maushi, put her hands on Maushi's knees and looked excitedly into her eyes. 'And Aai, when the baby is a little older, I will put her in a crèche and join the college,' she continued with her excitement at the thought of the new, unfettered life before her bursting out of her. 'We met this Canadian couple on the Majorda Beach and she explained it all to me, how I can do it. She said she too had dropped out of college when she got married and after three children – *three*, Aai, – she decided to go back to college. And she did it. And now she is in publishing art-books, imagine Aai! I will also learn something exciting. I will also do something exciting.' Her eyes were dancing. 'But I won't be a negligent mother or wife, Aai,' she added primly. 'I will take good care of my baby. And of Alec too, of course. She said it was quite possible over there in Canada to manage the household and one's personal interests, both equally well.' She stopped suddenly remembering Alec's raised eyebrows at that.

Once they got over the initial embarrassment of having a 'live-in son-in-law' for however short a time and for whatever the reason, the whole family was surprised at how easily and thoroughly Alec assimilated himself into the family, its routines, and its rituals. Alec, who before marriage had watched the household as an outsider, now wholeheartedly plunged into its customs. Alec, who before marriage had been embarrassed when Bhiku had tried to strap his sandals for him, now got used to being served all the time, to ordering Bhiku and Datta and even Anu – without embarrassment, almost as with right – to fetch him whatever he wanted, to do for him whatever he needed to be done.

In the mornings he too bathed at the well following Baba and Gajanan. He would sit very comfortably on the stone slab by the well as Bhiku scrubbed and washed his back and poured lota-fuls of water over him while Baba performed his daily puja of the red stone Ganesha at the base of the audumber tree. Then wearing a dhoti and with sandalwood paste finger-stripes drawn on his forehead, he would join Baba and Gajanan in circumambulating the audumber tree with a lota full of water, sprinkling it on the tree and the red stone Ganesha idol as Baba and Gajanan chanted the mantras. 'Good that he hasn't at least tried to recite the mantras while making the rounds of Lord Ganesha,' Gajanan said sourly to Baba. 'Given his accent, he would make them sound like the chatter of a monkey.'

But Baba enjoyed teaching, explaining and debating all these rites with Alec. 'Yes,' he said. 'Like you, many foreigners find the idea of an elephant-god difficult to accept. But His significance is at many levels. There is the merging of human and animal bodies signifying the one universal consciousness that pervades all living things. Then elephants are earth-bound beings, not flighty, and considered to be very wise. And God Ganesha is the God of Wisdom as well as the destroyer of all obstacles to human endeavours. He ensures success in everything one undertakes. You ought to pray for speedy processing of your passport during your morning rounds of Him.'

Alec was charmed, not so much by this roly-poly, lovable elephant-god, but more by the worship of the audumber tree, by this whole concept of nature worship. In the mornings when he woke up early enough, he watched Baba and Gajanan offering prayers to the rising sun and Anu had told him how a new-born baby was shown the moon on the day of its naming ceremony, the twelfth day of its birth. Baba and Gajanan circumambulated the audumber tree every day while women worshipped the holy basil every day and the banyan tree in the month of Jyestha in summer. Prayers to rivers were offered on the first day of the month of Shravan in the monsoons and baths in the river had religious significances. Coconuts were thrown into the sea to appease it on the full moon day in the month of Ashwin in autumn. 'But of course!' Baba said. 'Most of the early hymns in the Rig Veda are in praise of nature and most of our early gods were nature gods. We live very close to nature, in kinship with it.'

Here, in this land, Alec too felt the closeness to nature, the kinship to it, was equally in awe of it, and made his rounds of the audumber with equal reverence, without any inhibitions or self-consciousness or embarrassment, as if it were innate to him also.

After a breakfast of pohe—mildly spiced pounded rice—that Maushi served him garnished with grated coconut and chopped coriander and which he ate with such relish as to raise giggles in the kitchen, Alec went on the rounds of the family's farmlands and coconut and cashew orchards with Baba and Gajanan. Baba liked to have him around; he was more mature than Gajanan and Vinayak, not as rigid as Gajanan or as flighty as Vinayak. At mid-morning when they rested under the coconut trees surrounded by the farm supervisors, and while young boys scurried up the swaying coconuts as agilely as chimpanzees to fetch them green coconuts with sweet water, Baba discussed the farm management with him. Baba found him a good listener, quick in understanding and prudent in suggestions. He asked the right questions and took his time to digest the answers before responding. At times Baba wished he would stay around permanently.

On Tuesdays, the days of God Ganesha, when Baba, instead of Maushi, performed the puja of the idols in the gods' room after that of the stone Ganesha under the audumber tree, and when all the family members had to be present, Alec would also join in, sitting at the back with his hands joined before him and his eyes closed. 'Advaita Vedanta tells us that this whole world is maya—an illusion—created by the Brahman, and only within ourselves will we find the truth. So think of the puja as meditation, not religion. Just close your eyes and leave your mind free to go with the flow,' Baba had said, and Alec found himself noticeably relaxing while listening to the monotonous, hypnotic chanting.

There was an array of idols in the carved rosewood temple in the gods' room: Saraswati, the Goddess of Learning and Knowledge, made of silver, which was given to every woman on her marriage by her mother, and which Maushi had brought with her; Goddess Ekvira, made of brass, whom Gajanan's wife prayed to for the safety of her family; and God Vitthal, sculpted out of black stone, whom Vinayak's wife prayed to for the boon of a son. A practical concept, Alec thought, to be able to choose a personal god or goddess as per one's requirements and wishes.

Tuesday was also a day of weekly fast for the family and Alec, prepared to go to Panaji to have his fill on the first Tuesday of his stay there, was surprised at the feast prepared for the day. 'Only women fasting on the vrats or other religious days aren't allowed to imbibe anything at all, not even water,' Vinayak told him laughing at his confusion. But for the weekly fast, different rules applied. They only meant that certain foods could not be eaten on those days, Vinayak explained. Grains were not allowed, sago was allowed. Vegetables were not allowed, sweet potatoes were allowed. It was bland food and Alec badly missed those extremely bitter fresh fenugreek wadas that Maushi so lovingly cooked for him with a lot of jaggery and tamarind pulp and ground spices and which nobody else in the family would eat – only he and Maushi – and both enjoyed it. He also exhorted Maushi to cook him those bitter karelas stuffed with sweet and sour stuffing which also nobody else in the family would ever eat.

He was now accepted as a member of Bhau-log and was expected to behave as such, not only by spending time with them to the exclusion of women – to the irritated exasperation of Anu who had asked angrily, 'Where do sisters fit in their scheme of the world, except as hand-maidens?' – but also by being there for them, sharing everything with them, and helping out whenever required. In return, Alec found what a great comfort it was to be able to unquestionably rely on others, not to have to justify oneself but to be accepted without reservations, to take the family support for granted.

He enjoyed being part of the Bhau-log, going out to watch local cricket or football matches with them sitting on the grass or on stone walls, strolling on the river bank, or just sitting lolling around in the garden as they tutored him, with great hilarity, in the ways of managing Hindu women. Many evenings Siddharth would come over to discuss some complicated legal cases with him. Siddharth too took Alec's help for granted now that Alec was a family member. Then Alec played the role of the teacher and senior advocate explaining intricacies of law to Siddharth the novice.

Most afternoons after lunch, he and Anu would disappear from the house for the rest of the day. They spent the afternoons swimming and relaxing on beaches and spent the evenings in hotels and restaurants dancing and mixing with other foreign tourists. And although Alec should have asked Baba's permission before going out of the house, giving a full explanation of where and how long for and for what purpose he meant to go out of the house, he never did and Baba made allowances for him since he was a vilayati and a son-in-law – who is always treated as a god in Hindu families. Anu of course now was only under the orders of her husband or the eldest male in his family if he were around and not accountable to anybody else, and the family smiled fondly and indulgently at her that her husband cared so much for her that he should want her to accompany him on his jaunts. 'These vilayatis,' the women said shaking their heads with a smile and with a little jealousy too.

But some afternoons when visitors were expected, Anu had to stay in the house as it was her that they were coming to visit. Hordes of relatives kept on dropping in, some from even far distances, now that it was known that she was pregnant. Anu's aunts and cousins were of course frequent visitors coming almost every second day, bringing her the foods she craved. As was the vaisin who also came regularly to check her progress and slyly suggest – whenever Maushi was not around – the jadi-bootis to take or charms to wear for all sorts of purposes such as ensuring a son or holding on to the love of a husband and Anu laughed on her face.

'It's a big baby for four months,' she observed clinically while massaging Anu's stomach one day.

'And you are well-experienced in delivering vilayati babies, are you?' the old aunt, who was also visiting that day and who was now sitting next to Anu caressing her cheek and giving her advice picked out from her age-old wisdom, asked sarcastically at the same time quelling the vaisin with a look of derision. 'Just look at my grandson-in-law,' she added proudly. 'How tall he is!'

Alec too had to spend those days sitting in the men's room, making polite talk with the accompanying male visitors about London and Canada and fending their queries about his future plans, his family, and his income. Every once in a while he would find an excuse to walk down the passageway to the inner room to peek at Anu and give her an affectionate smile. This was how he liked to see her: surrounded and being pampered by all her relatives.

Other afternoons Alec just preferred to spend in the house, sitting on the back veranda on a chair that they brought out for him from the men's room, and watching the women at their daily tasks, and later in the evenings, listening to the children recite the shlokas, being very impressed with their memory and clear pronunciations, and said so to Baba.

'There is more to it than that,' Gajanan told him haughtily. 'Reciting shlokas destroys all sin and produces virtue.'

Baba glanced at him. 'There *is* more to it,' he said. 'Every sound affects one's body especially the nervous system. The shlokas and the mantras create very beneficial vibrations in your total nervous system rejuvenating the whole system. Try saying Om, you will find your whole body vibrating.' And sitting in lotus position on the ground, Baba intoned Om in such a way that it sent tremors down Alec's body. But however much he tried, he couldn't match Baba's musical pitch of saying Om.

'Not Ooooom,' Vinayak said laughing. 'It's Aaauummm.'

'Patience,' Baba said when Alec again produced a grating sound. 'Patience is also a Hindu virtue. Our sages practised asceticism for decades before realising any benefits from it.'

Afterwards listening without understanding to Maushi telling a story to the goggle-eyed and totally enrapt children, he thought of his childhood, and his grandmother who lived alone in her mansion and who had tried to instill proper manners in him. There had been formality in his relationship with her, propriety even in their confidentiality. Neither had she ever told him any story, either from the Bible or any other book. She had also refused to fund his higher education leaving him to fend for himself. And though she had been fairly religious – she always had the Bishop over for the Christmas dinner and had taken him to church every Sunday as a little boy – religion or any religious rites had not played a major role in his life especially after he grew up, except at weddings and funerals.

He was so fascinated by all these daily rites and rituals that on the Hindu new year day, he helped the boys as they fixed a pleated red silk cloth to one end of a long bamboo, strung a garland of marigolds around it, capped the end with a silver lota and then raised and tied it to one of the front veranda posts. 'This is to applaud the gods who will be passing in the sky commemorating their victory over the demons,' Siddharth's son told him. He also helped in stringing the welcoming garlands of mango leaves over the main door and even ate the little ball of ground bitter neem leaves, one of those that Maushi was making everyone eat, and which all of them, even Baba, gulped down with a glass of water without tasting. Afterwards, as everyone went around showing off in new clothes, Alec appeared in a silk dhoti and kurta.

Now whenever Alec was in the house, the whole family clustered around him, acquainting him with other rites, showing him the right way of performing them, and delighting in his efforts. Anu watched it all with morbid fascination, the same fascination with which she had once watched a snake slithering towards her.

'Don't you find anything wrong in all these rituals, in this system, in the way women are treated here?' she asked him once. 'Don't you find it wrong that women always have to eat after men? Here Aai makes sure that there is plenty of food in the kitchen but in many other homes, including my elder uncle's, there is very little food left for women after they have plied the men with it. Or that I always have to walk a few steps behind you when we go out of the house? Or that the women are hardly ever allowed out of the house except to visit other relatives in the village or to go to the temples and that too rarely? And always escorted even there? Or that we can never sit together or even talk together in this house except in our room and that too only at night?'

But Alec of the conquerors' and rulers' race, and used to the system where wives made small talk together while men stood apart in a group and talked of important issues, found nothing wrong with it. The more entrenched he became in the family routine, the more furious she got. Yet in that Baga hotel before marriage it was *she* who had described her family and the family customs and the rites and rituals that they followed so fascinatingly to him!

'What are you proposing?' she confronted him one day. 'Are you going to become a Hindu and stay here forever? Why don't you go to Mumbai and pursue your passport formalities? When are we leaving for Canada? I have to check in in a maternity hospital over there and soon it will be too late for me to travel.'

But Alec held her chin in his hand, tilted her face up to his and looking into her eyes said with all earnestness, 'I want my daughter to be born in this land.'

Anu gave in ungraciously. Maushi gave in resignedly. Rest of the family accepted it delightedly as the best solution. Even if Alec's passport formalities got completed in near future and they left immediately for Canada, Anu would soon have to come back to her mother's house for her delivery anyway as was the custom, and since Vinayak couldn't go all the way to Canada to fetch her, Alec would have to escort her back. Best then would be to stay on rather than travel back and forth.

'You should be happy to stay on with your family,' Alec said noticing Anu's dissatisfied manner.

'Whose family?'

'What?'

'This is *not* my family any more, this is *not* my home. You and your family are my only family now, don't you understand?' she said angrily. 'We are living under sufferance.'

She sulked, even refusing to go to the village square next full moon day to worship the banyan tree. Women of the family, attributing her tantrums to her pregnancy, offered to bring back a branch of the tree for her to worship at home since Watsavitri Puja was an absolutely essential rite for a married woman to ensure that she may never be widowed.

'You know what boon they ask of the banyan tree?' she asked Alec with a giggle when he also tried to coerce her to go. 'Long life for the husband, which is quite all right, I will pray for that, but also the same husband in the next seven lives!'

'I would very much like you as my wife in the next seven lives,' Alec said kissing her neck as he pulled her up and guided her to the door.

He and Vinayak escorted the women to the village square, all decked out in best of the saris and jewellery and carrying silver thalis that held kumkum and turmeric boxes and little silver lamps and flowers and fruit and the bundles of silk thread required for the puja. They stood watching as the women smeared the kumkum and the turmeric on the tree trunk, sprinkled the rice grains and flowers on it, and started winding the sacred thread around it circumambulating it for one hundred and eight times. But on noticing Anu's condition, the priest who was sitting under the tree chanting prayers and blessing the women after the puja told her that seven times around the tree would be enough for her. So she sat on a low stone wall by the riverside waiting for others to finish the rounds, revolve the oil lamps before the tree, and distribute the fruit that was offered for puja.

Walking back, Alec was totally mesmerised by the scene: the bright sunlight bouncing off the rocks, the deep blue-green shimmering river, the red earth, the lush green trees, the heady scent of the flowers, the enchanting chirping of the birds, and those brightly dressed women in their gold jewellery and nose rings walking with that undulating walk, laughing musically. And Anu fit perfectly into this setting, was an indivisible part of this scene.

'You are made for all this. This land, this house, this family, these customs. I wouldn't dream of taking you away from all this,' he said to her quite truthfully when they got back.

'This all is exactly what I want to get away from,' Anu retorted. 'You have no idea how oppressive it is to a woman over here.'

But Alec, newly introduced to the rites and rituals of Hinduism, not only found nothing wrong with them but defended them with the zeal of a neophyte.

Then the rains came.

14

Then the rains came; huge bucketfuls pouring non-stop for days on end, drenching everything—the fields, the plants, the animals. All windows were tightly shut for the monsoons; the back veranda was partially enclosed with dry palm fronds; depressing shadows lurked in the corners of all the rooms even during the day; and the house suddenly became claustrophobic. Flies swarmed in all rooms, bugs clung to the walls and ceilings and frogs appeared in the garden. And crows' umbrellas sprouted under the kadua tree.

And Alec became restless.

He found the confining atmosphere of the house more and more irksome as the days passed and the rains continued without a respite but there were not many outside places left to go to. The continuous heavy downpours inevitably wrote off the beaches. Tourist spots were impossible to get to. Most of the restaurants had closed for the monsoon. Only the luxury hotels were functioning. Alec found himself descending into a strange melancholic mood.

He was not the only one though; he found everybody in the house also affected by the monsoon. All of them moved around either dreamy-eyed or with a forlorn expression, even Baba was subdued and Gajanan had become mellow, and Gauri and Shanta hummed mournful melodies when doing their chores.

Coming back to the house one afternoon Alec walked on to the back veranda to find all the women sniffling and dabbing at their eyes with their pallavs and even Vinayak and Gajanan sitting around looking wistful. Worried and also a little afraid as to what might have happened, Alec gestured Vinayak to come to the men's room. 'It's that monsoon song that they are playing on the radio, based on Kalidasa's *Meghdoot*,' Vinayak told him, his voice heavy with emotion, pouring out the poignant story. 'It's about a young man who has gone to a foreign land and is forlorn without his lover and is cajoling the clouds to take a message to her. You will find her on the terrace of her house pining for me, he tells the clouds,' he stopped suddenly and gave a sheepish grin as Alec's lip curled in derision at this inane display of emotions at a mere song. 'All monsoon songs are sad and full of longings,' he continued defensively. 'This is the season for romantic love, for intense passions, for dreaming one's dreams. A season of longings, of nostalgia. We say showers of Ashadh—the month of monsoon—are the showers of yearnings.'

Now Alec too remembered and yearned for his dream.

Walking on the main market street in Panaji one day, he saw in a shop window the mannequins dressed in Western clothes—tall, slim and beautiful Western plaster models that stood haughtily turning their plaster noses up at the passers-by—and Alec was reminded of the time that he, a young lawyer's clerk, had been walking down the Bond Street in London, looking into shop windows just like this one, when a young woman had come out of one of those expensive shops and paused for a moment in front of him. She was tall, slim and dark, elegantly dressed, and her haughty glance had merely passed over him without registering him while he in his off the rack two-year-old suit had gaped at her. He had never been able to forget her. She was handsome, but that was not it. She was obviously rich, but that too was not it. She was stately! In a daze, Alec had walked on to the corner pub to meet his petite, blonde wife.

And the dream that he had pursued since and was so close to attaining: Alec in tails standing by his gleaming dark blue Bentley with a tall, dark and stately woman beside him with her arm linked through his, dressed in a designer evening dress that few women could get into and still fewer could carry off, two young boys in shorts and blazers – tall like him and dark like her – holding on to a couple of Alsatians in the foreground, and a three-storied town house with the butler still standing at its open door in the background.

And Alec became homesick. Languid Vagator Beach receded into background and busy skyscrapers of London rose in its place.

Now he longed for those bustling courts, those heated arguments, those accolades after a favourable judgement, those glittering banquet rooms, those assemblies of tail-coated men and women in pearls, that subdued laughter with emotions held under control and those conversations laced with typical English understatements.

Now he missed those walks in Lincoln's Park at lunch time on a summer's day, that pale sunlight, that light London rain—the clouds scudding across the sky, a light drizzle, and it's over before you know—that gentle rolling land. He thought nostalgically about sitting near the picture window in his study high up above Regents Park on a winter's day watching a white world below with a Scotch in one hand and a meerschaum in the other while Mozart played in the background. It never snowed in Goa.

He could barely stand to spend any time in Baba's house any more. Everything there irritated him. The lack of privacy: here everybody walked in and out of all the rooms; no closed doors were allowed in the daytime. The rigid routines of the house: he longed for the lazy Sunday mornings with Sunday newspapers and breakfast in bed. And the strict discipline: Baba's strict control over everything – you are only a link in the chain, Baba had told him, there is nothing like individualism allowed to Hindus. Virtue lies in subordinating one's will and individual needs to the interests of the family, he had said.

He also started finding faults with everything, particularly in Datta, Bhiku and Shanta's services. None of them did anything properly, or with pride. Datta ironed his shirts all wrong even after he had shown him at least three times how he wanted them, and Bhiku left too much polish on the shoes and would not spend that extra energy to bring a mirror shine to them no matter how many times Alec made him do it, and Shanta left too many corners unswept and too many surfaces undusted. But they all smiled and bowed when they brought the clothes and shoes to the family and their servility was all that the family seemed to require to please them. He also doubted their honesty. A couple of times he had found money missing from his wallet and one day he couldn't find his watch. But when he mentioned it to Baba and Gajanan, both had said that he must have counted his money wrong and left the watch somewhere else.

He started cutting Baba off in his elucidation of greatness of Hinduism and the cultural and moral superiority of Hindus. No, he was no more enamoured by the moral and spiritual superiority of Hindus; actually now he totally mistrusted their definitions of morality and sincerity. They did not fulfil even the smallest of their promises, he had found to his annoyance. Much of what they promised was either promised on the spur of the moment without proper consideration – they did mean it, he had to concede, but only for that particular moment – or it was just a formality with no intention of ever keeping their word though they always had good excuses for doing so. Ananta, one of Anu's cousins, had looked at Alec with absolute incomprehension when Alec had asked him the previous week whether he had brought those papers that he had offered to get for Alec from Margaon.

'Yes, yes,' he had said making an effort at recollection. 'I will definitely be going to Margaon tomorrow to pick them up.'

'That's what you said last week and the week before too,' Alec had reminded him with annoyance.

'Well, I had to go to Mapusa the whole of last week for that bank work. And the week before that...'

Alec had stopped listening. He never got the papers.

Now he kept away from Bhau-log and avoided Siddharth when he came to discuss his cases with him. But Siddharth, failing to notice the change in Alec, accosted him one morning and pulled him into a corner of the men's room for a discussion of the case of their cousin who was indicted on a charge of fraud. The men's room was dark like the rest of the house and the forty-watt bulbs only helped to emphasise the darkness making the large room seem cavernous and gloomy. Alec, feeling cornered, listened with only half his mind until what Siddharth was saying penetrated.

'You are going to defend your cousin knowing that he *did* cheat?' he asked in total disbelief.

Siddharth flipped a hand in the air. 'He is a cousin. Of course I have to defend him.'

Just then Anu, now ungainly in her pregnancy, came into the men's room with plates of pohe and Alec looked at it as if he had never seen anything like it before.

'I will have just toast and tea,' he said brusquely.

'Children finished the bread you brought,' Anu said miserably. 'Aai thought since you like pohe so much...' she stopped in mid-sentence seeing his clamped lips and the eyebrows beginning to rise.

Siddharth, unaware of Alec's anger and keen to expound his strategy, waved her off. 'So I thought of asking my maternal uncle to give an affidavit...'

'An affidavit is a statement given under oath,' Alec broke in shocked. 'Your uncle will be lying under oath?'

'The family has to stand together. We can't let Pratap go to jail,' Siddharth said.

'And you think that he will be acquitted just on the strength of that one affidavit?'

'Of course. Govind-bhatji has been holding a yajna for him for the last three days, that's a major puja with prayers to the holy fire, you know. And all the elders' blessings and everybody's prayers are with him. Of course he will be acquitted.' Siddharth said with total conviction as Alec stared at him in incredulity. Familial contract was inviolate.

No wonder Indians have never got anywhere in these modern times, he muttered afterwards to himself, mired as they are in their past and superstitions and emotions and family loyalty. They have none of the social morality or pragmatism or efficiency that is required to progress in today's world. He felt the gap between him and them widen day by day and now he watched them from an immense distance wondering how he could ever have envied them for their heritage, how he could ever have strived to be a part of them, how he could ever have wanted to belong to the family.

He couldn't stand the family any more. He now found it an overbearing, rigid, oppressive monolith. The adulation of the women in the family that he had basked in, now reeked of obsequiousness to him and suffocated him. Bhau-log, he thought, spent too much time just lolling about or chitchatting instead of doing some hard work and he was peeved at their taking life so casually.

He became particularly short-tempered with Anu. Now he felt a repulsion at all that she did and all that she was though that was exactly what had attracted him before. Now he found her too impulsive when she should be cautious, too carefree when she should be serious. He felt she was too exuberant, too spontaneous and too friendly with the tourists they met on their outings and he pulled her away in embarrassment. Now he frowned at her vivaciousness and liveliness and sentimentalism in public and avoided taking her to the hotels and restaurants with him. He berated her all the time on her behaviour. He stopped buying books for her and pulled her up whenever he found her with a book reminding her of his needs that needed attending to. He particularly minded that she was much more widely read than he, that her knowledge of the world – though bookish – surpassed his, that she, a village girl from a corner of India, knew more about England than he, an Englishman, a Londoner. And that she was, he secretly suspected, more intelligent than he. Now he took to belittling her before everyone, putting her down at every opportunity, ridiculing everything she said. If Anu, in a happy mood, made some remark about anything at all, he would raise his eyebrows in such a way that she wilted immediately. Just her presence around him had him raising his eyebrows, clamping his lips, and looking at her down his nose with that English hauteur of his, before turning away. Now a disapproving silence became his way with her. Now he started avoiding their previous light-hearted banter and the serious talks of their future at night in their room, or even any intimacy between them, by coming late to the room and immediately turning on his side away from her pretending to be asleep.

Anu, first bewildered and then rattled, then became fraught with anxiety at this inexplicable behaviour of his and tried to cajole him, appease him, adjust herself to his moods. The more solicitous she became towards him, the more irritated he became with her. Nothing she did pleased him any more. Her laughter started becoming rare, her eyes became haunted, her manner nervous.

'Could I come to Panaji with you today?' Maushi heard her ask him one morning as she was passing the open door of their room and stopped in her tracks hearing the pleading tone in Anu's voice. 'I want to do some shopping over there,' Anu explained nervously. Dumbstruck, Maushi glanced in at Alec. He was puffed up with the power she was acknowledging in him but was also looking down his nose at her, with scorn.

Maushi passed on considerably disturbed in her mind. She had known Anu's rebellious tones, her pert tones, even her saucy ones when she was trying to cadge a favour, but never had she heard her use that pleading tone of voice before, not even with Baba when she was persuading him to allow her to go to a college in Panaji, though that was how most women talked to their husbands. Every requirement was asked for as a favour. Every need was begged for as an obligation. No wonder men look at us with derision and treat us with contempt. But Anu had always been so confident of herself, so audacious, rebellious even when cornered.

What's happening, daughter, what's happening to you?

Just take her to Canada quickly, she wanted to say to Alec, just take her away from here and she will be fine. She will make her own life once she is free of the confinement of these walls, she will manage to regain what she has lost because she is capable, and she will stand on her own two feet and she will do well. She will even learn to manage her life with you, to live with you on equal terms. Just take her there quickly before she loses any more of her self-confidence. And what is happening about the renewal of his passport?

'Why is it taking so long?' she asked Baba. 'The marriage should be registered soon, Anu being pregnant.'

'There were hundreds of witnesses to the seven steps they took around the holy fire; the marriage can't be denied,' Baba said. 'And you know how slow our government offices are. Alec is doing all he can to hurry them up. Don't create more pressures on him.'

Maushi's uneasiness increased just as Anu's apprehension increased day by day.

But Alec deliberately seemed not to notice it at all. He took Anu's obsequiousness as his due, hardly paid any attention to her, hardly talked to her. Most of the time that he spent in the house, he now spent with Vinayak rather than with Anu. He also took to going out by himself without even telling Anu where he was going.

'When will you be back?' she asked him once while adjusting his coat collar.

'Do I have to report to you all that I do?' he asked irritably in return and walked out of the house ignoring her eyes that were beginning to fill with tears.

'He is a man. He has his own tasks to attend to. You can't expect him to hang around the house all the time,' Baba said when Maushi mentioned Alec's frequent absences from the house to him. 'And Anu is so big now. Surely you wouldn't allow her to go to Panaji with him?'

No, Maushi thought, but he could spend a little more time with her, go visiting with her.

Nowadays it was Vinayak who escorted Anu when she went visiting her aunts and cousins. And it was Vinayak who asked her whether she needed anything from the market when he went out rather than Alec who almost always forgot to bring her whatever she had asked for.

He was also not present at the celebration of the seven months of Anu's pregnancy. Though it was only a women's function, many of the men of the family including Baba and Gajanan and Vinayak and a few of Anu's cousins also had stayed back in the house to watch the ceremony. Vinayak had also gone through a lot of trouble to get the flowers – they were rare in the monsoons – to bedeck Anu and to twist around the ornate brass chains of the carved and painted timber swing that Maushi had made her sit on in the inner room. As her aunts and cousins and sisters-in-law sang the songs wishing her many honourable sons and beautiful daughters while they gently rocked the swing, Anu burst into tears for no reason at all.

Maushi watched helplessly as her daughter languished before her eyes. The sparkle had gone out of Anu's eyes. She had stopped humming around the house.

Alec now frequently spent time in Panaji or even in Bombay ostensibly to follow up his passport formalities. He sat in hotel lounges and bars reading English newspapers and talking to the English visitors there. The tourist season was long over and there were hardly any English tourists in the Panaji hotels, a few more in Bombay – mostly businessmen rather than tourists – but Alec still spent time with them talking about London and avariciously listening to English being spoken in the British accent while Anu waited in the village house.

Walking into the Panaji hotel one day he found the assistant manager in a heated argument with an English couple and was suddenly overcome with a comradely feeling towards his co-nationals that made him intervene, 'What's the problem?'

'Well, hello. You are British?' said the gentleman as the assistant manager gave him a nod and a smile of recognition. 'Do you know these hotel personnel?'

'I have stayed here before,' Alec said. 'Are you having a problem with them?'

'Are we! When we booked this hotel from Bombay we were told that we will be charged non-seasonal rates. But now that we are here, this gentleman informs us that they don't give any non-seasonal reductions and we will have to pay full rates.' The Englishman explained indignant at being cheated while the assistant manager looked embarrassedly at Alec and gave a silly giggle.

After the matter had been settled favourably, the Englishman shook his hand and introduced himself. 'Bill Rogers. This is my wife Fiona.'

Fiona Rogers was tall and dark, had violet eyes and wore a dress to match them.

'Thanks very much for helping us,' she said in a well-modulated voice offering a manicured hand to him. 'These Indians are such cheats!'

They invited him to join them for a cup of tea.

They sat on the tea veranda that was now enclosed with clear plastic sheets in timber framing watching the rain pouring off the plastic sheets, obscuring the view outside. Bill Rogers turned out to be a consultant with Greysons in Regent Street and came down often to their branch office in Bombay on business. 'Chris Norton is our manager in Bombay. A good chap. If you should need anything while you are there...'

He had insisted on Fiona joining him on this trip even though it was monsoon and the wrong season for India, but, he said, he had to return the hospitality of his hosts here who had treated him on many occasions and it was useful to have a wife to make small talk with other wives at dinners and cocktails while he clinched the business deals. Fiona had not enjoyed the trip at all.

'We have had a terrible trip,' she complained. 'Bombay was dirty, filthy, and the beggars... ugh!' she shuddered delicately. 'And shopping was no fun either. These Indians! They cheat and lie about everything. So when there was a break in the weather I thought we could at least soak up a bit of sun in Goa, but look at it! I can't wait to get back to London.' And Alec sympathised with her with all his heart.

The tea arrived – brewed not boiled, accompanied by thin cucumber sandwiches and scones. Over tea, Bill asked Alec about his area of work. 'Our London office is looking into having other counsels on panel,' he said. 'Jeffries, Henderson and Chase are our primary counsels but sometimes they can't handle our work due to conflicts of interests.' As they digressed into a discussion of the cases that Bill's company was fighting, Fiona lit cigarette after cigarette and watched the rain with a blank expression. Glancing at her out of the corner of his eye Alec thought to himself, I need a suitable wife right now to make small talk with her.

On the way back, Alec was totally depressed by the incessant rains, by the dim yellowish light, by the dismal atmosphere. The normally blue-green river that had given him so much pleasure was now overrunning its banks with thick, dirty ochre-red water and every depression in the ground was filled with the same thick, heavy-looking ochre-red water. It ran along the roadside, gurgled along all the slopes, and roared down the hillsides that were covered with lush greenery. Wild yellow-green creepers had proliferated everywhere, growing over everything, covering everything—barbed wire fences, shrubs and low trees, and rocks—blurring all the sharp edges and individual branches, and turning everything into one lush, amorphous, smooth, lumpy mass. Every inch of the ground was covered with the same wild creepers spreading in all directions; they had even climbed up some of the large riverside trees festooning them, hanging into the river. The large dark green trees standing at the back and sedately waving their branches had a dignity. This continuous, smoothly undulating, yellowish-green lush lump was repulsive. It was too profuse, too bright, too obscenely lush.

On the top of the hill, just before the road started winding downwards, in a lay-by under some thorny babul trees was a low, square brick and plaster platform with two eyes painted on it in black paint with a big solid red circle in between them and some other strange red paint markings on it. Once, a long time ago in spring, Alec had seen a group of young fisherwomen with their saris tucked tight between their legs dancing on the ground before it in a circle with their arms around each other's waists, heads bowed, moving back and forth slowly and rhythmically as in a trance. It had been a beautiful, enchanting scene for him but he had seen only fear in the eyes of other passers-by as they went past the site.

Alec's driver as usual took the tiny detour and slowed the car enough to allow him to throw a couple of coins on it before speeding on again, a ritual which Alec usually watched with disdain. Alec had once asked him what it was. 'It's a site of tantrik rites, of the worship of Mother Kali,' was all that his driver would say. Even Baba or Siddharth or Vinayak would not tell him anything more than that the tantriks were worshippers of Goddess Kali—a frightening demon-slayer goddess—and were supposed to derive great powers from their worship of the Goddess.

Kali, the wrathful goddess – a bell rang in Alec's mind.

'That's a cult that considers the female principle to be the highest, even higher than Lord Shiva,' Baba said reluctantly. 'There are many different sects even within the tantriks and they are not all frightening though they believe in satisfying all their senses as a path to moksha and at times can be rather wild and uncontrolled. There are hardly any of them here in Goa. These illiterate villagers are scared for nothing.'

More information came from an unexpected source. On one of his jaunts to Panaji, Alec came across Lisl waiting for transport to the airport. 'I have to go for business to Berlin,' she told him. 'But I will be back in October for nine days for the Durga Puja festival in Calcutta.'

'Ah yes,' Alec said sitting by her side. 'You are a devotee of some of those goddesses, aren't you? Also of Goddess Kali if I remember right.'

'Kali, yes. The frightful beheading and blood-drinking goddess that emanated from Parvati—the loving, placid, mother-goddess.'

'Why?'

'Why? Because it was her time. Only she could kill all those demons.'

'Tell me about her. What's she like?' Alec said.

'Kali? She is black, with three eyes, four arms; and her bloody tongue hangs out of her mouth. She carries a bloody sword in one hand and holds a severed head in the other and uses the other two to bless her devotees. She is naked with only a girdle of dead men's arms around her waist and a garland of skulls around her neck and her body is covered with ashes and blood. She is always projected as dancing with one foot on the breast of her supine consort Shiva. That's Kali, the frightful goddess.'

'What does she signify?' Alec asked feeling sick.

'She is a life destroyer but also a life giver, Alec. She teaches that without death, there can be no life. Without destruction, there can be no creation. She is the sacred cycle of all existence, forever destroying and forever becoming.'

'So what's her attraction?'

'Her boon is freedom. She makes her devotees accept the realities of pain and horror and sorrow and decay and destruction and then let them go, confront them and then be free of them, be able to sing and dance, enjoy life to the full. And most importantly, she wipes out their karma and fulfils their desires. She releases them to life. Her devotees call her Mother Kali, call themselves her children. But she demands a price for the freedom that she offers.'

'Price?'

'There is always a price for everything, Alec.'

'What price?'

'Sacrifices. Bloody sacrifices. And she wants her children to dance with her in the blood, eternally intertwined in the dance of destruction and creation; the dance of being.'

'What bloody sacrifices?' Alec asked fascinated.

'Chickens and goats mostly. Some say even humans sometimes. I have not seen it.'

'Why the foot on her consort's breast?'

'Some people they tell me that it's to show that she is Shakti, the primal energy. Not only the source of life but life itself – all-creating and therefore, all-consuming. I rather like that, don't you?'

Now Alec shivered as he passed the platform with the black eyes and the red marks painted on it and averted his eyes.

Dusk had fallen when he returned to the house. The dim lights in the house further accentuated the gloom. Sweet cloying smell of incense clung to the corners of all the rooms. The house was noisy as usual. Baba was talking loudly with some men in the men's room; he could hear some raised women's voices in the inner room;

Anu was scolding Shanta in the dining room; Maushi was telling something to Gauri in the kitchen; Gajanan was leading the shloka recital on the now enclosed back veranda. Enough of this mumbo-jumbo, Alec thought listening to the incomprehensible chants. I am weary of all these rituals to which I do not belong. I am stifled by these people and their emotions that I cannot cope with. And I am frightened of the mystique surrounding them. As soon as my daughter is born, I will go back to London.

Long ago, when Anu had first told him of her pregnancy, before they were married, even before she had lured him to visit her ancestral house by the riverside, that sprawling, tiled house with the holy basil in an internal courtyard and antique flooring in all rooms and with flowers and bumblebees in the garden and with a large stepped well and with old mango and tamarind and audumber trees, he had decided it would be a girl.

'What if it's a boy? I would very much like a son. A son just like you,' Anu had said to him in that Baga hotel. She was bending over him and had coyly pulled a handful of her hair across her face while the rest of her long black tresses had cascaded around his face curtaining around both their faces and creating a private dark world of their own. Her eyes were sparkling like fireflies in a dark night out of the black hair covering her face and surrounding it and Alec had stared into them bewitched.

'It will be a girl. A girl just like you.' He had said, a little throatily, a little huskily, holding her with trembling hands.

I stayed too long over here, I got too involved, I lost myself, he thought with sudden clarity remembering Anu's allure; remembering those enchanting times with her; remembering that ravishing, sensual, passionate Anu in the Baga hotel, that radiant, golden Anu on the beach rising out of the sea like a sea-goddess, that vivacious Anu in the bar-restaurants that he had delightedly laughed with and at; remembering the great time he had spent in Baba's house visiting the farmlands and in discussions with Baba and Siddharth, as well as those relaxing and hilarious times he had spent with Vinayak and the Bhau-log. It's fabulous here as long as I come here for short visits and keep a distance, he thought with sudden nostalgia for this lifestyle, for Goa, for Anu, now that he knew he would be leaving soon. However irked he was with it all at the moment, he knew that soon on his return to London he would start missing Anu, start missing Goa. He was now forever captivated by Anu, by Goa, by the exotic lifestyle here, all intertwined together, all acting together as one entity, none of which could exist independent of others. A fling on a beach had escalated into a serious obsession.

No, he will not be taking either Anu or his daughter back to London with him. But he would not be deserting them either. He already looked forward to coming here again, to seeing Anu again, to watching his daughter grow; of course he will be visiting Goa quite often. And of course he will pamper Anu whenever he visited here—take her to the beaches, take her to the restaurants. Her and his daughter. Perhaps when his daughter had become a young lady, he would bring her to London, when his wife of that time could accept her with equanimity and when his professional reputation would be high enough to absorb a scandal such as this.

It was during that week of his visits to Baba's house, before he had made his offer for Anu, that he had decided on the way he would organise his life—both in England and here in Goa. A tall, dark and stately English wife and sons in England; a golden, willowy Indian wife and a daughter in Goa. A centrally located town house in

London; a riverside farmhouse in Goa. A busy, active lifestyle that stressed him to the peak of his performance in London; frequent restful interludes to unwind in Goa. It was time he started the procedures to that end, he thought, both here in Goa and in London too, as soon as he reached back. Both needed drastic re-organisation. In London, he needed to divorce his present wife who was unsuitable to his present lifestyle and find a wife more compatible with his current status; in Goa, Anu had to be settled.

Goa first.

Here, I will buy a piece of land nearby and build a house on it. He mentioned it to Vinayak. Vinayak laughed. 'If you decide to live here,' he said, 'Baba will give you that riverside land in dowry.'

'Oh, not live here permanently,' Alec hastened to correct him. 'But I'd like to come here often. May be every few months or so.'

I have deferred it for too long, he thought, I should have settled Anu long ago. However excited she may be about going to Canada, hadn't she also described to him her house and garden and well and her family and their customs in absolutely glowing terms in that hotel in Baga? Of course she would prefer to stay here in an environment that she is born to rather than in Canada—a place strange to her. And doesn't this society treat being a second wife and her staying back in the village as an acceptable custom?

I will ask Baba for that riverside land, he thought. I will provide enough money to build a house – a house just like this with verandas and a tiled roof and a gods' room and a garden. My daughter will be brought up there among the flowers and the butterflies. She and Anu will stay there, near her family – they are such a close-knit family – fondly cared for by them all. I will visit here every few months, may be even every couple of months. When I have reached the top of my profession, I could come here very often indeed!

This is what he had decided during that first week of visits to Baba's house, but now he was not so sure as to how it will be received by the family. These Hindus, they behave so contradictorily, so unpredictably, so mystifyingly! And they have those ancient Vedas and the Gita and the Manusmriti behind them to back them up!

I will deal with it long distance, as a fait accompli, he decided. I will get a broker in Bombay to settle everything with Baba. I will talk to Chris Norton. He will understand. He will arrange it.

Then Elizabeth came to Goa.

15

'Then Elizabeth came,' Pundlik said.

You are the one who should know, Maushi thought to herself, you brought the news. Couldn't stop yourself from following Alec about, could you?

Pundlik had come to see Maushi the day after Anu's engagement was announced. His normal manner of self-righteousness and self-importance had gone, his eyes had a desperate look in them, and he had such a terribly dejected air about him that for a moment Maushi had forgotten her happiness in the feeling of pity for him. She knew that he had spent the whole of the previous day futilely trying to convince the elders in his family to make a marriage offer for Anu. Firstly, he was too young to think of marriage, as was Anu, they had said, secondly, a Mangli girl, and thirdly, a girl with a reputation of being wayward even though they had known her from her birth...

'A vilayati, Maushi!' he had tried to convince her. 'It's not necessary that she be married to a vilayati just because she is a

Mangli. There are pujas to perform that can alleviate its mal influence. And gems to wear that counteract it. Surely Govind-bhatji can suggest something,' he had said. 'Or because she is a spirited girl. She is just too young. She will mellow down after marriage, once she has children. She will forget all her wild ways and settle down to the family. She only needs a strong husband to control her. Surely you could wait a few years for her marriage. May be a better match will come along,' he had added with a false hope.

He had looked so woebegone that Maushi had felt sorry for him in spite of knowing what he actually meant though he himself might not have realised it. She had always known that Pundlik was madly attracted to Anu because of her wild spirit, her unconventional attitude, her exuberance. But to him, her spirit was a challenge. Like all other men he too didn't want to nurture it, he too wanted to subdue it. He too wanted to see her tamed. But only by yourself Bhacha, not by anyone else, Maushi had thought to herself, and not immediately, but after a few years of marriage. You all men have only one vision of a woman before your eyes, she thought remembering a picture from a book of paintings that Anu had brought from her college. A woman sitting with some pots and pans and a cat at her feet, a parrot on her shoulder, a baby in her arms, and a self-satisfied, smug smile on her lips. 'The whole world could pass her by and she wouldn't even notice it,' Anu had said with derision looking at it over Maushi's shoulder.

But that's how a woman was supposed to be in this men's world. Anyone wanting something beyond these cannot be, would not be tolerated. She would have to be curbed, tamed, brought under control. And it will be in your power to do so, Bhacha, if Anu were to marry you. Our society gives you that right. Physical violence is not even necessary, or even locking her up. Scornful looks, contemptuous remarks, sexual rejection—they all are enough to subjugate a woman. And the more abject she becomes, the more contemptuous of her you will be. You are exactly what she is trying to escape from, Bhacha, Maushi had thought as she sadly shook her head.

She had watched him during the marriage ceremony as he sat across the holy fire from Anu and Alec as if to check that the ceremony was really taking place and glared with murderous hatred at Alec when the priests raised their voices to a high pitch to chant the last of the ritual shlokas and Anu and Alec garlanded each other. And she had seen him afterwards standing behind the tamarind tree near the well, leaning and sobbing against the tree, and then trying to take control of himself. Anu was now permanently out of his reach. But he still couldn't control his terrible jealousy of or his unwarranted fury at Alec. His envious eyes watched Alec's every move. He dogged Alec's steps.

Pundlik came one rainy night, rather late and quite agitated, banging on the main door, demanding to see Baba. Maushi came out to see what all the ruckus was about but it was Gajanan who opened the door to Pundlik and took him into Baba's room. Then he came back and closed the doors, main door as well as the one to Baba's room.

It was three days afterwards that Baba called Maushi to his room and told her that Alec was not yet divorced, that his wife and son were here in Goa, staying in a hotel in Baga.

'His wife and son? Not yet divorced?' Maushi asked in confusion. 'And they are in Baga? But Alec said he was staying in Panaji to follow up his passport formalities...' she stopped in mid-sentence seeing the 'you should know better' expression on Baba's face.

'What do you expect him to say when he finds himself in a bind?' he asked coldly.

Maushi tried to collect her wits. 'Did you know that he was married?' she asked.

'A man like him is bound to be married.' Baba shrugged. 'That's not important. But obviously his marriage to Anasuya cannot be registered and her name entered on his passport unless he divorces his first wife. And Gajanan has found out that Anasuya cannot get a visa to Canada otherwise.'

'What does Alec say?'

'Poor Alec,' Baba commiserated. 'He said that that marriage had been a mistake. They had got married by themselves when they were students – always a mistake. He has been asking her for a divorce for a long time now but she is being difficult. What's this "asking" business? I asked him,' Baba's voice started rising. 'Why *ask* her for anything?' he continued angrily. 'Just go ahead and divorce her, send her back to her parents, I told him. But he says it's different with vilayati women. She has to consent to the divorce or she will contest it and create problems for him, not just accept it. He says he hasn't pressurised her because she has been chronically depressed for some years. Well, depressed or not, we are going to talk to her now. With our connections here we can get an uncontested divorce pushed through very quickly. And even the waiting period for remarriage after that can be waived. Don't tell anyone else in the house.'

And so they went, the three of them, Baba, Gajanan, and an important looking Pundlik, whom, at that moment, Maushi hated more than all others including Alec, while Maushi waited in the gods' room.

Young Pundlik, jilted suitor, sworn to secrecy by Baba in front of the Ganesha idol, was bursting to talk. 'She said, "Your daughter isn't the first, nor will she be the last,"' he reported to Maushi in a hushed voice.

'What did Baba say?'

'He shrugged. He said, "That's the natural tendency of men. Men do these sorts of things. Our women are brought up to deal with it and still keep the family intact. You Western women do not know how to handle men. You have no subtlety, no finesse. You demand everything. You demand your rights. You demand equality. Without being ready to pay the price for it. Without being ready to give up something else in return."'

That is true, Maushi thought. You cannot demand anything if you have nothing to bargain with. A confrontation never gets you any of what you want when you start from a position of powerlessness.

'So Baba told her that it was too late for her now to try to save her marriage, that the time had come when divorcing Alec was her only option. Western women are supposed to be independent, aren't they? And she is still working in some office.'

'And then?' Maushi asked.

'She answered back to Baba, Maushi,' Pundlik said in an awed tone. 'She said, "You don't know anything about what our life has been like, do you? When we were young? We were happy together at one time." She said she gave up her studies, her prospects of a promising career, and took up a job to put Richard – she called him Richard – through the Law School. She said she had struggled to make ends meet while living on a pittance and suffered with him and for him in all those early years of his practice. "And now you come here and ask me to leave him?" she asked.'

'Why did she call him Richard?'

The rookie policeman expanded his chest. 'I checked his police registration form,' he said proudly. 'His name is Richard Alec Harrington-Wells. They have two first names you know. They don't use father or husband's first name as middle name like us. Maybe they call him Richard in Canada,' he stopped suddenly. 'And I had always thought his last name was only Wells,' he said dubiously. And then his chest collapsed. 'Maushi,' he said in an uncertain, confused tone, lowering his voice still further, 'his address on the form, and also that of Elizabeth, is only of London, England.' He looked at Maushi as if she could provide an explanation.

Maushi looked stupefied for a moment. 'He only said he was *going* to settle in Canada,' she said at last, thinking, Alec the lawyer ever.

Pundlik digested that information and continued his narration of the meeting with Elizabeth. 'So Baba told her that he will personally ensure that she and her son will be well provided for, if that was what was worrying her. She laughed a little sadly then. "Please understand that I *love* him. I loved him then and I *love* him now. I suffered with him and for him only because I love him. I can't live without him, I really can't. I love him too much," she told Baba.' Pundlik was quiet for a moment. He could very well understand and sympathise with unrequited love. 'So Baba told her that if she really loved Alec, then she should be thinking of his happiness and not hers,' he added in a virtuous tone.

'What did she say to that?' Maushi asked.

'She said, "Richard is not really in love with your daughter. I know him. He is only infatuated with your daughter and though I'm sorry for her, it will wear off in due course. It always does." But she was totally devastated when Gajanan showed her the marriage photographs and told her that Anu was seven months pregnant.

Didn't speak a word after that. She looked so shattered, Maushi, like a fragile china statuette—all cracked up.'

Maushi's face had gone ashen, her eyes were lifeless. 'What does she look like, this Elizabeth?' she asked.

'She is like a doll, small and delicate, Maushi,' he said. 'Like that English doll that Anu had. Like that princess in all the fairy tales that we used to read about? The one who came from beyond the seven seas? She has the same blue eyes and she has that same golden hair and her cheeks are like – like those roses you have in the front garden, those little pink ones, and...'

But Maushi had stopped listening. Princess, she thought cynically, Alec's two princesses! remembering Alec coming to talk to her when his marriage offer for Anu was accepted, with his hands joined in a namaskar and with Vinayak translating: 'He says our Anu is like a princess, Aai. He says this just doesn't feel real to him. It's like a dream, a mirage.' Alec got married in a dream and both his princesses will now be paying the price of his infatuation. Both will be shattered like fragile china statuettes.

Shattered! I know what can shatter Anu—the prospect of spending all her life marooned in a village like this—but what shattered you, Elizabeth? A second wife? An expected step-child? Not an unknown phenomenon over here. Quite a few men here have liaisons, some even openly maintain a second home and a second family. Divorce is not common amongst us and so both the wives are always accepted in the society with due respect. Especially if they are in two different towns. And the Western society is supposed to be much more permissive sexually, much more easy-going on marriage contracts, isn't it? Gajanan had lectured her on that when hippies were news in Goa, and Vinayak and his cousins, when young, had whispered the stories from the Western movies to her in between embarrassed bursts of laughter after their sneaky visits to cinemas in Panaji. A first wife—divorced or extant—and a stepson wouldn't worry Anu at all as long as Alec took her to Canada with him and the first wife stayed in London or some other city. No, a liaison or a second marriage is not enough to devastate or shatter a woman, Maushi thought, though the heartache that went with it could be wrenching at times.

'Men do these sorts of things,' Baba had said.

Yes, men do, Maushi agreed bitterly remembering the past.

In the last year of Baba's father's sickness they had kept a nurse for him, a young, rather sassy woman. The nurse was not quite a servant and therefore was allotted a room at the back of the house. It was a joint family then with Baba's brothers and their wives and children all living under the same roof and Baba's nocturnal forays to the back room were known to all. Men—Baba's brothers and even Maushi's brothers—had shrugged it off with a little embarrassed smile saying, 'Men do these sorts of things'. Women had consoled Maushi saying, 'At least she is not within the house. You are still the mistress here. When your children get married, *you* will be the one sitting next to Baba before the holy fire.' Maushi had swallowed her humiliation, anger, jealousy and hurt, and had smiled in public and also for Baba. Baba was the eldest son and she knew nobody would dare to chastise him.

One day Baba had come back from the market with a string of aboli flowers for her—the little peach-coloured ones that she so loved. She had accepted it gracefully with a smile and wound it around her bun, and then watched the nurse parade around the inner courtyard with a similar string of flowers wound in her hair and smiled at her. Later, alone with the women of the household, she had furiously wrenched it out of her hair and thrown it on to the rubbish heap.

She looked up and saw Pundlik watching her with concern. 'And now?' she asked him.

'Baba is going to talk to Alec. He says it will be up to Alec now to get her to agree to a divorce. He was quite angry. "What kind of a man is he that he can't control his own wife?" he said.'

Later, after Anu's death, as he lay on his bed suffering from high fever, this was the sentence Baba was to remember.

Maushi never knew what Alec said to Elizabeth. That night, at midnight, Elizabeth walked out of their hotel room and into the sea off Baga Beach.

PART THREE

16

'Why don't you send Meera to Gajanan's in Belgaum?' Pundlik asked. 'Colleges and education are much better there than here in Goa.'

Maushi almost laughed aloud remembering the last encounter between Gajanan and Meera. When Meera had turned fifteen, Gajanan had taken it upon himself—against Maushi's strong advice—to lecture her on the conduct befitting women. 'You are a young woman now. You have to dress properly, behave properly. You shouldn't mix with boys any more. Walk with your eyes cast down. Don't look men in the eyes,' he had said. 'Men are animals. Women have to protect themselves with their modesty.' He had just stopped himself from adding, 'Look what happened to your mother.'

Meera, in turn, had started addressing his wife as 'zoo-keeper' which had made Vinayak laugh, but Gajanan had turned red with fury.

Maushi wiped the tears of suppressed laughter from her eyes. 'They are not on talking terms,' she said. 'He can barely stand being in the same house as her when he visits here.'

'Then how about to Vinayak's in Mumbai?'

'It's Ronnie's coming here that is worrying you, isn't it?' she asked.

'I understand he has almost become a fixture in this house,' Pundlik said dryly and not without envy. Since Gajanan's and Vinayak's departures and the rest of the family's estrangement, he had taken over the responsibility of looking after Maushi and Baba. Whenever he had any time, he made the rounds of the storehouses with Maushi. He ran errands for them, kept a check on their farms and plantations, looked after their welfare, and saw to it that they were not inconvenienced in any way. Actually he was behaving like a son towards them and in return considered himself to be the only outsider to have full rights to their house as an accepted family member, to be the only one who could rightfully walk into the house at any time of the day or night.

Then one day he had walked into the house as usual and found Meera and Ronnie sitting close together in front of Meera's computer. 'Pundlik Mama, this is Ronnie,' Meera had introduced him quite casually and Ronnie had smiled up at him and said, 'Hello Pundlik Mama.' He had been too shocked to respond but neither of them had noticed it as they had turned back to the computer and their animated discussion.

He was still more shocked when arriving at noontime another day he found Ronnie at lunch with Baba in the dining room. Baba had never used the dining room since his sickness even though Vinayak had the dining room set-up replaced with a dining table and chairs so that his wheelchair could be brought right up to the table. Now here he was sitting and eating at the table with Ronnie while Ronnie bantered with Maushi. 'No,' Ronnie was saying, 'No. I won't eat unless you also join us, Aaji. Gauri can serve us.'

'Eat,' Baba said pointing to his thali. 'She will eat later in the kitchen.'

'It's silly,' Ronnie said, 'her eating later all by herself.'

'Eat,' Maushi said smiling at him as she served him stuffed bitter karelas that Baba never ate. 'You have a very big mouth. You like these, so just concentrate on eating.'

'Don't give him any more of those if he talks again,' Baba said with mock severity.

'Where is Meera?' Pundlik asked Maushi more so as to break this atmosphere of bonhomie around the table; he was already feeling like an outsider.

But it was Ronnie who answered him. 'She has an afternoon class. She will be home in a couple of hours.'

'Where did she meet him anyway?' an exasperated Pundlik asked Maushi later. 'And why has she become so friendly with him?' not daring to ask why Maushi and Baba too had taken to him so, why they too were treating him like a part of the family, why they had allowed Meera to bring him home in the first place. That innocent, bubbly, outgoing child makes friends so easily, he thought, but she is also so naïve. And Maushi has done nothing to instill the feminine caution, the proper Hindu reserve in her.

'You have indulged her too much, Maushi. You have let her grow up in too much of that Christian atmosphere right from her school days. She has hardly any Hindu culture,' he said with frustration welling inside him; frustration at Maushi being in sole charge of Meera, at his not being allowed to guide Meera into Hindu proprieties, at his not being allowed to act as surrogate father to Anu's daughter. 'Look at the way she dresses: in jeans all the time;

or her friends: all Christians; or even her manners: all vilayati,' he finished peevishly.

She does what she is comfortable with, Maushi thought. And what has our Hindu culture given to us women? Kept us under strict control, defined our wants and wishes for us, offered us nothing but enslavement; sometimes with love and affection, sometimes with care and concern, sometimes even with reverence, but enslavement all the same, meted with exaggerated respect mixed with contempt. Maybe, once, we were honoured and respected as equals; maybe, once, we had freedom to make and follow our choices; maybe, once, a long time ago, in the Vedic times? Or did we? Did we ever enjoy a position of honour and equality? Aren't even our Vedic goddesses subordinate to gods? And what about us, the rest of the women? She wondered remembering those stories from Mahabharata and Ramayana, stories from tens of centuries ago. Even highborn princesses had not escaped being treated like pieces of personal property, allowed no freedom of thought or action beyond the perimeters prescribed by men, punished for no fault of theirs. Princess Madri, for whom patriarch Bhishma had paid a very high bride price and brought her over to marry his nephew Prince Pandu, and who knew not till later that Pandu was not allowed to have sexual intercourse as it would kill him. Or Princess Gandhari, whom Bhishma had brought to marry Prince Dhritarashtra, another of his nephews, who also knew not till the eve of her marriage that Dhritarashtra was blind! Or Ahalya, the innocent, guiltless wife of great Sage Gautama, whom her husband had cursed and turned into a rock for being treacherously seduced by God Indra. And they all had accepted their fate without any protest. Madri had borne twins from another man on her husband's orders, Gandhari had bound her own eyes for her lifetime so that she would not see what her husband couldn't, and naïve Ahalya was in no position to object to anything having been turned into a rock. No, it may be a great culture but not for us women, not now, not then, not at any time, she concluded. It's time somebody rebelled.

'What's wrong with Meera's dress? It's appropriate for the active life she leads. And what's wrong in her mixing with Christians? Don't the scriptures teach us that all different paths lead to the same God?' she said now getting impatient with Pundlik's peevishness. 'What matters is that Meera has absorbed the important teachings of Hinduism, the important ethics of our dharma.'

'Such as?' Pundlik asked, still irritated.

'Such as? Such as she is diligent, she respects elders, she has concern and compassion for all living beings, she is truthful and straightforward and conscientious and she is not selfish or covetous.' Maushi recited with equal irritation. And no, she wanted to add, she will never be subservient, or submissive, or self-sacrificing, whatever the dharma might say.

'She didn't show much concern for you or Baba when she thought of going abroad for further studies,' Pundlik, who had strongly opposed the idea, said fussily. But Meera had concerns. She had discussed it endlessly with Maushi and Baba and even Vinayak, and to Pundlik's chagrin, Maushi and Vinayak had encouraged her wholeheartedly and even Baba had agreed surprising Pundlik. Well, not exactly. Over the last almost two decades, he had watched the change in Baba's attitude. From his always-respectful manner towards Maushi to his seething rage at her at the time of his sickness – 'How dare she! How dare she!' Pundlik had heard him murmur – that had bewildered all. From his autocratic traditional rule over the whole family to his grudgingly accepting and never opposing Maushi's totally unconventional and at times even outrageous upbringing of Meera, and then, strangely enough, to his taking great pride in Meera's accomplishments, even more than in those of his grandsons. Maushi's support to Meera had, of course, been expected. 'Did I bring you up the way I did to then keep you tied to my pallav? Go. Go and experience that big wide world,' Maushi had said to her unconsciously using Anu's phrase.

But that had been before Ronnie had come to Goa. Now Meera and Ronnie reviewed their subjects together, discussed other fields and researched other possibilities on the net also together. Now she and Ronnie planned together. And Pundlik had flinched every time he had seen them engrossed in a discussion. But he had no authority over Meera. He couldn't even advise her any more; she had stopped asking his advice on anything since he had told her that her ambition of becoming a scientist was unsuitable for a girl, that, at most, she should think of becoming a software programmer, though she was always respectful towards him.

Now Ronnie dropped in all the time: morning, noon and evening. He came to pick Meera up to take her to college on his hired motorbike. He came to drop her home. He came even if Meera wasn't at home, even if she was going to be in her classes all day, spent time with Baba and Maushi, or just lolled about, sat surfing on her computer, kept asking Gauri to make him bhajias. He made himself at home. And Baba and Maushi not only tolerated him but encouraged him, pampered him, treated him like a cherished family member.

Then there was that time when Pundlik had come in and found Ronnie cajoling Maushi to go to a bhajan that was being held in the temple on the hill.

'Meera tells me all her aunts and grand-aunts are going and that at one time you also used to very much enjoy going to listen to them,' he was saying while Maushi kept shaking her head and Baba watched with an impassive expression. 'It's not right that you don't go out of the house at all these days, Aaji. I will bring a car and take you.'

How can she go anywhere with her husband lying disabled at home? Pundlik wanted to shout at him. Don't interfere in what you don't understand, boy. Don't meddle in the affairs you know nothing about. These are our customs, our traditions, our dharma. Self-denial and self-sacrifice by women for their menfolk are the foundations of our dharma.

'He is getting too familiar, Maushi,' Pundlik said as a warning chafing at all that he couldn't say. Why have you encouraged this friendship? Why have you welcomed him in this house with love? Why haven't you thrown him out the very first day he came here, forbidden Meera to see him again? Don't you see the danger, he wanted to ask Maushi, don't you sense it, the two of them researching topics together, the two of them comparing notes? Can't you see where it could lead to? Can't you imagine the consequences?

Maushi looked thoughtfully at the river. A couple of village boys were fishing in the bend, whirling their nets over their head in graceful arcs before dropping them in water. A pond heron circled over them equally gracefully, its white wings flapping against the brown of its body, and a bulbul was singing plaintively in the gulmohar tree now bereft of any of its blood red summer glory. A pair of lapwings zoomed to the riverbank to forage and then flew off together with their find. It worries you what the two of them will find out together, doesn't it? she thought watching the lapwings; it worries you what the two of them will ferret out together. Did you really expect them to forever stay ignorant of each other's existence? You and Gajanan, both of you had always thought that Meera would forget all about her father as she grew up, especially as Meera had stopped asking any more questions about him by the age of ten. Didn't it occur to either of you that she has stopped asking about him simply because she thinks that nobody in the family has anything more to tell her? I know what you both have been hoping for, Bhacha, she thought, but it's a futile hope, Bhacha.

Because Maushi had always known—from the day that Baba had sworn Gajanan and Pundlik to total secrecy about Elizabeth and Ronnie from even the rest of the family, from the day that Gajanan had burnt all the photographs that had Alec in them—that she herself would be telling Meera more about her father when she would grow up. That he was a lawyer in London and not in a Canadian city. That he was already married and had a son when he married her mother. She would tell her about Elizabeth and Ronnie. Just that much, nothing more. And only when Meera would turn eighteen, not before. And she had hoped that Meera would be able to deal with it.

But lately Meera had been talking of going to Canada for further studies, had even applied to some universities there, and it was obvious that she meant to look up her father. It was time to apprise her of the facts.

Then Ronnie had come to Goa.

'I would have told her in just a little time,' Maushi said to herself. 'I would have prepared her about Ronnie. If only Ronnie had come just a little later...'

If only!

No use speculating on what might have been, Maushi thought, it has happened already. One has to act as circumstances demand.

The news of Ronnie's arrival in Goa had initially disturbed her deeply though she had hardly expected him to run into Meera.

Ronnie walking on to the back veranda behind Meera had been a great shock to her – he evoked the past, but more than that, he challenged the present, he forced the future. But pushing him away or forbidding him from the house was never a possibility she would even think of. He was Elizabeth's son. And then he had joined his hands, bowed his head, and had said, 'Namaste Aaji' with such an open, pleasant and yet vulnerable smile! Elizabeth's traits? He certainly didn't have Alec's hauteur or his patronising manners, or any of his bigoted opinions. Except for that habit of his of raising his eyebrows when questioned. So like Alec. But Alec did it to belittle the other person; Ronnie did it to express his perplexity. For one moment she had wished he would bend down and touch her feet in the Hindu way so that she could place her hand on his head and bless him.

And he had turned out to be such a lovable, affectionate, charming boy! Even Baba, who had initially withdrawn from him in shock, now waited for him to come, lost his grumpiness in his presence, treated him like a grandson, lectured him, joked with him, and laughed with him. Gauri too smiled at him and cooked his favourite foods when he was around. And, most important, he and Meera had become such good friends, though both had different areas of interests. But they were also so much alike: both were serious in their interests yet had a sense of humour. They understood each other, nurtured each other's interests, and took care of each other. Maushi watched it with mixed feelings, with an unquietness she would not admit even to herself, postponing the moment of her decision. Yet, in a way she was happy that Meera and Ronnie had met, had come to know each other, and had formed a friendship before knowing the relationship. Now she felt comforted that he and Meera would always be there for each other—a family at last for both of them, somebody to unconditionally and totally depend on.

Yet Ronnie running across Meera had not been a part of her initial worry. Even if he hadn't met her, could she have let him come here, to Goa, and not talked to him? Not told him the truth about Meera, about Meera's mother, about his own mother? No, Ronnie also had to be told. He and Meera, both had a right to the truth. That was never in question. The question Maushi had been struggling with was when to tell, how much to tell, and how to tell: Meera and Ronnie separately or together. They both will need time and space to understand the past, to come to terms with it. But recently she had also been very much aware that time was running out for her, that she couldn't delay it any further. And it wasn't only because of the possibility of Ronnie's imminent return to London. She turned to the river again searching for the pair of lapwings but they were not to be found. Instead the bulbul still sitting on the bereft gulmohar branch gave another mournful cry and Maushi felt the time rushing her.

'Why does he come here so often?' Pundlik continued irritably.

'Meera has many friends. They come here all the time too,' she temporised.

But Pundlik would not be put off so easily. 'They move together everywhere. He even goes and waits for her in her college library while she is attending her classes,' he said in a warning tone.

Maushi turned and looked at him with unbridled hostility. 'Meera is just a child, not even eighteen yet,' she said curtly. 'And Ronnie will be going back soon. He is here just on a holiday.'

The danger! The danger! Pundlik's mind screamed. You very well understand the danger lurking behind this close friendship of theirs even if you won't acknowledge it to me. You know it. You know there is a danger whether they find out the truth about each other or not. Either way it's a highly treacherous situation and could lead to a catastrophe. It's a situation that should never have been allowed to develop; it should have been nipped in the bud.

'The rains have already started, what's he still doing here? This friendship could become a matter of real worry, Maushi. Meera is growing up. In fact she is already a very attractive young lady.'

17

'Well, well, well. You would never believe it,' Ronnie said. He was lying on his stomach on a flat stretch of ground at the base of an almost vertical cliff reading from the book he had laid in front of him. Meera was sitting a short distance away on one of the rocks that had sprouted out of the sea, dangling her feet in the water, watching the tide coming in. The waves that had just tickled her toes a while ago were now playing around her ankles.

'What?' Meera asked watching the waves.

'It's a poem by William Wordsworth. Just listen to this,

Two voices are there,
one is of the sea,
one of the mountains,
each a mighty Voice.

He of course didn't know it, but he was writing about Goa.'

'You ever think of how the seas die and the mountains grow, Ronnie?' she asked looking at him over her shoulder.

Ronnie laughed.

Meera frowned. 'No, seriously. Himalayas grow five centimetre every year.'

'Really?' Ronnie asked surprised.

'Sure. I know. I am studying rock strata and water molecules and all sorts of other things to decide my future direction. One thing is definite, I am going to be a scientist,' she said standing up and throwing her hands high up and pirouetting on the rock, her face glowing and eyes sparkling just at the thought of it.

Ronnie turned on his side, rested an elbow on the ground supporting his head on his palm, and looked up at her. 'You are not serious enough to be a scientist,' he said with a mock frown. 'All the scientists I know have these long, furrowed faces and they wear pince-nez and have no sense of humour at all. Or any feel for fun. You had better join me in studying the nature, conserving it and writing poems about it.'

Meera laughed and then sat down facing him. 'It isn't such a dry subject, Ronnie,' she said earnestly. 'Actually it's terribly exciting when you decipher something or discover a new way of doing something. It's... well... I can't quite describe the feeling, but it's as if every moment is leading you towards that cry of *Eureka* and a run down the street.'

'Naked?' Ronnie asked with a naughty smile. 'Now, that should create a sensation even if your discovery doesn't.'

Meera bent down, scooped a handful of pebbles, and threw them at him. 'You never know what I will discover. May be I will discover a way of harnessing all this energy that's going waste,' she said gesturing at the waves now beginning to crash on the rocks that they had been caressing only a little while ago.

'Ya? Then I better be around to put some poetry in your ventures to ensure that they don't go dry. And to see that you don't harness *all* the nature.'

'And I better be around to put some reins on your nature conservation or we will all be covered with greenery in no time at all. It could work you know: a kind of symbiotic partnership,' Meera said drawing out the word symbiotic.

Ronnie laughed and put his head down on his folded arms. 'Does Aaji want you to be a scientist?' he asked after a while looking sideways at her thinking of his overbearing father and his rigidly enforced rules as to what Ronnie should be and should not be.

Meera shook her head. 'She doesn't mind what I choose to do,' she said. 'She says do whatever you like, but then do your best at it.' She turned to watch the restless sea. 'She has never minded my doing anything as long as it isn't harmful to anybody or anything, particularly the plants,' she said reflectively. 'Or do anything that violates any of her proprieties. She has driven me hard, rejoiced with me in my successes, but...'

'But?'

'Well, does she have a terrible temper when provoked! And I guess I had got rather bigheaded at one time, kind of disrespectful and sassy to my aunts and uncles, derogatory to my cousins, you know. Whew! Did she chew me out then!'

'Punished ya, did she?' Ronnie asked recalling being sent to his room on those innumerable occasions, forced to miss dinners, cricket games and TV shows, punished for wanting other things than what his father thought were proper for him to have, punished for not getting good grades in the subjects chosen for him by his father, punished for insisting on different interests.

'No, not like your Dad,' Meera said shaking her head. 'She reasoned with me whenever she thought I was in the wrong. Just badgered at me until I saw the light. She said I don't have to be under anybody's thumb but that's no reason to be mean or nasty to them.'

'But besides that she always let you do whatever you wanted.' A statement, not a question, remembering the books on environmental studies that he had had to read on the sly. He had told Meera about them and about his intense interest in environment and all about his Dad too, all that he couldn't talk to Hilary about.

'At least you had a father around, Ronnie,' Meera had said.

'You miss your father very badly, don't ya?' Ronnie had asked looking sideways at her.

'Terribly.' Meera had said. 'Aaji and Ajaa love me so much. Especially Aaji. She has really gone out of her way to do things for me. But it's not the same, is it?'

'I don't know,' Ronnie had said looking into distance. 'Dad was never a real father to me. All he ever did for me was to discipline me.'

It had seemed so natural, telling her all about his childhood and his dreams while sitting there close together on a rock on one of the high ridges of Western Ghats with white clouds swirling around them and that limitless expanse of the land laid out far below them: miles and miles of deep green forest with silver rivers and black roads snaking in between and towns rising out of it every once in a while—an awe-inspiring landscape. 'What a sight!' Ronnie had said overcome by the majesty of the forest below.

'It's already diminishing. You can see those patches of red earth in between,' Meera had said. 'Loggers, you know. Illicit logging.'

'Kill the bastards!' Ronnie had shouted jumping up and throwing his arms wide. 'Avenge the trees!'

'Then they are gone, without having faced the consequences of their actions,' Meera had said. 'Aaji says killing the perpetrators is never an effective revenge. They must live to repent.'

'That's Christian way of thinking,' Ronnie had said looking down at her.

'That's also Hindu way of thinking,' Meera had said.

'Yeah,' Meera said now. 'She badgered me to get all the info, discuss it, think about all the pros and cons, but then she would just leave me alone to do whatever I chose to do—to make my own mistakes and learn from them. Or not learn, but live with them. But she also taught me to laugh and enjoy it all through everything.'

'No wonder you view everything that happens and everything that you do with a sense of excitement,' Ronnie said.

For some time they both stayed quiet with their thoughts—Meera watching the waves, Ronnie watching the clouds.

Then Ronnie turned on his back with a sigh.

'Don't you want anything more in life, Meera? Other than being a scientist?' he asked after a while.

'Oh ya, a lot of things!' Meera exclaimed expansively, turning and throwing her arms wide. 'Lots and lots and lots of other things.'

'Me too,' Ronnie said wistfully. 'Lots and lots and lots of things. I want to travel; see the Amazon jungles, cruise down the Nile, walk on the ridges of the Pyrenees.'

'I do too. Travel, I mean. Go to a lot of different countries, meet and talk to a lot of interesting people, understand what's happening in other different fields.'

'Both can be done together,' Ronnie said.

'Unh hunh,' Meera said in agreement.

The sky had gone dark and a few drops of rain dropped heavily splattering around them. Ronnie put his hand out and caught a couple on his palm.

'The rains have been so considerate up to now,' he said watching the raindrops on his palm. 'Showers only in the night, sun blazing away all day. And yet the beaches are deserted. Almost all of my old gang have already left.'

There were hardly any foreign tourists left in Goa, only a handful of die-hards. He knew that Hilary was still around; he had seen her once with a couple of English boys in Anthony's—one of the bar-cafés open even in the monsoons—and they had exchanged friendly smiles and warm greetings and had talked together for a little while, but their paths hardly crossed any more. Ronnie had climbed high up into the crags of Western Ghats with Meera, walked through the Devil's Canyon—the impressive deep gorge of the Dudh Sagar waterfall, had taken boat-trips up the Mandovi and Zuari rivers, and had even gone up one of the tributaries in a small, narrow fishing boat deep into the dense tropical jungle, into those narrow waterways lined with lush green trees with branches overhanging so low that he had had to duck to avoid being scratched by them. He had spent hours on the unlimited, wide expanse of the Morjim Beach watching the sea turtles come in to lay the eggs and on the Chorao Island watching the birds in the bird-sanctuary. Rest of the time he spent with Meera's friends at their haunts in Panaji or in her house in the village.

'These are only pre-monsoon showers. Wait till the monsoon starts,' Meera said pivoting to sit facing him.

'Quite heavy ya? Guys say that the monsoon here is awful,' Ronnie said watching a flock of plump sandlingers with their long thin bills scrounging in the sand, playing in the waves. They jumped back as the heavy waves came in pounding the shoreline, scurrying away on their long thin legs, and ran back to wade in the low waters to peck at the exposed tiny shellfish as the waves receded. They know how to live with nature, he thought.

'Oh it's beautiful, Ronnie,' Meera said leaning forward excitedly. 'It comes down in sheets and sheets and sheets, absolutely non-stop, as if the whole sky is cascading down. You have never seen anything like it, Ronnie, it washes everything, cleans the whole world, rejuvenates everything. Everything perks up. You see the difference during the dry spells in between. The sun shines brighter, the sky looks bluer, the rocks gleam, even the air is scrubbed clean. Every inch of ground becomes green and silver waterfalls cascade everywhere. And the peacocks dance. And so do we all. You have to see our rain dance to know what the Goan monsoon is all about.'

'Wow! For a budding scientist, you are pretty lyrical,' Ronnie said. Just then a thread of lightning slashed across the black sky and a low growl of thunder followed it.

'When will the monsoon start?' he asked.

'Now,' Meera said as another growl of thunder sounded louder this time.

'Right now?'

'Unh hunh,' Meera said laughing.

Ronnie jumped up. 'Then let's split before the heavens do,' he said and looked at the sea that had become almost ferocious. 'Look at those waves,' he said with awe. 'I have been watching them ever since I came here. They are so gentle on the sand, they just come rolling in, and yet the moment they come across rocks they change their character completely, become absolutely violent, as if they don't like any barriers to them, any restrictions imposed on them. They want to define their own boundaries. Just like you,' he said and ducked to avoid the pebbles that Meera threw at him.

'Neither are they ever satisfied with the rocks they defeat and overwhelm; they want to overwhelm all the rocks. That's also like you,' he continued while still ducking around the rocks, protecting his head with his arms from the pebbles she kept raining at him. 'And however determined you are about keeping your seat on that rock, that huge curly one is more determined to swallow it up.'

Meera stopped scooping up the pebbles and turned to look at the sea and jumped up as the wave came in roaring and curling its foaming crown and crashed on the rock she was sitting on, sending huge sprays at her, falling just a little short of swallowing the rock. Meera watched it recede in defeat, and then stood on the rock facing the sea and spread her arms wide to include the expanse of the whole coast. 'All yours,' she said grandly offering her perch and all of the coast to the sea and scampered back as the sea came roaring in to claim it.

'Hey!' Ronnie shouted in alarm from the pillion seat while the motorbike careened dangerously to the right. Meera precariously navigated around a couple of puddles and turned left with a screech of tyres.

'Hey, look out!' Ronnie shouted again hanging on to his seat as a tree loomed ahead out of the pouring sheets of rain.

'I can't look out for anything in this driving rain until it's right over me,' Meera shouted back over the noise of the thudding rain and whistling breeze.

'I think this is the wrong time for you to learn to ride a bike,' Ronnie shouted close to her head trying to make himself heard over the cacophony surrounding him.

'Of course it's the right time,' Meera shouted back. 'If I can ride in this weather, I can ride any time, anywhere. And almost four months in Goa are like this,' she added gunning the engine and turning sharp right to avoid another pothole.

'Hey!' Ronnie shouted again as they careened again but to the left this time. The bike was almost aquaplaning on the waterlogged road, either riding with the ferocious thrust of the wind or trying to fight a way through it. Another tree loomed ahead, one that was almost a forest by itself, it seemed to Ronnie. He gave in to the inevitability and taking a hold on Meera, jumped off the bike with her.

'Damn! Damn! Damn!' Ronnie said lying on his back. He was spouting every four-letter word he knew and also some that he didn't know. Meera was laughing her head off. Ronnie sat up, shaded his eyes with his hand and looked around as much as the pouring rain would allow. He and Meera were lying in a ditch. Red, muddy water full of twigs and leaves ran over them like a river. Then heavily pouring rain and the running water of the ditch cooled Ronnie's temper, he ran out of the four-letter words, and also out of breath. Wearily he climbed out of the ditch feeling down in dumps and then bent down to pull Meera out. Meera too had run out of breath and out of laughter. The two bedraggled and shivering kids surveyed each other's dirty, muddy faces and hair festooned with weeds and grimaced. Meera stretched up and plucked a couple of twigs out of Ronnie's hair and then ran her hands on her hair. 'Ouch!' she said tugging at the twigs and leaves entangled there. Ronnie, still subdued, bent forward and pulled them out silently. But Meera couldn't remain quiet for long. Bursts of laughter escaped her every now and then.

'What are you laughing about?' Ronnie asked crossly. But that only made Meera laugh more and more. Helpless with laughter, she could only point at the tree that they had hit. 'It's a banyan, a banyan,' she spluttered in between bouts of mirth.

Ronnie shaded his eyes with his hand and looked at the banyan. It had a girth of at least twenty feet. With the aerial roots hanging around it, it would be at least fifty feet. His bike lay at the base of it. A bit of the bark of the main trunk had been skinned. He looked back at Meera. 'So?' he said.

'It's a banyan that we hit,' Meera said swallowing her laughter. 'Banyan!' she repeated emphatically.

Ronnie looked at her blankly.

'That's the tree all women worship to be blessed with the same husbands in the next seven lives,' she said between gasps for air.

'What?' Ronnie asked incredulously.

'Didn't you notice them two weeks ago on the full moon day walking to that old banyan in the village square? All dressed up and carrying those silver thalis with all the puja things in it? The flowers and the fruit and the little silver lamps and bundles of silk thread to clothe the tree?'

'Clothe the tree?'

'They wrap the thread around the tree.'

Ronnie thought about it. 'The same husbands as of now?'

'Well, if those women had worshipped the banyan seven lives ago also, they'd be the same husbands as then too, wouldn't they?'

'In all of the next seven lives? Won't they find it boring?' Ronnie said staring at her in amazement.

'And the next seven. And the next.'

'Don't the husbands have a say?'

Meera gave a hoot of laughter in response and a little burst of laughter escaped Ronnie also. They looked at each other and started laughing in bursts. Soon the bursts turned into uncontrollable fits of laughter. They laughed helplessly, leaning towards each other, supporting themselves on each other, until exhausted. Quietened at last, they walked unsteadily to the shelter of the banyan tree, their arms around each other.

'Aaji will fire me if I were to tell her I hurt a tree,' Meera said fingering the skinned bark. 'She loves all trees, plants, in fact, everything that grows.'

'Won't she worry about your hurts?' Ronnie asked pointing at the cuts and bruises on her arms.

'Oh, she will say I will mend easier. She will remind me that while I am not even eighteen as yet, this tree is probably hundreds of years old.'

'And she knows enough English to berate me too,' Ronnie said glumly. 'Where did she learn it, anyway?'

'From me. When I started school, I had to sit with her every evening after school and teach her what I had learnt that day. She said she wanted to be able to understand exactly what the vilayatis say all by herself, without a translator.'

They looked at each other for a long moment and then wordlessly held hands and started towards the bike, both thinking of Meera's father. They rode towards the beach in silence, this time Meera riding the pillion.

All the beach dhabas were closed for the monsoon. Most had been dismantled and the crudely knitted coconut fronds that their roofs and walls had been made of lay scattered on the sand rustling in the wind while the ones still in place were torn into shreds by the gushing wind. Only the stark bamboo frameworks stood on the beach looming upon them out of the rain, suddenly and eerily.

It was still raining heavily and Ronnie and Meera were drenched to the bone and chilled to the marrow as they straggled on to the beach dragging their feet in the wet sand. There was no shelter on the beach; nor the hot cup of tea that they had looked forward to.

Ronnie's anger was rising. Anger at Meera's father who had left her behind without a thought, anger at his own father who had shown no interest in him except for his education. And at both their mothers for dying when they were both so young. He felt dispirited, overwhelmed by the situation that they were in—both Meera and himself. Totally miserable, he sat down and pulled his legs to his chest. My father kept too tight a leash on me, he didn't let me learn how to manage anything myself, all I have ever learnt is how to protest and rebel, and right now what I want is someone who will say, 'It's okay, kid, it's okay,' he thought, and throwing his head back, 'I want to go back,' he screamed to the sky not knowing whether he meant back to England out of this downpour or back into his childhood when daddy-and-mummy was one warm and protective two-headed animal who took care of everything. He sat encircling his knees with his arms and lay his head down on them to escape the rain lashing at his face.

Meera's voice reached him through the pounding of the rain. 'So you don't like our rain, hey Ronnie? You don't like our lovely Goan rain, hey? You don't like our rain dance either, hey, Ronnie, hey?'

He could hear the teasing laughter in her voice and looked up to see her dancing wildly on the wet sands. Her hair was plastered to her skull, her white cotton shirt was sticking to her body and she had taken her jeans off. In her red panties she was jumping up and down while kicking out one leg at a time and waving her arms about. 'You look like a monkey,' he said.

'I do, ya? So you want to go back, hey Ronnie?' she said still kicking her legs out and prancing in the rain. 'So you want to go back, hey? You would rather go back than dance in the rain, hey?'

Ronnie laughed, pulled off his jeans, jumped up, and standing before her jumped and kicked one leg high up into the air and waved his arms about. Then he planted his feet in sand and threw his head back and arched his back and howled and she threw her head back and arched her back and howled. Then she swirled and bent forward and brayed and he swirled and bent forward and brayed and they continued monkeying about on the wet sand.

Two innocent kids romping on a beach in rain.

18

'Ronnie and Meera,' Pundlik said with a tight face, refusing with a flicking gesture of his hand the cup of tea that Gauri was holding in front of him.

He had arrived quite some time ago, had helped Bhiku take Baba on a turn of the garden in his wheelchair and had spent quite a bit of time in his room discussing the local political situation with him before coming to sit on the front veranda with Maushi. But he had been tense all the while, wheeling Baba's chair too fast so that Baba scolded him, taking contrary sides in his argument with Baba until Baba told him to go and cool his head. He has something to tell me, Maushi had thought watching him, I can sense it, but he is purposely dawdling. It is as if he is dreading to talk to me, she thought waiting for him on the front veranda.

'Ronnie and Meera,' Pundlik began again and stopped abruptly and looked at the river. He was sitting rigid, his face impassive, but his shoulders were bowed down under the weight of the betrayal he was about to commit, betrayal of his promise to Baba of maintaining a secret. He had spent two sleepless nights struggling in his mind, trying to find a solution to his dilemma, and had at last given in to the inevitable. There was nothing else to do. Not now. It was too late already. He looked entreatingly at Maushi, entreating her to understand what he could not say. 'You will have to tell Meera,' he finished lamely.

Maushi turned away and looked into the setting sun. The sky was pink, red, blue and purple in streaks and the river was a myriad of those reflected jewel colours. But her garden was grey, full of dried grass and dusty weeds, and strange-shaped dark shadows flitted over it, cast by the wavering trees. She shivered and pulled her pallav tightly around her.

Pundlik waited; waited for some response, something, anything. Maushi stayed looking at the setting sun, her face blank. Then Pundlik pulled himself together. He was a police inspector after all. He straightened his back and squared his shoulders and looked straight at Maushi. 'You will have to tell Meera,' he repeated authoritatively, 'about her father.' Never before had he used that tone of voice with her.

The babbler birds suddenly flew out of the neem tree screeching loudly. Maushi kept staring into the sun. Those strange shaped dark shadows were now playing on her face.

'What!' Meera said in total bafflement. She was standing in her room with her back to the window facing Maushi standing rigidly at the door to her room. Her room was dim on that heavily overcast morning. A weak, diffused sunlight struggling out of the bank of black clouds came in through the window behind her and hardly reached up to Maushi's feet. Maushi had not come into her room but had just stood at the door and had coldly pronounced her dictate. Suddenly a few rays of the sun escaped the clouds and lit up the whole room and Maushi's face too was briefly but sharply lit up against the shadowy veranda behind her and Meera had never before seen her look like this: her eyes were hard and flinty, her mouth was compressed into a thin line, and her face was set in a tight mask. Meera had known her anger before but never like this. This anger was frightening; more so because it was not being expressed. Usually Maushi just let fly her temper; today she was as terse as never before. And what she had just said was bewildering.

'Not meet Ronnie, not talk to Ronnie, and then not even think of Ronnie? What do you mean by that?' Meera asked indignantly, forgetting Maushi's anger, now concerned only with what she had said.

'I meant exactly what I said,' Maushi said through clenched teeth standing absolutely still in the shadows that had again flooded the room and covered her face. Only her eyes were blazing like burning coals in that semidarkness.

'But why?'

'Because I said so,' Maushi said turning away stiffly, the matter closed as far as she was concerned.

'There must be some reason, Aaji. You never get angry without any reason. What did he do? What did he say? Tell me, Aaji, tell me. You have to tell me. You can't expect me to stop seeing him just like that.' Meera said entreatingly to her back, following her to the door.

'You will do it because I said to do it,' Maushi said in a tone that would brook no further argument, already walking away.

But Meera was not brought up to accept dictates without reasoning. This was the first time Maushi had *ordered* her to do anything; and that too without explaining it, with no apparent reason *and* it had to do with Ronnie. 'You are not making any sense,' she declared turning away, quivering with resentment.

Maushi stopped in her tracks and swung back into the room. 'What did you say?' she said walking furiously up to Meera, glaring balefully at her, her anger which had been simmering throughout the night now reaching a boiling point. 'Is that the way you talk to your grandmother? Have you no regard, no respect for elders? No proper manner of behaving with them? Have you learnt nothing at all from me in all these years? Gajanan and Pundlik are right. You have no Hindu culture at all. It's that half-vilayati blood in your veins...'

'Vilayati ya!' Meera cut in, her eyes flashing, her face suffused with anger at this illogical order, becoming illogical herself. 'I have heard you and Gajanan Mama and Pundlik Mama talking about vilayatis. You hated my father because he was vilayati, didn't you? That's why you kept me away from him. That's why you would never even talk to me about him. And now you want me to keep away from Ronnie because he is vilayati too. You never cared for my mother or me. You never cared for her happiness or mine. You must have made her life hell for her and now you want to make mine...'

Maushi raised her hand and gave Meera a resounding slap. The force of it as well as the unexpectedness of it sent Meera flat on the floor and she just lay there looking up at Maushi with tears in her eyes and complete incomprehension on her face. Maushi glowered down at her for a moment, then turned and went out of the room without a word leaving a numb Meera still lying on the floor staring tearfully at her back.

'But what did you say to her?' Ronnie asked. He had arrived at noon to find a despondent Meera sitting in a corner of the back veranda dangling her legs and kicking aimlessly at a pile of fallen leaves that had collected below the veranda.

The tamarind tree near the filled-up well rustled suddenly, noisily, and the bunch of crows sitting on it flew around frantically, black wings flapping against the background of a dull grey sky, cawing raucously. Ronnie and Meera looked up at them momentarily startled by this ominous sign.

'What do you mean by she is not talking to you? What has made her so angry with you? Didn't she explain anything?' Ronnie asked when the crows had settled back on the tree to again wait silently. Meera too was again sitting silently with her head bowed, kicking at the leaves, not responding to his questions. 'What exactly did you say to her?' he asked after a while rephrasing his question.

Meera flicked her hand and shook her head to indicate that it was of no significance. 'I was rude and nasty,' she said dejectedly. 'I apologised but she won't even look at me.'

'That doesn't sound like Aaji,' Ronnie said perplexed. This was not the Aaji he had come to know, the caring, loving Aaji, the patient, reasonable Aaji. He had seen her anger too and experienced her temper also, but it wasn't like her to not explain anything to Meera, to just stop talking to her. No, not like Aaji at all. 'Didn't she explain anything at all?' he asked again.

Meera didn't bother to reply. Ronnie looked at her meditatively. 'There must be a reason for it,' he said at last.

Meera sighed, shook her head in exasperation, and gave a vicious kick to a dead weed. Ronnie smiled and tenderly pushed back a loose strand of hair from her cheek. They sat in silence watching the dead leaves flying in the wind.

In a while Gauri came out on the veranda carrying some banana leaves, glanced apprehensively at them, went to the opposite corner of the veranda, laid two banana leaves flat on the floor and squatted on the floor waiting, looking pointedly at the floor till Maushi came out of the kitchen carrying pans of rice and dal. Ronnie and Meera turned to look at her but she didn't even glance at them. Going straight to the other corner she handed the pans to Gauri and bent down to serve the rice on the laid out banana leaves.

'What's she doing?' Ronnie asked.

'She is serving a meal for our ancestors,' Meera said turning away.

'What?'

'Whatever we are to eat, we have to offer it to our ancestors first. When a crow comes and eats it, we can have our meals.'

'A crow?'

'Unh hunh.'

'She does it every day?'

Meera nodded distractedly.

Ronnie turned to look at Maushi who had served the rice, perfectly moulded in half spheres from a silver bowl, on both the leaves and was now ladling dal over them from the pan that Gauri was holding out to her.

'Why two leaves?' he asked.

'Ancestors are *male*,' Meera said frowning and tilting her head to look at him from under her lashes. 'She always serves a separate one for my mother,' she said turning away again.

Ronnie watched Maushi ladling the dal for a moment longer and then got up and went over to where she was still bending over the banana leaves.

'Will you do it for my mother also?' he asked.

'What?' Maushi asked pausing with the ladle still in her hand, startled by the question.

'Whatever you are doing for Meera's mother. Will you do it for mine also?' Ronnie said.

'No!' Maushi snapped straightening up, glaring at him.

'Why not?' Ronnie asked in surprise.

Maushi glared at him for a moment longer with her lips pressed tightly together and then exploded making the ladle go clattering along the veranda floor.

'Because her mother is *dead*,' she burst out. 'Your mother is *insane*.'

Ronnie took a step back. Meera jumped up. The crows burst out of the tamarind tree again cawing ominously but none of them noticed them.

'Your mother is in the Home for the mentally infirm at Santagao,' Maushi added harshly.

'But my father said...' Ronnie faltered, his mind in turmoil, icy fingers crawling up his spine.

'Your father! Your father! Your father was a liar and a crook.'

'How do you know?' Ronnie snapped back.

'Because he was *her* father also,' Maushi said flicking her chin at Meera.

Meera stood frozen.

'I don't believe you,' Ronnie said but his voice was weak; he already believed it.

'Gauri, bring the photographs,' Maushi shouted.

Ronnie traced his father's figures in the photographs with his index finger as if to make them more believable. His father in a silk dhoti and kurta and a shawl around his shoulders with Anu in her wedding finery in front of the holy fire, ladling ghee into it with his hands linked with hers; his father tying mangalsutra around Anu's neck; his father leading Anu around the holy fire, with the end of his shawl tied to her pallav; his father looking at Anu with so much love, so much love... 'I loved her so much,' a deathbed confession echoed in his mind – said with eyes looking far, far away, beyond the horizon. 'I really loved her.'

With a heart-rending scream of a wounded animal Ronnie threw the photographs down and ran headlong along the veranda, through the garden, out of the gate, down the road.

Meera unfroze and without a word ran into the house. Maushi found her later, sitting in a corner of the gods' room, hugging her knees with her face buried in them.

PART FOUR

19

'It was an accident,' Baba said. He was lying supine on his bed in his room staring at the opposite wall with the only lamp in the room on the wall above his head throwing dark shadows on the lower half of his face, with Maushi sitting near his bed on a rug on the floor holding her head in her hands and Anu standing in the corner with her head turned to look out of the window. Outside, it was dusk. The river was a ribbon of darkness. A dull grey light had enveloped Maushi's garden turning all trees into ghostly dark shapes that whistled eerily in the occasional gusts of wind. A bevy of little dark shapes flitted across the window: the little brown babbler birds were returning to their roost in the neem tree.

'They pulled her out of water but she has lost her mind. Not only that she hasn't spoken a word since, but she doesn't even recognise Alec or even Ronnie. Just keeps standing at the window staring at the sky. Gajanan is helping Alec to move her to a Home for the mentally infirm.' He glanced obliquely at Maushi from under his eyelids. 'Doctor Gomes doesn't think there is any chance of her recovering her mind.'

Maushi's mind was whirling. That's not it. That's not all. You are not telling us all the truth, the whole story. Nobody loses his mind in a drowning accident. There is more to it. Something more happened. Something more happened that Elizabeth's mind couldn't bear any longer. Something happened that left her feeling totally helpless and desolate and despaired.

What happened, Elizabeth, what happened to you, that you ran out of your room at midnight, in the pouring rain, to seek the only solace you could find – the all-enveloping, embracing, comforting sea?

'Of course Alec can't take her back to England in her condition,' Baba continued in a matter-of-fact voice, his words ringing hollowly in the ghostly dim light in the room and echoing over their heads before dissipating in the darkness above. 'Divorce too is impossible in this situation. In either case, he will have to tell the whole story. His reputation, his career, all will be ruined. And our family name, family honour will be ground in mud.'

Family honour, family honour! Family honour – to be inherited from the ancestors, to be preserved and protected at any cost, to be handed down to the descendants. Family honour – more sacred than the dharma, more cherished than the family members! Looking at Anu's profile etched against the white wall, her face raised to the window, chin held high with a determined slant to it and not an emotion on her face, Maushi had a sudden premonition of further tragedy to come. Don't berate her now, don't push her away now, she pleaded to Baba in her mind, give her some understanding, some pity, a little sympathy. Give her love. Or lie here on your bed forever, as you have done for the last three days, and leave me free to take care of her.

'This wretch has brought nothing but dishonour to our family,' Baba said.

Anu kept looking out of the window. She didn't say a word nor did she shed any tears. Ten days after her daughter's birth she jumped into the well hugging a stone to her breast.

20

Two days after Anu's death, on the twelfth day of her birth, the baby had to be named. This time there was no crowd of well-dressed women in the inner room, no children running about the house, no merriment, no laughter. There were only Gajanan and Vinayak's wives in their everyday saris and Gauri and Shanta besides Maushi. Men's room was empty. Vinayak was sitting alone on the back veranda.

Shanta had put a few strings of flowers on the cradle and Gauri had made one thali of sweet cakes at Maushi's behest and both were sobbing uncontrollably. Maushi, dry eyed and stony faced, was the only one rocking the cradle and singing cradle-songs until Vinayak's wife joined her in a tremulous voice. Then, since the baby's aunt was not present, Maushi bent down to whisper the baby's name in her ear and to give her a lick of sugar from her finger. Straightening up she announced loudly, 'Meera', named in memory of the other Meera, a sixteenth-century queen who had unflinchingly followed her own faith in defiance of her family, her community, the whole society, even at the cost of being ostracised by them all, and Vinayak clapped from the door. He also accompanied Maushi and Gauri when they went to the river to immerse the flowers from the cradle.

They could only wade in knee-deep and the flowers that they threw in came back with the current to wrap themselves around their legs. Gauri uttered a horrified cry at this ill omen and tried to wrench them off her ankles until Maushi quietened her with a stern look and said, 'They will find their own flow,' and walked away without a backward glance. But Gauri, looking back, saw that the flowers had indeed disentangled themselves and found their own flow.

The house felt deserted and desolate to her when Maushi returned to it. Her both daughters-in-law and the maids were sitting silently in the kitchen, all their heads bowed down to some minute chore requiring their total unmoving concentration. Male servants had made themselves scarce. There was nobody working in the garden. There was not a sound, not a movement anywhere. The birds were quiet, the trees stood motionless, even the air was still. Yet the house was only empty of men, which happened all the time. But this time there was no expectant air to it, there was no energy radiating out of it. It sat solid and inert, its silence heavy with the air of a house of death; but there was more to it than that. It also had the air of a house awaiting death.

She heard the baby crying its head off as she unlocked the door to her room. 'Don't cry little one,' Maushi said. 'I am here to take care of you.' But looking speculatively at that bawling, kicking, red-faced infant, she added, 'Are you crying because you just got a foretaste of the life to come?' She could envision exactly the life the little one would lead, if she were allowed to live, a motherless girl forsaken by the father. Baba will call her a wretch, others an abhagan—evoker of ill fate. Relatives will despise her and treat her with contempt; playmates will treat her with derision and avoid her. Everyone in the family will insult and humiliate her, treat her as an unpaid servant, lade her with the chores nobody else would want to do, and expect her to be forever grateful for the food and shelter that they would grudgingly provide. Any sign of enjoyment of life, or of ambition, or of independence on her part will be frowned upon and squashed in the cradle. She will teach herself to become unobtrusive and subservient; and grow up meek and cowed down with bent shoulders and dead eyes. And she will always, without questioning or reasoning, accept every blame as her deserved due. With mute resignation she will watch the world go by and her dreams will be as unfruitful as her mother's. She will never laugh or sing or dance. Born in pain and shame, she will live in pain and shame.

If, Maushi thought looking at that tiny infant, if they allow you to live. A girl, unwanted to begin with; and then born to an as good as deserted mother, left by her to a fate she couldn't prevent and could not bear to think of. Which family would put up with her and the blot on the family name that her presence would be a constant reminder of? Which family would bear the shame of rearing her? Who would shoulder the almost impossible task of finding her a household that will accept her as a daughter-in-law when she grows up?

Maushi shook her head. 'You stand no chance against them, my little one,' she said unemotionally, stating a fact of life. 'At stake here is the family name, the family honour. And they will not only have the whole family's sanction but also that of the whole society to back them up. An age-old tradition set against a twelve-day-old baby – so defenseless. How long can I look after you like this? How long can I keep you out of their hands?'

The day waned but Maushi still sat by the cradle. When the night came and Gauri made the rounds with her incense pot, Maushi was still sitting by the cradle and when the day dawned again and Shanta came to sweep the room, she found Maushi still sitting by the cradle watching the sleeping infant – 'With her eyes red as those of a witch,' she reported to Gauri.

21

The days after Anu's death were of total haziness for Maushi. She hardly absorbed any happenings around her and except for caring for Meera, whom she had moved into her room, she remained totally in a cocoon. She had mutely stared at Baba when he had told her that Anu's death had to be announced as death from fever – right after Gajanan had pulled Anu's body out of the well, while Maushi was sitting on the back veranda holding Anu's head in her lap, when nobody else had yet been woken up, only Mahesh, Baba's doctor nephew, had been fetched by Gajanan and was in deep conversation with him. Suicide was detrimental to family honour, and would raise further questions. The baby was not even mentioned as if she had already stopped existing.

Only one fact kept ringing in her mind, reverberating like temple bells: the information that Pundlik had brought to her in an accusatory tone—Alec's passport had been valid all along.

Alec had never intended to take Anu away from here.

And Anu had realised it. Anu, whose one overriding desire had been to escape from here; Anu, who dreaded living her whole life in this suffocating village; Anu, who would have soon died here anyway pining for the freedom and the thrilling opportunities existing out there. She had in fact died the moment she had realised that there was no way she could leave here, that Alec had meant her to live here, imprisoned in this village.

She shuddered and shivered so much every time she thought of Anu's last ten days after the birth of her daughter that she had to be covered with a blanket even in that warm weather. 'You knew, my daughter,' Maushi said to her in the silence of her mind with her head bowed, 'you knew your fate was sealed; you knew you had no future left. And how you must have dreaded the thought of the fate of your daughter. That she too had no future left before her. You knew, my poor Anu. With your deadened eyes but still holding your chin up. Clutching the little girl to your heart, afraid to loosen your grip even for a moment lest she be snatched away into oblivion. What a torment you must have endured those days until you could bear it no longer.' But no tears would come to Maushi's eyes; no sobs would break from her lips. She felt inundated, drenched and parched, all at the same time as if all the waters of the river outside her garden had flown over her and yet left her bone-dry.

She flitted in and out of the times and places trying to make sense of what had gone amiss with Anu's life. All the child ever wanted was to live her own life her own way. When, at what point, did the fate turn its back on her?

Memories kept flooding her mind. Singing rhymes to an infant Anu happily gurgling in her cradle. Running after a crawling Anu to stop her tumbling off the edge of the veranda. Holding her hands and helping her take her first tottering steps. Teaching her to draw Goddess Saraswati, the Goddess of Learning, on her new slate, compulsory before starting to learn the first alphabets. Preparing for her and even feeding her the boiled rice and curds in sickness. Boiling the herbs and forcing the concoction down the throat of a newly teenager Anu to clear her complexion until a sixteen-year-old Anu started asking for it voluntarily. Combing the tangles out of her thick, long hair after the weekly ritual of washing it with Anu complaining and even screaming in pain. 'Why can't I just cut it short like Vinayak's?' she had once asked screwing up her face and holding her hands to her hair to stop Maushi from pulling the comb through it. 'Hush, girl!' Maushi's sister-in-law sitting nearby had hissed – only widows had their hair cut off – and slapped Anu's face. 'Evoking ill fate!' she had muttered as Maushi had wiped Anu's tears and patted her comfortingly on her shoulders. Years and years of wiping Anu's tears and comforting her. Through all the ages. So much tending, so much caring, so much nurturing – twenty years of nurturing. And now she was gone!

Why?

Images of Anu kept floating before her eyes. She had been such a happy child. Maushi vividly remembered her, a toddler with a big grin on her face, standing next to a golden dahlia almost as big as her face competing with it for sparkle and beauty. A three-year-old Anu, trustingly putting her arms around Baba's neck and giving him a contented smile before going to sleep in his arms. A four-year-old Anu, dressed in new clothes, importantly bustling around at the pujas as the grown-ups smiled fondly at her. And then a six-year-old Anu, fighting with Vinayak for a stick that they used to play gilli-danda with. Vinayak was hauled off but it was Anu who had ended up getting a resounding slap from Baba. That was when the problem became apparent, Maushi thought. For both: for the family and for Anu. That was when the differences in their attitudes surfaced and grew wider and wider as Anu grew. Anu, who would not abide by any rules that she was expected to keep to as a girl. Anu, who had hankered after the freedom of choice and variety. Anu, who had yearned for something exciting and interesting in life.

'Surely there is something more to life than just this,' Maushi remembered her saying. She was standing on the veranda of the inner courtyard, gesturing at the women cleaning grain in a corner, women sewing baby clothes in another corner, knots of women sitting and gossiping with their heads held close together, women running after children crawling or toddling all over, and young girls applying kohl to their eyes and stringing strings of flowers to entwine in their hair. Anu, a teenager, who had just been ordered by Baba to put her book aside and go and help the women in the inner courtyard in whatever chores they were doing.

Anu at fifteen, an avid reader now accomplished in eluding Baba's watch on the household, coming to talk excitedly to Maushi. 'And in England, Aai, they do this and in France, they do that.'

'What's France?' Maushi had asked.

'It's a big wide world out there, Aai, with so much exciting happening there, so much to do.'

Yes, there certainly is, Maushi thought sighing, but what access did you have to it my daughter? For you also, like all the rest of us women, the only way to get anywhere, to attain anything, to fulfil any wish, was through a man. You too, my daughter had to rely on a man, his wishes, his whims, and his intents. And your life was finished because a man that you trusted let you down. Alec!

Alec had never intended to take Anu away from here.

This total dependence on men for everything is what has kept us in their control, Maushi thought angrily. This is what we have to get away from if we want to become our own persons. We have to learn to stand on our own feet, not lean on a man. We have to make our own opportunities. But how does one make opportunities? How does one find out about options? And how does one avail of them? For that we need training, we need to equip ourselves with different skills, we need to develop different attitudes, especially different attitudes. We need different motivations. We have to learn to depend on ourselves. Or we will always be let down. By some man. Like Alec did.

Alec had never intended to take Anu away from here.

'She had so much looked forward to going to Canada, had set her heart on it; it was the high point of her life; she thought it would lead to the fulfilment of all her dreams,' Maushi said aloud, her voice hoarse, her eyes red and puffed. 'And how much she had loved him. Her eyes never left his face. He was the one she had been waiting for all her life. Someone to talk to, someone to love, she had said. He was the prince charming of her dreams.'

Anu's dreams.

Anu kneeling before Maushi, excitedly telling her about her dreams in life. My poor Anu, talking of taking up a job. Anu thinking that going to Mumbai would solve all the problems for her. Anu crying in her room because she wasn't allowed to go to the science college. 'I could even become a scientist,' she had said with a giggle. 'Wahwah,' Maushi had said shaking her head in wonder, having no idea what a scientist was but still awed to think that her daughter could become one.

'What is a scientist?' she asked Pundlik after Anu's death.

As he explained, a sudden surge of rage coursed through Maushi's veins. Rage at the family who wouldn't let Anu become a scientist but also at Anu who had said it with a giggle. She never took herself seriously, Maushi thought to herself. My daughter never took her own ambitions, her own wants seriously. But then she was taught not to. From childhood all and any of her ambitions and wants were always derided, remembering a tearful four-year-old Anu coming to hide in her lap when Baba and Gajanan had laughed scornfully at her some childish ambition of becoming a policeman or such. 'Are you a boy to want to become something more than a wife?' Gajanan had asked her derisively. No wonder she could not get a focus on her interests or develop the self-confidence required to pursue them. Self-confidence. Absolute necessity for self-reliance.

'It has to be taught in infancy,' she said loudly startling Pundlik and interrupting him in his discourse on what the scientists did.

'What?' he said looking at her bemusedly.

But Maushi was not listening. Another image came to her mind, of Anu and Vinayak tumbling together out of the guava tree, both bawling away. Baba had scolded Vinayak to stop crying, 'boys don't cry,' he had said, and at the same time had picked up Anu, tenderly wiped her tears, and consoled her saying, 'poor girl', and told her not to climb a tree again. Everybody did that. Everybody coddled her and restrained her. Everybody loved her and just wanted to protect her. For her own good. All the restrictions, rules and regulations were for her own good. So that she didn't make any mistakes and hurt herself in the process.

This eradication of freedom to make mistakes, of any initiative, of her confidence in herself—all had been so gradual and subtle and done with so much love that it had been impossible to know or check. Anu had not even realised when and how she had got indoctrinated into the system, when or how she had accepted the fact that she needed to be protected from making her own mistakes, that to get anything she wanted she too had to depend upon the largesse of a man. But she had. To the extent that had sealed her fate. She had no faith left in her own ability to attain her goals.

It has to be taught in infancy.

No wonder she was fluttering her eyelashes by the time she was three years old. Cadging favours out of Baba by pouting. Learning the coquetries to get her will. Waiting for a prince charming to fulfil her desires. She was brought up to depend on men to get whatever she wanted; on their pleasure, on their goodwill, not on her own capabilities, not on her merits. No matter how much independent natured she was, it was all curbed and channelled in her childhood, she was taught not to question but to accept. Her directions were decided in the cradle, her attitudes were formed before she could walk or talk, and she had never learned to dance in freedom.

'You didn't dance my dear daughter, you only moved like a marionette to the set tunes,' Maushi said aloud again. 'The more you struggled against them, the more entangled you became in the strings that had been tied to you. You never learned to dance in freedom, in abandon; you never learned to dance on your own.'

It has to be taught in infancy.

And I didn't realise it either; I too didn't know; I was helpless too; I couldn't help you, my daughter. I couldn't care for you, couldn't shield you, couldn't protect you. But more than that I couldn't teach you to take care of yourself, couldn't open any doors to any opportunities for you, couldn't point the right directions to you. 'Lie on your bed forever and leave me free to take care of her,' I had pleaded silently with Baba watching your impassive profile. But he didn't and I couldn't. And by then it was too late. And now you have gone leaving Meera in my lap. Now there is Meera. What about Meera? What about Meera?

Maushi felt far removed even from herself as if she were looking down upon the whole household from a great height, impassively watching the whole house and the people in it, herself included. From far above she watched the men sitting on the front veranda and pompously discussing the politics of the day – the death of a daughter already relegated into the background. She watched the women on the back veranda servilely bustling about. She watched young girls adorning themselves. She watched a red-faced infant bawling in its cradle in a back room. And she watched a helpless elderly woman sitting on the back veranda wrapped up in blankets – a woman who had resigned herself to the fate: to her own fate, to her daughter's fate, and now perhaps even to her granddaughter's fate? All entangled together in an age-old web of traditions and customs and proprieties. All under one umbrella of dharma.

What can I do for you, Meera, what can I do? How do I fight the traditions and the customs and the dharma? How do I fight against myself? Am I as helpless as it seems? What means do I have? What *means* do I have? What means do *I* have? An old woman in a village! Dependent on the well-being of her husband for survival!

When at last Maushi closed her eyes, the image that came before her eyes and just wouldn't go away was that of an infant Anu happily gurgling and kicking in her cradle mixed with that of lifeless Anu laid out on the veranda floor after Gajanan had pulled her out of the well; but she couldn't discern whether the infant gurgling and kicking in the cradle was Anu or Meera.

22

Maushi was sitting on the back veranda leaning her back against the wall, looking over the activity in the backyard without really seeing it, when Baba came out to talk to her.

It was the thirteenth day after Anu's death, the day when final religious rites had to be performed for the soul of the departed ending in a meal for the relatives and the villagers. So many times had Maushi supervised preparations for the thirteenth day rites – for her father-in-law and mother-in-law and the old sister-in-law and the young nephew and also for the infant daughter of Baba's youngest brother. That death had always bothered her – the presence of the vaisin and the muted sound of the drip of the silent tears of her young sister-in-law by an empty cradle.

But this time, thankfully, the family had left her alone. Nobody had bothered her after Gajanan's wife had asked her whether there should be kneaded flour balls or cooked rice balls in the puja thali and Maushi had looked blankly at her as if she could not understand her language. Only Vinayak's wife had come out with a cup of tea for her and had sat with her for a while trying to say something but had ended up crying silently herself. Maushi had watched her impassively, without any response, and without any tears, and she had soon fled into the house overcome by the coldness of Maushi's grief.

All over the backyard preparations for the religious rites and the following meal were in full swing. Sitting with her back to the veranda wall, Maushi watched them numbly. The big pots and pans had been taken out of the storeroom and three cooks with their helpers were busy cooking the thirteenth day meal in a specially erected cooking tent at the back. A huge amount of vegetables were being cleaned, stringed and peeled and already a pile of chopped potatoes and grated coconuts had accumulated near the cooking tent. On the other side, in another tent, women of the household were laying out flowers, rice, camphor and sandalwood sticks in silver plates and preparing oil lamps in little earthen bowls that would be required by the priests. There were so many people around and so much hustle and bustle that Maushi hadn't even realised that Baba had come out on the back veranda and was standing before her until she heard his voice.

'You have what? Called Alec over to Anu's thirteenth day rites and meal?' she asked in total disbelief.

Baba looked at her strangely. 'As Anu's husband, he has to perform the rites. What will the people say if the son-in-law of the house is not present?' he said, his tone implying that it shouldn't be necessary to tell her this, she should know it by herself.

Maushi did not answer; did not protest. She was flabbergasted at this comity of men for protecting the family name; even in death. Family name – father's name – husband's name – man's name – it took precedence over everything. They supported each other to protect it and expected women to sacrifice themselves to preserve it or to eradicate themselves when their presence threatened it. Like Sita, like Sati, like Anu. And like Elizabeth who was deemed as dead while living.

Baba watched the cooks at their tasks and the women at their chores for a moment and then turned to go into the house, a patriarch walking tall, keeper of the family name, upholder of the family honour, one whose word can never be disobeyed by anybody.

Maushi watched his retreating back with a twisted mouth. You killed her, she said to his back, you and Alec both together. Neither of you ever took her seriously. Neither of you cared for her as a person. Neither of you tried to understand her, her aspirations, her ambitions. Both of you only cast her in the moulds you had in your mind for her. For both of you, her yearnings, her desires were such that could be disciplined out of her. Both of you, individually, by yourselves, decided what was in her best interest, what she should do, what life she should lead. But she would not abide by your rules. She transgressed the parameters you had set. She aspired for something more, something different. And that could not be tolerated. You both made it impossible for her to live. You both killed her, killed her jointly, as if you had pushed her into the well yourselves. With four hands. And now you will sit together and feast together on her thirteenth day! Maushi turned her gaze away from the activity in the backyard, past the cooking tent, towards the well near the tamarind tree – the well that she had not been able to look at or even think about all these days. She stared at it now, stared at it without blinking; and without flinching.

'Aai, you should come inside now,' Gajanan's wife said, far more gently than ever before, squatting before her. Maushi did not respond to her; did not even look at her. Gajanan's wife frowned at her. 'You should lie down for a while, Aai,' she said grasping Maushi's elbow to pull her up. 'Take a little rest. Soon Alec and rest of the relatives will be here.'

Soon Alec will be here. Soon Alec, an accepted, honoured, loved and cherished as a member of the family, will be here. Alec, who had made this his home for four months, will be here. Alec, who had never intended to take Anu away from here. Alec, who all the while had been conspiring to incarcerate her here in this village. And we all watched it and accepted it even if tacitly; even after he had talked to Baba about the riverside land and Baba had exulted and Anu's eyes had gone blank never to come alive again.

'What will they all think if they see you sitting here like this?' Gajanan's wife said.

What will they all think? We women too worry about what people will say; we too keep up a face, we too cover up our own degradation, we too contribute to our own subjugation; perhaps more than the men do, Maushi thought. She became aware of the pull at her elbow and glared at Gajanan's wife until she relinquished her elbow and retreated inside the house. It's not your fault that you too believe in this system, that you are also a staunch enforcer of it, Maushi wanted to call out to her. We, all of us, all the women, have internalised this system until it seems right to us. We too, all of us, have believed in the natural superiority of men and our own worthlessness except in servility to them. We too, all of us, have believed the patriarchal system to be the divinely ordained, to be inviolable, and so degraded ourselves. We ourselves have done it to ourselves. Since the Vedic time. Since before the Vedic time. For too long have we resigned ourselves to the status men delineated to us. For too long have we allowed them to play with our existence, with us as persons, with our essential beings. Now they don't even have to demand our self-subjugation, our self-annihilation. Our dependency on them is such, our belief in our own insignificance is such, that we leave ourselves with no alternative. Like Anu. Like Elizabeth.

Anu, Elizabeth. One to be incarcerated, other to be discarded. Now Elizabeth is incarcerated, both in mind and in body, and Anu is dead. If Anu was sacrificed on the altar of Hindu prudishness, Elizabeth was sacrificed on the altar of Western permissiveness. In both cultures, women were the expendables.

Anu, Elizabeth. Both of you chose water as the last solace for you. You ran to the infinite sea, Elizabeth, but Anu, my poor Anu, who all her life had yearned for the big wide world, had to end her life as she had been made to live it – within the narrow confines of a well.

Elizabeth. What happened to you Elizabeth, what happened to you that made you lose heart totally, that made you despair so much? What happened to you that made you give up on life? Maushi tried to visualise Elizabeth – golden hair, blue eyes, cheeks pink as roses. Elizabeth saying to Baba, 'Your daughter isn't the first, nor will she be the last.'

'She will be, Elizabeth, she will be the last,' Maushi said aloud. 'I promise you that.'

The cooks were shouting loudly to the helpers to pour the cut vegetables into the pans on fire. Meal preparations were over. Women had finished laying out the puja materials and had gone inside the house. The priests would be arriving shortly. The light went out; a deep dark shadow enveloped the backyard. Maushi looked up at the sky. Black clouds had spread over the whole sky. The tall trees in the backyard stood still and etched against the dark sky. Groups of crows waited silently on the branches of the tamarind tree. A storm could be expected later. Maushi watched it dispassionately. Her herbs were covered with a tarpaulin to protect them. Her flowers were long gone without leaving a sign. A storm, when it passes, leaves marks behind it. Flowers, when they go, leave no marks behind. Only memories, only memories... Maushi closed her eyes.

'Maushi, should I press your legs a little?' Maushi opened her eyes and startled at seeing the vaisin squatting before her, snapped, 'What are you doing here?' before realising the inanity of her question.

But the vaisin smiled understandingly. 'Maushi, Anu's thirteenth day! And I won't be here?' She bent one of Maushi's legs and began to knead the calf. 'You are absolutely worn out, Maushi. Just look at you. What a face yours has become. All drawn out. How much burden can you carry all by yourself? Why didn't you send for me? They tell me you massage and bathe the baby all by yourself. That you won't let anybody else even prepare her milk bottle, leave aside getting a wet nurse. Why are you doing this to yourself Maushi?' She straightened the leg and laid it down, then bent the other one. 'She is a cranky baby too, they tell me. So she should be. Hardly any babies born so much before their time survive. It's a miracle this one has lasted this long.' She gripped Maushi's leg in both her hands and looked up into Maushi's face. 'Doesn't matter. Now you relax. Now I am here. I will take care of everything, don't you worry...'

Maushi snatched her leg out of the vaisin's hands as if they were on fire and stood backing away from her glaring at her with so much venom that the vaisin, who had fallen back on her haunches, didn't utter any reproach, just gaped at her with fear in her eyes.

'She came out of the baby's room, collected the garden tools, and went straight into the garden,' Gauri told Shanta later. 'She washed and ground all those roots and vegetables and made those special spicy wadas for her husband and her son-in-law all by herself, wouldn't let me help, in fact, I don't think she even heard a word of what I said. Just kept on mixing and moulding and frying with a frightening concentration with her eyes burning red and yet her face, it was so calm; but a strange sort of calm, you know, like the calm that comes after a storm, after one of those particularly devastating, destructive storms.'

PART FIVE

23

For three days Meera sat in the corner of the gods' room without speaking, without crying, and with her face as blank as Anu's had been in her last ten days. She sat there hunched encircling her knees with her arms, almost without moving, sometimes even sleeping with her head resting on her bent knees. She sat there watching Maushi at her daily puja in the mornings and afterwards watching the silver, brass and stone idols in their carved temple, watching the flickering of the metre-high brass oil lamp with brass elephants supporting its fluted base and a brass peacock on top, the lamp that burned day and night before the temple, and listening to the tinkling of the little brass bells that hung from the red and black plaited silken cords on the sides of the temple. She ate there – whatever little she ate – and slept there. Except for bringing her a quilt and a cushion, covering her when she slept, and bringing her food, at times even feeding her herself, Maushi let her be. Only when she slept did Maushi sit by her, stroking her hair and gently patting her on her back and shoulders, sometimes even crooning softly to her.

On the fourth day as she sat caressing Meera's bent shoulders, Meera raised her head from her knees with a wrenching cry, looked at Maushi with a wounded, vulnerable look, and then, with a surge of lost and lonely feeling, threw her arms around Maushi and buried her face in her lap. Maushi continued gently caressing her shoulders, stroking her head, and murmuring soothingly to her. Meera clung to her like a child, sobbing and shaking, shedding the tears she had not shed since the age of ten, the questions she had not asked since then now looming large in her mind. Up to now everything had been understandable and acceptable and excusable – excusable at least to a certain extent. Her mother was dead. Her father must have married again and though in Hindu tradition her place was in her father's house, it was possible that his second wife – vilayati, obviously – had objected to it. And so it was natural that her grandparents should bring her up. It hurt, and also made her angry, that her father had not ever visited her or contacted her in any way but she had formulated many excuses for him in her mind. Now the whole context had changed, the points of reference were different. She had to reconnect herself to the past, find new directions, ask different questions, and find the answers all over again. And they may not be so excusable any more.

Her mother had never belonged to her in spite of her intense longing for her. She had belonged to Aaji who had nurtured her and consoled her and had applied henna to her hands and feet and therefore could now mourn her. And she had belonged to Vinayak Mama who had laughed with her and had played pranks with her and had pampered her and therefore could now cry for her. She had even belonged to Pundlik Mama who now refused to talk about her but obviously had a right to miss her. But Meera could not miss her or cry for her or mourn her. She had no memories of her mother to recall in grief; she had not learnt her alphabets sitting at her mother's knee, she had not lisped the nursery rhymes looking into her mother's face, she had had no ties with her mother. And so she had desperately yearned for her father, all her life she had longed to meet him, to understand him, to form a relationship with him. Now not only he too was gone, not only he too had belonged to others, but there was something else, something far more disturbing, far more distressing, something difficult to come to terms with.

Her mind was in an uproar. He was Ronnie's father too. 'Ronnie's father too,' she said to herself trying to sort out the implications of that in her dazed mind, the implications that her mind refused to acknowledge. All that she acknowledged was that he was bound to both of them. Her father, Ronnie's father. And yet Ronnie had not known about his mother. Eighteen years, and Ronnie had not known. His father had not told him. The strict, unloving, unhappy father whose only interest had been his own career. Had he at all loved and cared for Ronnie's mother? And had he at all loved and cared for her mother?

After a long while she raised her tear-stricken face and looked up at Maushi and still clutching on to her asked, 'Did my father lie to my mother, to you, to Ajaa?'

'Hush, child,' Maushi said wiping her tears with her hands and patting her head. 'He didn't lie; he just didn't tell all the truth.' And Meera nodded at this fine distinction. After a while her sobs subsided and she let Maushi pull her up from her corner and Shanta run a hot bath for her and Gauri cook a khichadi for her.

Afterwards, much composed, she came and sat cross-legged before Maushi where she was sitting on the back veranda and putting her hands into Maushi's lap and looking up into her face with her still anguished eyes, said, 'Now tell me Aaji, tell me about him, tell me about my father, tell me who he was, what he was.'

'He lived here for almost four months,' Maushi said. 'He was very well mannered, very polished, a gentleman. He had the looks of a prince. He assimilated himself into our family without any demur, followed all our customs, enjoyed our food. He was very much interested in Hinduism, learning it from your Ajaa, discussing and debating it with him all the time. Everybody here liked him, even your Ajaa who is so particular and even Gajanan's wife who abhors vilayatis. At one time he was very much in love with your mother. He also eagerly awaited your birth and couldn't love you enough when he visited here, coming here every day though he was living in Baga at that time with Ronnie and his mother. But then, at one time he must have been in love with Ronnie's mother also and must have loved Ronnie also the same way.' She paused, reflecting. Meera was sitting absolutely still, absorbing every word, listening intently to any nuances. It was as if she had blocked out all other senses, as if she was totally unaware of anything else except Maushi's voice.

'When we found out about his first wife and son,' Maushi continued after a while, 'that was just before your birth, he told your Ajaa he was planning to divorce her and take your mother and you to Canada to settle there. Then his karma intervened. Ronnie's mother was pulled out of the sea and lost her mind. Your mother left this world.'

So her father *had* lied, if not directly then obliquely, but lied all the same, Meera thought.

'Did he lie to us?' Maushi continued. 'He told us his name was Alec. In England he was known by the name of Richard. Both were his names. He said he was planning to settle in Canada. Was that the truth? Perhaps. He told your Ajaa that the death of your mother and the accident and hospitalisation of Ronnie's mother had forced him to change all his plans. He said he was going back to London because he couldn't bear going to Canada without your mother. He asked if we would care for Ronnie's mother, since, he said, he was too devastated emotionally to care for anybody, and to which your Ajaa and Gajanan Mama agreed wholeheartedly, even with alacrity.'

And yet, Ronnie's father had not told him about his mother. *Her* father had not told Ronnie either about his mother or about her.

'That was the story he told us.' Maushi continued looking into Meera's still turned down face. 'Perhaps it was the truth. There are others who will tell you other stories that he told them, and perhaps they too might be true. There are many truths, child, and only God knows the whole and absolute truth.'

This was the father she had dreamt about too much. This was the father she had yearned for too much. Now Aaji was telling her she must not hate him too much.

'Karma, your Ajaa said to him when everything went wrong with his plans, your last birth's actions are what you are paying for now. But there are two types of karma, child, so the Karmawada, Code of Karma, tells us, dependent on the type of one's actions. With Sachita karma you see the results of it in your next life but with Agami karma you see them in the same life, and for all his interest in Hinduism, your father did not appreciate this difference. Nor did he believe in karma. He did not believe even in the cycle of death and rebirth. He believed only in the present and lived only in the present; he had disowned his past and thought he could control his future. He did not expect to pay for his actions, others had already paid for them, very heavily, and he thought he was left free to go on with his life, that that was the end of it. But it never is.

One's karma always catches up with one; when one is unsuspecting, unexpecting and unprepared; unless one acts knowingly, in full awareness of one's actions. Your father acted like a nastik—an unbeliever. Hinduism is not something you learn in a few months. It runs in your blood.'

So her father had not worried about the consequences of his actions on others. He had forsaken her and Ronnie's mother also because they were both impediments to his plans. He had other goals. And he had tried to reach those by any means even if it meant trampling over other people or discarding them by the wayside.

'Ronnie's mother,' she whispered with her head still turned down. 'Did she mind it badly? My... his marriage to my mother?'

Maushi sighed. 'Yes child, she did.'

'She was broken-hearted,' Meera whispered to herself. 'And my mother?' she asked hesitantly. 'Did she too die broken-hearted?'

Maushi was startled into silence. No, she thought, certain truths cannot be told. Neither to you nor to Ronnie. Certain truths about Elizabeth, and about Anu, and some others too. Not because of the scandal they will cause but because neither of you should be made to bear them all your lives. And there is nothing you can do to alleviate the agonies of those times, those miseries. They happened and now they have to be kept hidden behind the cupboard doors and I have to take them to death with me.

She evaded the question. 'She didn't mind a first wife,' she said. 'Here we take these things differently, more casually; karma, she would say, and live with it.'

'We are all ruled by karma,' Meera said tonelessly lapsing back into stupor.

'No child,' Maushi said. 'Karmavada also tells us that we, each of us, can affect our karma by our actions. That though karmic forces set the pattern of our lives, we still have the freedom of action and we should choose our actions in awareness, knowing the benefits to be received or the price to be paid for every action of ours. That's why there is the Code of Dharma – to keep us on the right path.' Maushi paused, musing pensively. The silence prolonged. Meera's head was still turned down. She sat looking at her hands in her lap and did not break Maushi's silence.

'Yet there are times when one has to act against the dharma, act in full consciousness of one's actions, act knowing that there will be a price to pay for one's actions, but still act against the dharma because one believes in one's goals and one is limited in one's actions due to the circumstances.' Maushi spoke at last in a low hushed voice. 'Because there is no other real choice. Options aren't options at all. So you do what you have to do and you pay what is asked of you.'

She was almost talking to herself and Meera, startled out of her stupor, looked up at her face but Maushi had forgotten her. She was sitting absolutely still, her eyes blank, looking through the emptiness of the veranda. Her silence started ringing in Meera's ears but there was no silence in Maushi's mind. She was hearing the bawling of a red-faced infant kicking in her cradle, she was hearing the cackle of the vaisin reverberate on the veranda, she was hearing the exploding bursts of the bubbles in a well, and she was hearing a pathetic voice saying with bravado born of desperation, saying over and over, 'He is only infatuated with your daughter. He will get over it. Then he will come back to me, back to me, back to me,' until someone stifled it for ever.

They could not break out of the circle of karma. They had not learned to be their own persons, to sing and dance for themselves. They did not know how to help themselves and then it was too late for them, Maushi reminded herself with her eyes still blank, still looking into the far distance. So you did it. You did it because it had to be done and because you were the one who could do it. You did it for Anu and for Elizabeth and for Meera, and to bring song and dance into Meera's life even though you knew that the price would be high.

Meera, bewildered, watched her face for a moment longer and then leant forward and grasped her hands tightly. After a long while Maushi turned her head and looked at Meera. 'Don't let the karma get you down ever, child,' she said with urgency with that faraway look still in her eyes, 'your own or anybody else's. Past actions are past. They have already been paid for. So let the past lie, don't let it stop you from acting in future. You act, child, you act as you believe, even if you act against everybody's notions of right and wrong, moral and immoral; even mine, child, even mine. You act as you believe, and if there is a price to pay for it, remember that it has already been paid, but never accept, child, you act; act as you believe to be right. That's the true dharma, child, not what the priests tell you. And never, never forget how to sing and dance. Dance, my child, dance for yourself, and for your mother, and for Ronnie's mother also.'

Then she bent forward and took Meera's face in both her hands and looking intently into her eyes asked, 'Do you understand child?' and Meera nodded dumbly.

What she understood was that she had to be aware of her past and come to terms with it but not let that knowledge rule her mind or dictate her future actions. She should let her father be, let him remain as part of her memory and not as an obsession. Nor should she let her father's karma affect hers and her karma was in her own hands. She had to know her own aims, her own goals and follow them steadfastly and regardless but only if she truly believed in them and that she should act as per her beliefs and not as per any set rules.

My goals, my ways, my life.

She is leaving me free to live my life my own way, Meera thought. Bending forward she hugged her grandmother.

'I love you Aaji,' she said.

24

Ronnie walked up and down the beach kicking aimlessly at the stones that littered it while Hilary sat on the sand a distance away watching him.

The sky was heavily overcast. Everything—the sky, the sea, the sand, the rocks, the trees—was dark hued from grey to dark grey to black; Hilary a darker patch on a dark background. A howling wind was racing up the beach, palms and clumps of bamboos were rustling noisily, waves were heaving on to the beach with a vengeance and could be discerned only by their furiously foaming white crowns, but Ronnie walked along the beach totally oblivious of the waves and the wind.

He had been walking since early that morning, a morning that had not dawned at all but crept out of the night, dark, damp and close. It had been claustrophobic and oppressive and Ronnie's breath was getting caught in his throat when he walked out of the Home in Santagao for the first time in ten days. Ten days of caring for

Elizabeth, spending time with her, sitting before her and telling her how much he still loved her, while she looked at him with blank eyes and preferred to stand at the window and watch the sky and the trees. Ten days that had totally drained him. He walked without realising that he was walking, one foot in front of the other, not knowing where he was, not knowing where he was going. At some point, without a conscious decision, he just stopped and sat down in the middle of the road holding his head in his hands, incapable of any thought.

There was a flash on the horizon and a noise like heavens breaking apart and another flash that lit the whole countryside. Ronnie watched from between his fingers as a green hill rose before him. Midway up the hill, momentarily lit up like a beckoning beacon, was a white church with a wide white flight of steps leading to a terrace. A light rain began to fall. Ronnie got up.

The church was empty. Its tall, wide doors stood wide open. Inside, the church was dimly lit but its tall stained glass windows glowed in multi-coloured splendour even in that dim light, its massive vaulted roof with heavy criss-crossing ribs and its soaring fluted pilasters with Corinthian capitals still cast an aura of overbearing awe and dwarfed the worshipper. Ronnie sat in a back pew shivering in the cold, musty atmosphere, his head bowed down to his chest.

'Son,' Ronnie looked up to see an old white-robed priest bending over him. 'Son, I am Father Britto. Are you in need of confessing?'

'I am not Catholic, Father,' Ronnie whispered. 'My parents were… are… Church of England. I am not religious.'

Father Britto bent further and looked at him closely. 'You are a soul in distress who has come to His door seeking help. Come,' he said helping him up.

He led Ronnie to an anteroom, a stark white room with just a desk and two chairs in it and an oiled timber cross shining black on the rough white wall behind the desk. He gave him a towel to dry his hair, made him sit on a chair, and put a glass of wine in his hand. Then he pulled the other chair and sat facing Ronnie and leaning towards him said, 'Now tell me son, what has distressed you so deeply?'

Ronnie sat hunched in the chair, holding the glass in both hands. He had gulped half of the wine in one shot and now some colour was creeping back into his face. A sense of stillness, of tranquility was descending on him; the kind of tranquility that comes from knowing that you are not alone, that you can unburden yourself to somebody, somebody with compassion, somebody who will understand, somebody you can trust, somebody with authority.

'My father…,' he said looking into his glass, 'my father,… he told me and everybody in England that my mother died here, drowned – washed away – while swimming…' he stopped. Father Britto sat silent. 'She didn't die,' Ronnie continued in the same monotone still looking into his glass. 'They saved her life but she has lost her mind. She has been here in a mental hospital for the last eighteen years.' Father Britto leant forward and put a hand on Ronnie's hands holding the glass but said nothing, just waited with infinite patience.

'He left her here for dead!' Ronnie burst out at last. 'Never visited her, never cared for her, kept me also away from her! How could he do that? How?' He put his face in his hands in anguish, tears rolling down his cheeks, the first tears he had shed since Maushi had told him about his mother.

Father Britto didn't say anything. He let Ronnie cry his heart out and when he had quietened, got up and gave him the towel again. Ronnie wiped his face and picked up his glass. Father Britto poured him some more wine and sat back in front of him. 'You just found out?' he asked gently.

Ronnie nodded.

'Where is your father?'

'He died some months ago. In London. Of heart attack,' Ronnie said looking at his hands.

'Who looks after your mother here?'

'My...my sister's family.'

Father Britto kept looking at him, waiting. At last Ronnie looked up into his eyes and saw no disapproval, no reproof, no judgement. Nothing but kindness and understanding in those eyes.

'My father married another... an Indian lady here. I have a sister,' he said at last.

'And her mother?'

'She died soon after my sister's birth. Of fever.'

Father Britto got up and went to stand against the window looking out at the dark sky, at the silent rain.

'My father never mentioned my sister, never visited her either,' Ronnie said to his back. 'He deserted her. Just as he deserted my mother also.'

Father Britto kept looking out of the window. His astute mind had already divined the situation in totality. He turned and looked at Ronnie, at his drawn face, at his haunted eyes. 'Sins of fathers – ' he squashed the thought; that was uncharitable. This youngster had probably venerated his father and was now finding out his feet of clay. He had come to God's house in great distress bearing his father's cross. The least Father Britto could do was give him some support to ride over his distress, not lecture him on theological precepts, but dispense some of God's compassion and charity. He glanced at the cross on the wall, bowed his head and crossed himself. Then he came to sit before Ronnie and took both of Ronnie's hands in his.

'Son,' he said. 'Your father has sinned—sinned against God and the Church, sinned against his wife, and against his daughter. He has sinned through his actions and also through his inactions. He freely chose his relationships but then reneged on the contract that goes with every relationship: the contract to love and care. He denied his responsibilities towards them. He left those for others to bear.

'But we are not concerned with him right now. We are concerned with you, my son, with your capacity to deal with the legacies he has left behind for you and your state of mind towards him and through him towards yourself. You are pained by the plight of your mother but you are also consumed by the anger at your father. You detest him right now, son, but soon you will turn this anger against yourself, you will detest yourself. You will destroy yourself, son, unless you learn to leave judgement and condemnation to God.

'Forgiveness is a very big word, son. So just accept your father for what he was, with all his faults and frailties and his inadequacies and his limitations. And then let him be. He has left behind responsibilities for you to bear and in the words of a long gone poet, "Bear them you can and bear them you must." Of course he was referring to the penalties that went with too much wine,' Father Britto said with a conspiratorial grin.

Ronnie smiled back weakly.

'But God also made man in his image and gave him the gift of love, the gift of laughter and the gift of enjoyment. To reject the joy of life is therefore also a rejection of Him, son. So fulfil your responsibilities but also live your life to the full; enjoy it, love it; love the life for what it is: a gift of light out of darkness.

'And remember son, not to consider yourself responsible for your father's actions, not to carry the guilt of your father on your shoulders, not to let his past control your present and your future. Let him bear his own cross. You have your own life to live.'

After a long time, Father Britto escorted Ronnie to the terrace and down the flight of steps and stood looking at his retreating figure going down the hill. 'Go with God,' he said, 'and may He protect you and keep you in His care,' and made a sign of cross as he turned back to his church.

Ronnie automatically squared his shoulders as he walked down the hill towards the road. 'I don't believe in God, Father,' he had said to Father Britto, aware that he had not told him everything that had been worrying him, that he would have to carry his own burden on his own shoulders and that God was of no help, but still there was a firmness in his walk now and a confidence building up in his mind. He could and would deal with the situation. He would not wallow in blaming his father or in his past, or disregard his responsibilities. Now he felt capable of making the necessary decisions. It will take time for him to come to terms with it, but he could do it. Without knowing, he walked towards the shore, past the shops and bar-cafés, past the dhabas that were still open to the few tourists who had stayed back in Goa to enjoy the monsoons.

He had not been able to talk to Hilary at all, had only stared dumbly at her when he had accidentally come face to face with her near a dhaba, but one look at his face and she had fallen in step with him without asking any questions and now sat watching him spend himself on the stones on the beach. But Ronnie walked along the beach unaware of her, his thoughts on a blank faced woman in a Home for the infirm.

Mum. What should I do with you, Mum? Should I take you to London with me now? But Dr Gomes had said, 'All she does is watch the sky and the trees. And she is used to this sky, these trees.'

Perhaps I should talk to Giles first. And then get a second opinion. And a third one if necessary. Only then should I decide my course of action.

He stopped pacing and stood facing the sea. The roar of the white crested dark waves was calling 'Meeeera'. Over his head the thrashing palms were screeching 'Meeeera' and behind his back the rustling bamboos were sighing 'Meeeera'. Even the wind that was beginning to whirl the sand in a whorl was howling 'Meeeera'.

Meera. My sister.

With a menacing crackle, a lightning lit up the whole hemisphere – in sheets, with tentacles that extended sideways and downwards, a momentous display that lit the sky, the sea, the palms, the bamboos.

Thunder and lightning. Ronnie looked up enthralled, everything else forgotten for the moment. A storm was building up, winds ruffling the bamboos and the coconuts.

Bamboos and the coconuts. Coconuts stand tall and unyielding, get uprooted in the storm. Bamboos bend to the wind, they survive the storm. I am glad I will be studying nature.

With a roar the rain came down in huge sheets of water. Ronnie turned his face upwards, spread his arms wide, and stood with the rain running down his face. Then Hilary came over running, caught his hand and tried to pull him towards the shelter beyond the coconuts and the bamboos, but Ronnie gave her a lopsided grin and shook himself free, and then, standing alone under the dark sky, jumped high up in the air swirling and kicking out one leg at a time and wildly waving his arms about, dancing his last rain dance.

25

'Ronnie went back to London yesterday,' Pundlik said watching a lapwing flitting around, searching for its mate. 'A girl called Hilary went with him.'

Ronnie had steadfastly refused to meet Meera or Maushi or Baba. 'Not now, not yet,' he had said with the pain for his mother still in his eyes and with the fury at his father—Meera's father too, he had reminded himself—still in his voice even though Maushi had repeatedly sent him messages through Pundlik to come over, to come and stay in the house. 'Not yet, not yet,' he had said, and in the end they had sorrowfully accepted it and respected the space he had asked for.

'The lad grew up fast,' Pundlik thought remembering his last meeting with Ronnie when on behalf of the family he had offered Ronnie any information, any explanations, any help that he required. 'No, Pundlik Mama,' Ronnie had said. 'I don't want to understand anything from you. There are some things that one has to understand, act upon and bear alone. I will need your help though, when I have decided my course of action.' And Pundlik had stared at him in bemused surprise. This wasn't the same easy-going young lad of a couple of weeks ago. This was a mature, grown-up young man speaking. A young man ready to shoulder his responsibilities. 'You have grown up,' he had said and Ronnie had given him a wry smile before turning away, a smile that gave away his sorrow at the loss of his innocence.

'And Elizabeth?' Maushi asked.

'She is still here.'

Maushi nodded looking at Meera's back where she was sitting on the riverbank watching the moorhens darting in and out of the cover of shrubs, wading in the shallows. She still spent most of her time sitting by the riverbank watching the water birds or lying on the back veranda with her head in Maushi's lap watching the black woodpecker that preferred to peck at the mango tree and the whirring flight of the nightjars in the evenings. 'Ronnie loves watching birds,' was one of the few sentences she had spoken in all those days.

Occasionally she asked a few more questions about her father but she asked them unemotionally and nodded impersonally at Maushi's answers. She still moved in a daze, her eyes were still bewildered and wounded, and all her actions were automatic but Maushi knew she was getting over the shock when three days ago she had insisted on going to see Elizabeth and so Pundlik had put both her and Maushi in his car and driven them over. Meera had sat in front of an unresponsive Elizabeth talking to her for a long time while Maushi had sat on a chair in a corner of the room and Ronnie had watched from the door. After a long time Meera had got up and gone to stand in front of Ronnie. He had looked at her for a while in silence and then putting his arms around her had buried his face in her shoulder. Maushi could hear his sobs where she was sitting. Meera had let him cry his heart out, and when he had quietened, had pulled up his head holding it in both her hands, and looking into his eyes had wiped his tears with both her hands. They hadn't spoken a word to each other but when Maushi had turned to look back from the gate when they were leaving, Ronnie was still watching Meera from the porch, his face a picture of loss and grief.

Maushi had tried to reconcile this Elizabeth with the picture she had of hers in her mind formed from Pundlik's description eighteen years ago. A doll, he had said. With golden hair and pink cheeks. Maushi averted her eyes to hide her sorrow.

Pundlik still wondered at Maushi's empathy for Elizabeth. She had insisted that he visit Elizabeth regularly and report to her. She had insisted that he meet Dr Gomes regularly to check on Elizabeth's treatment. She had insisted that he ensure that Elizabeth did not lack for anything. She kept sending clothes and food to Elizabeth, even flowers, remembering Alec saying that Western women enjoyed receiving flowers.

Pundlik himself had always held Elizabeth responsible for Alec's wanderings and for the break-up of their marriage. Blamed her for being a working woman. A woman's place is at home; she should have made Alec's and Ronnie's welfare her goal in life. Men stray, men lose their bearings and their directions. It is up to women to maintain the equanimity, to forgive and to protect the sanctity of the family with whatever sacrifices that may be required of them.

'Did Ronnie say anything about taking Elizabeth to London?' Maushi asked.

'He is just a young lad. He will have to discuss it with his family back home,' Pundlik said.

And they will have to consider the resulting impact on their family name, on their family honour, Maushi thought.

'Dr Gomes had a long talk with Ronnie before he left, mainly about Alec. Ronnie told him that his father had become impotent on going back from here and...' Pundlik stopped in mid-sentence. Did he just see a smile flit across Maushi's face? I must have imagined it, he decided.

He turned to look at the barren yard. Black clouds had amassed in the sky and a damp and restless wind ruffled the weeds in the garden and blew the dead leaves of the neem tree around them. At places water collected from the last shower had turned to slush. The dull grey light that the day cast over everything further added to the drab and dismal feel of the yard, even the few trees left standing looked grey and eerie rather than providing any relief to the depressing landscape. His gloomy mood intensified.

How beautiful it had all been till eighteen years ago. Huge red and yellow dahlias, pink roses, white roses, even black roses, pink-and-purple madhumalti and wispy powder puffs, all swaying in the breeze with red silk cotton and flame of the forest soaring high above them. Butterflies of equally beautiful colours flitted over them. The air so fragrant with the aroma of jui, chameli and keora. In the night tuberoses would add their scents.

'You must have been missing your garden,' he said.

Maushi didn't respond.

'There were those jai, jui and madhumalti creepers climbing the veranda pillars. As also that deep purple krishna-kamal, the king of flowers, which bloomed only once a year. What an occasion it would be when its first flower appeared. The whole village would come over to view it,' Pundlik said reminiscing. 'Then there was that temple champa in the corner with its trumpet-shaped white and pink flowers and the golden champa with those golden ones shaped like half-closed claws.'

Maushi still didn't respond. She was looking at the river but she hardly saw it. There was a faraway look in her eyes.

'And that kadua tree near the gate with those wild multi-coloured fungi growing at its base and all over its trunk in the monsoons. It offered at least some colour, some semblance of a relief on a murky monsoon day like today even though all those fungi were poisonous.'

'It fell.' Maushi said.

'It had such delicate beautiful flowers. White with orange pattern on the inside. But no smell at all.'

'It fell,' Maushi repeated.

'There was a rumour that eating its roots caused impotence in men.'

'Just a rumour,' Maushi said.

'They are also supposed to be very bitter. That's how it gets its name – kadua.'

'Just a rumour,' Maushi repeated.

Suddenly Pundlik sat up straight as an age-old memory tumbled into his mind making an unexpected connection, creating an upheaval, and he looked once again at the dull and gloomy corner where the delicate kadua tree with its branches sagging under the load of pretty blossoms used to stand. 'At that Anu's thirteenth day meal, you made those special wadas for Baba and Alec only. You didn't serve them to anybody else,' he said with his policeman's instinct working overtime. 'Not even the priests.'

At that meal they had sat exactly the same way as they had sat for Anu's wedding feast. Baba, Alec, the priests, and the family elders separately in the place of honour, on the paats laid on the veranda, and being served only by the women of the household while servants bustled around with buckets of curry and dal and huge copper thalis of puris serving others seated on long durris in the tent.

'Priests eat only the sweets,' Maushi said.

'And the bitter ones, you served those only to Alec.'

'Nobody else in this family eats anything bitter like karela or methi. Alec loved them. I used to make those wadas all the time for him.'

'That day even Alec complained about their bitterness though he ate them all since you told him that particularly on that day he had to leave a clean thali.'

'What would Alec know?' Maushi said.

'Leave your thali totally clean today, don't leave even a tiny bit of food on it,' she had told both Baba and Alec bending before them on that dark and gloomy day eighteen years ago, a day just like this day, as she herself had served the wadas to them, 'or Anu's soul won't leave in peace,' which Gajanan had brusquely translated to Alec.

Equally suddenly Pundlik sat back on the bench. 'Anu jumped in the well, didn't she?' he said. 'That's why Baba had it filled up.'

Maushi didn't reply. But Pundlik didn't need her to. He had always suspected it; rather, he had always known it and suppressed the knowledge in his subconscious mind. After all he was the only other person besides Maushi, Baba and Gajanan who knew about Elizabeth and Ronnie. He was also the only one besides them who was aware that Alec could not take Anu to Canada on his passport and Anu could not get a visa on her own. And they were the only ones present at Anu's death. And Mahesh, the doctor nephew of Baba. Of course, that was the only way out left to Anu – what other alternative did she have once it was clear that Alec could not take her away from here? A first wife would not have mattered at all if only Alec could have taken her away from here, settled her somewhere else. But as things stood she had nowhere to go. And which family of Baba's standing would allow a married daughter to live permanently with them? Or allow a scandal such as this to surface? Which family would bear such a shame on the family honour, tolerate a deserted wife amongst them? No, Anu had been left with no other recourse but to jump into the well. Baba knew that. Gajanan knew that. And he also knew that. He had suppressed that knowledge all these years because he was afraid to accept that Anu, whom he loved, that lively, exciting woman who lived every day of her life in glory, had been reduced to such desperation.

Pundlik's eyes became misty with melancholic grief as he at last confronted his emotions that he had suppressed for so long and he bowed his head to hide them.

And Meera? What about Meera? If Maushi had not taken charge of her and alienated the whole family, the whole village, all of the community in the process, what would have been Meera's fate? Pundlik pushed that thought far down into his sub-conscience and closed his mind to it as he had done with Anu's suicide. For eighteen years.

Alec! A vilayati with vilayati morals. But were they really any different from ours? He had also loved Anu. He had also wanted to watch his daughter grow up. And he had also wanted his life in London with his English wife and son. Is that any different from what we want? And he had also wanted to protect himself, like all of us. Sure, he lied. About Elizabeth. And about his passport. And Canada was also probably a canard. Still, it was drastic to feed him those kadua root wadas...

Pundlik stopped thinking like a policeman and looked at Maushi, looked at her strangely as if he had never known her, never seen her before. Is this the same Maushi who had always been a fountain of love? Maushi, who always healed and never harmed? Maushi, the earthmother who accepted any and every deed of men and suffered in silence and still loved? Maushi, who in his eyes, was like a goddess, a goddess who could never be pitiless, or merciless, or unforgiving, how could *she* do it? How did *she* ever become retributory? How did *she* ever become so wrathful, so revengeful like Goddess Kali? Maushi, whom he had worshipped like Goddess Parvati. Maushi, whom he had revered from his childhood. Maushi, by whom he had loyally stood even when she did wrong in the eyes of the society. He had stood by her when she took over as the head of household against all the customs and conventions. He had stood by her through all her decisions regarding Meera even though he had strongly disagreed with almost all of them. He had stood by her when one by one all the village families had started ostracising Maushi and Baba and Meera. Even the villagers had taken a lot from her and still stood by her until Meera's behaviour had gone totally out of bounds and Maushi had still refused to control her; in fact, Maushi had actively supported her.

Pundlik sat up again.

Maushi could not have taken over as the head of the household and certainly would not have had any say in Meera's upbringing if Baba had not been disabled.

Something exploded in Pundlik's mind. His stomach began to churn. A great lump of bile rose in his throat. He couldn't swallow, his breath came in gasps, hair on his neck prickled, but his policeman's mind was racing ahead at speed.

'And Baba - Baba – those special wadas you made for him – those wild fungi, those monsoon fungi, those poisonous, debilitating fungi...' he faltered. His mind couldn't accept any more – not about Maushi. Maushi, the paragon of wifely virtues. Maushi, the epitome of womanhood. Maushi, the dutiful, the devout, compared to Sati-Savitri. Maushi, whom he had revered more than his own mother.

He couldn't pick up his eyes, couldn't look at her face; instead looked wildly around the yard but that dark and depressing yard offered him no comfort, its eerie trees exuded no solace, its gloom seemed to swallow him up.

'Baba knew,' he said at last when he could speak. 'That's why he didn't want a doctor – no doctor could have helped him anyway. That's why the uprooting of the garden, the cleaning of the house; he was searching for the hidden fungi; a wild monsoon rodent indeed! He knew and he never said a word to anyone.'

What could he have said? And to whom? Maushi said to herself. The family name, the family honour that men always hold aloft to keep women under control, the family honour that dictated that Anu should jump in the well and that her suicide be covered up, that same family honour tied his tongue and sealed his lips.

In fact Baba was the only one who had understood and appreciated, even if momentarily, why she had done what she did. Once and only once had he mentioned it. After his fever had passed, after he had the whole garden uprooted and the whole house turned upside down, after Maushi had forced Gajanan and Vinayak to leave the house, when Meera was already growing up into an independent, confident child. 'You had no other recourse,' he had said to her without any reference but with an involuntary look of admiration in his eyes as he looked at her. Just once. And they both had understood. At that moment she had felt a surge of sympathy towards him. And pity too. And at that moment she had at last forgiven him for all that he was. But he never forgave her.

Pundlik, devastated by her betrayal of his trust in her virtues, was still watching her, his eyes still accusing her. 'Your own husband!' he cried in agony.

'And Anu's father. And Meera's grandfather,' she said coldly.

Pundlik felt as if he had been kicked in the stomach. His eyes glazed. His breath came in gasps. But on another level, his mind was working very clearly in the contrary direction. This was to be expected, he acknowledged to himself. All this time we have been dispensing with the lives of our women as we liked, with little regard, and as convenient to us. For centuries we have been sacrificing them for the protection of our honour, of ourselves. Why do we feel incensed if they do the same to us to protect and preserve themselves? We did oppress them for too long a time, for too many centuries, in most unjust ways. There has to be a rebound—for life, for freedom, for power. A reaction to every action. Even if that too takes centuries. We suppressed their ambitions, erased their identities, and reduced them to mindlessness. We pushed them to the brink. And when they do fight back, what other weapon do they have?

Every man must unconsciously be dreading being poisoned by his wife, he thought, his stomach knotting so badly that he had gone grey in face as he remembered the times he had glanced suspiciously at his wife when something in the thali had not tasted quite right. He had not thought consciously of poison then. But now?

That's why widows are blamed for becoming widows. That's why the stigma attached to widowhood, the shaving of the head, the banishment to some ashram, or living in some relative's house working like a slave, eating like a dog. So that every woman remained deathly scared of becoming a widow. To ensure that the husband's welfare remained the primary goal of all women. That's why the worship of the banyan tree. That's why all those vrats to be kept for the long life of the husband. All instituted by us. All for protecting ourselves.

Why? Why have we been doing that? What are we scared of? Why this need to subdue a woman, to put her in her place? Why do we perceive any sign of independence on a woman's part as a direct threat to us?

Pundlik's head started spinning. He shrank back from the implications of his reasoning and shook his head from side to side to clear his thoughts, to bring them on line, to focus on the present reality: Baba's cherished family honour that had worked against him, shambles of Alec's dreams, Gajanan's thwarted ambitions, destruction of a way of life.

'Maushi,' he said in a pleading voice, bending forward, leaning towards her. 'Maushi, what you did, it was done in a state of shock, in a moment of... of... high tension, brought about by Alec's... by Anu's... well, by everything, wasn't it? I mean it was just an aberration that you have since regretted, wasn't it? Wasn't it?' He was desperately trying to absolve Maushi and thereby all of the womanhood of any deliberate intentions of rebellion, of revenge, of self-preservation. 'I mean you still look after Baba so dutifully.'

Maushi was looking at the river. 'It's my duty as a wife to look after him,' she said tonelessly.

'But what you did... I mean it was not to... not to...'

'Meera's very existence was at risk,' she said cutting him short.

'And wouldn't that have been the right thing to do?' he asked bristling with belligerence.

Right? Right for what? Right for whom?

'So I had to make a choice,' she continued stonily still looking away from him.

'Choice? Choice? What choice was there? How could there be any choice? He was your husband! There was one and only one way out of that situation,' Pundlik was almost shouting in aggression. 'Then your sons and grandsons would have been here. Your husband would have been hale and hearty, head of the whole family, the patriarch as he deserved to be with the family honour kept intact, with no scandals or shame on family name. Then nobody would have dared to ostracise the family and life would have gone on as always, as it has done for centuries.'

'Yes,' Maushi said with a twisted smile. 'Yes, that's how it would have been. Unless someone broke that circle.' She got up and went to the door.

At the door she paused and turned to face him. 'That's the choice I had, you see Pundlik,' she had addressed him as 'Pundlik' after a very long time and he stared at her sensing her acknowledgement of the abyss that had opened between them. 'The choice of letting the life go on as it has done for centuries or breaking that circle. And I exercised it,' she said and then turned and went into the house leaving him sitting there, still leaning forward, his eyes red, stomach knotted and mouth slack, staring at her back.

PART SIX

26

'Baba passed away peacefully,' Pundlik said. He was sitting on the front veranda of Maushi's house holding a cup of tea. It was early morning and the light filtering through the mist surrounding the trees was soft and unreal, the trees being just dark-grey hazy shapes on a hazy background, the sounds from the village were muted, even the birds were quiet, and at times an eerie silence seemed to engulf them, to smother them. Maushi was watching the cloud of white fog that hung over the ribbon of the river. Pundlik was sipping his tea looking into his cup more so that he wouldn't have to look at her face. Her face, without the large red kumkum on her forehead that he remembered from ever before, seemed totally desolate to him. They had also taken away her mangalsutra and Gauri had broken her green glass bangles on a stone in the backyard leaving only the gold ones.

Pundlik had been a rare visitor to the house these days, and when he did come, he spent all his time with Baba pausing only to touch Maushi's feet while coming and going. It was after a long time that he was sitting on the front veranda with her. Maushi too hardly sat on the front veranda nowadays. There was nobody and nothing to wait for any more. She had fulfilled the purpose of her life: she had helped Meera mould herself into a confident, focused woman. Rest was up to Meera and Devachi iccha – pleasure of Gods.

'Yes,' she said.

'The house has emptied so suddenly,' he said. 'For some time it was buzzing almost like the old times, with Gajanan and Vinayak and their families, all being here.'

'They left right after the thirteenth day rites. Schools, offices, you know.'

'And Meera?'

'Vinayak took her to Mumbai with him. He will see her to the airport. Her plane for Canada leaves tomorrow.'

'So she is going,' Pundlik commented pensively.

'What else?' Maushi said. 'This is the age for her to experience the world, to learn from it.'

'She could have waited a little,' he said.

'For what? And miss her time there? There is nothing more for her to do over here.'

So she would have gone anyway, so the turn of the circumstances had not subdued her ambition or dampened her zeal for life, Pundlik reflected. She will do well in that Canadian university, he thought, she will put a shine on the family name; and reluctantly acknowledged the surge of pride he felt in her as if she were his own daughter. And why Canada still? Why not some other country? She has gotten over her father-obsession and this is her way of showing it, he decided. And England? Will she be going to London too? he wondered suddenly but did not feel up to asking Maushi. 'Will she ever come back?' he asked instead.

'This is her home,' Maushi said and Pundlik turned to look at her startled.

Of course *this* is Meera's home, he thought, no matter whom she marries or where she works, this is where she will always come back to. This is Meera's home in the way it had never been Anu's home; both, she and the family had been waiting for her to go to her home – her married home.

Maushi was still looking at the ribbon of white cloud over the river and Pundlik too turned to watch the white cloud.

'Gajanan wants to come back here you know,' he said after a while.

Maushi had noticed the way Gajanan had straightened his shoulders and picked up his chin when the priests had put the pugree on his shaven head during the thirteenth day rites declaring him head of the household; but everything had gone totally wrong when he had tried to reinstate the old traditions. At the evening time none of the children, including his own, could recite the shlokas properly. They had also fidgeted during Maushi's story narration after that, asking couldn't they instead watch the Batman and Spiderman video tapes that Vinayak's children had brought with them from Mumbai. He had vented his anger on his wife, who, servile to him until only a few years ago, had answered back – *answered back*! – saying that she was too distracted trying to cope without a cooker and a mixie to bother with the children and then had asked how long would they be staying in the village.

'His wife and children won't let him,' Maushi said.

They sat in silence for a while waiting for the light to strengthen, for the trees to regain their colour and the river its flow, but the light remained hazy, the trees remained grey, and the river remained covered in fog. Then Pundlik put his cup down and said, 'I have applied for transfer to South Goa, Maushi. I leave tomorrow. I won't be visiting this side for a time to come.'

Maushi nodded. They sat in silence again, both aware of the unsaid, 'and now you are all alone here,' hanging in the silence between them.

Then Pundlik got up to go and as he bent down to touch Maushi's feet, he looked into her eyes and asked, 'What did you ever want for yourself Maushi?'

Nobody has ever asked me that, Maushi thought. They have only expounded my duties to me and those have been adjustment, submission and sacrifice. Sacrifice for the husband and for the sons. Daughters and granddaughters are not to be sacrificed for. They too have to sacrifice. Or be sacrificed.

But she didn't say any of that to Pundlik. She merely put her hand on his still bent head and said, 'Sukhi ho, sukhi raha,' in blessing. Be happy, stay happy.

She watched him go down the garden path and through the gate. She watched him latch the gate and go down the road. She watched him, a hazy shape in the still hazy light, till he was lost in the haze.

Then and only then she turned and walked into the empty, silent house.

The front room, opening off the passage to the internal courtyard, appropriated by men. At one time there would be heated arguments – about politics or cricket or something – resounding from here, punctuated every once in a while by calls to Anu or one of the women to send more tea, more bhajias. No women had ever been allowed in here. Now cobwebs hung from the chains of its hanging lamps, sofa covers had frayed and left unmended, and its windows were murky with accumulated dust. On the other side, facing it, was Baba's room. From here he had ruled over the whole household, issuing his orders, enforcing his discipline with an iron hand, his voice reverberating in the whole house. Nothing that happened in the house had ever escaped his notice or comment. I am sad that you had also been lonely here, lying helpless on your bed, watching the world go by through your window, Maushi said to herself, but I couldn't have saved Meera's life or brought her up to become what she has without your cooperation, even though it were given reluctantly, under duress.

Around the courtyard, Gajanan's room next, now used just thrice a year, a week at a time. Gajanan, the strong-headed, tradition -bound, designated inheritor. How he had tried to emulate Baba in everything, including his way of treating women, but without having inherited Baba's understanding. He had always taken it for granted that he would be the landlord after Baba, looked forward to reigning here, continuing the age-old traditions. I am sorry my son, I had to make it all impossible for you by unbearably harassing your wife and children so that you were forced to take them away but it was your desire against Meera's life and that was no choice. Next, my Vinayak's room, also empty most of the time. The younger, affectionate, lively son who laughed at everything, whose laughter could be heard all over the house, laughter that still clung to the corners of the courtyard, still floated on the breeze along the internal veranda. How he used to exchange secret smiles with his wife whenever he thought nobody was looking. Also forced to leave here. An innocent victim. But I couldn't throw out Gajanan alone.

On the other side, my Anu's and later Meera's room. Full of excited chatter, of ambitious schemes, of dreams of an exhilarating future; first Anu's, later Meera's. Those dreams still permeated the air, hung from the ceiling, entangled any visitor to it in their magic. My Anu, my Anu. Caught in the cross-currents of ambition and tradition. You never knew what you wanted, my innocent, exuberant and yet courageous daughter, you only knew what you didn't want; but your daughter knows, my child, your daughter knows. She knows exactly what she wants and goes all out to attain it.

Then the dining room. Here Vinayak had incurred Baba's wrath for laughing out loud when Alec, in emulating Baba and Gajanan, had tried to pour buttermilk into his mouth from a lota held half a foot above and got it all over his nose and kurta and Anu had giggled from behind the kitchen door. Then this long veranda around the internal courtyard. Here the diners sat for their meals in a row on long durris when there was a large crowd in the house and the dining room proved too small, overlooked by the windows of the upstairs rooms used by the visitors, the windows that visitors waiting their turn – when the crowd was so large that many sittings were required – would lean out of to hold conversations with the diners, the windows that had now lain unopened for many years.

And now the women's domain. The inner room. All women's functions—haldi-kumkums, naming ceremonies, celebrations of pregnancies—were held here; and here Maushi had bustled about revelling in her role as the elder, the organiser, the supervisor. Women visiting in the afternoons were also entertained here. Its corners still held so many whispered gossips and bouts of suppressed laughter and giggles shushed from behind the hands when at times they had been too loud and Baba had shouted from his room, 'What goes on there?'

The storeroom on the side. Crowded with earthen pots large enough to store a year's supply of rice and wheat and lentils for the whole family, now lying empty, and pots and pans big enough to cook for forty people at a time, used at least once a week at one time, rarely used nowadays, dotted with rust spots, copper and brass showing through the tin anodising on the inside. Racks of silver thalis and bowls lying undusted. Here, under a sack of rice, I had hidden some of Anu's marriage photographs away from Gajanan's prying eyes. The kitchen next, where Gajanan's wife and Vinayak's wife had spent their mornings and evenings and which Anu had tried to avoid whenever she could. On festivals, even Baba's brothers' wives and daughters would be bustling in and out of here and the children would be squatting around Gauri crowding her as she sat moulding laddoos or preparing some other sweet, squealing in anticipated pleasure.

Then Maushi's room, at one time constantly echoing with the children's racket: their jumping on the beds, their pillow fights, their laughter, their quarrels, their complaints and their whimperings. They would sleep here with her since Anu refused to have them in her room.

Maushi walked from the eerie silence of one room to that of another, ghosts following at her heels, visions tugging at her pallav, until she stood on the back veranda, once the hub of the women's life. Here, once, Gajanan's wife had gloated and Vinayak's wife had cried. And here, once, Maushi's sisters-in-law had gossiped and their daughters had giggled behind their hands. And also here, once, Anu had sat leaning her back against the corner post humming a song of love, lost in her own dream world.

Now she will turn into the gods' room, sit on the paat before the temple, open the boxes of kumkum and turmeric, light the little silver oil lamp, and start the worship rituals. But before that, for one moment, just for one moment, she wanted to sit on the back veranda, rest her back, lower her shoulders. Just one moment for myself, she thought.

'Maushi,' Gauri called softly standing in the doorway to the back veranda but Maushi did not answer her. She was sitting looking at the tamarind tree on which flocks of crows waited silently in the all-enveloping haze, at the broken down lopsided swing hanging from it on a single rope, at the bare branches of the mango tree, but Gauri knew she was not seeing any of it, that she had not heard her. There was an unbearable ache in her eyes, an ache that all through the last eighteen years she had denied even to herself, and tears were streaming down her cheeks, tears that she had not allowed herself to shed even as she had sat here suppressing her memories, and a deep yearning was etched on her face, a yearning that she had not allowed to surface for eighteen years, as she sat alone on the back veranda of that silent, empty house, lost in the past, a past when the swing had two ropes, when the mangoes were in blossom and flowers bloomed in the garden, when the house had thronged with people, and when every corner had resounded with different sounds, different voices.

ACKNOWLEDGEMENTS

Dolly Thakore, who was the first to read the completed manuscript and who has given her wholehearted support to it.

Niyogi Books, particularly Madhuparna Banerjee, who took much interest in this book and put a lot of effort in it.

Sachin Desai, who showed me around his family house with two courtyards in Goa and introduced me to his eighty-seven-year-old grandmother who talked with me at length about her life in that house.

Siddharth Naik, who took me to talk with his friends living in a courtyard house and drove me to many different locations all over North Goa.

Vasumati Dhuru, who talked to me about life in a traditional joint family; Swatija Manorama for the information she gave me on traditional songs; and Sonal Shukla of Vacha Trust for giving me access to their library.

AUTHOR'S NOTE

The coastal stretch between the Arabian Sea and the Western Ghats from Dahanu in Maharashtra including Goa and up to Mangalore in Karnataka is called Konkan and the spoken language of this region is Konkani. Konkani has no script. Marathi is the state language of Maharashtra and the written language in Goa, though a few years ago, Goa declared Konkani with Devnagari script as its state language.

Culturally, Goa and Maharashtra are similar. Not only most Hindu Goans speak Marathi, but the literature, songs, even bhajans in Goa are in Marathi. Religious ceremonies and rites – with minor differences – are same in both states and are conducted in Marathi. The medium of education in schools is also Marathi.

The Christians in Goa are Catholics and are called 'Catholics' and not 'Christians' even in casual conversation. For simplicity, I have used 'Christians' in the book.